CHANTAL ROOME

Book Cover by Chantal Roome

2nd edition 2023

Print ISBN 9781777707606

ebook ISBN 9781777707613

To my Husband
You encourage me without knowing you do it.
You remind me about nap time (favourite time of day)
You're in my head so much it's freaky
And you always make me laugh
Thanks for your support and for giving us our second chance

Shitty Jobs and Shittier Boyfriends

Alex

"Son of a bitch." I stomp my way to my car after slamming the door behind me. I rip off my chef's jacket and throw it into the passenger seat, along with my knife roll. These assholes may have sent me home, but I should have left long ago. And not just for today, but permanently.

I've had it up to my ass with my latest clients, the dirty old pervert and his not-quite-young-enough-to-be-a-trophy wife. He keeps trying to grab my ass, and she keeps trying to blame me for it. I really need this job, but I'm not sure how much longer I'll be able to keep my mouth shut about the harassment.

I pull my hair out of its high bun and scratch my fingers along my scalp to help ease some tension. It's amazing the stress a tight hairstyle can cause. Once I'm mostly calm, I turn on some angry music to finish soothing me—what can I say? Angry music calms me—and drive home to the apartment I share with my boyfriend. Well, it's probably more accurate to say I live in his apartment, rather than share it with him, considering he's been there for years and I recently moved in. It doesn't feel much like mine since almost everything in it belongs to him, anyway.

I stop to check the mail in the lobby on my way in before taking the elevator to the fourth floor where our apartment is.

Since I'm off work early, I think I may as well put the time to good use. I'm distracted with thoughts of the hot bath I'm going to take and the amazing meal I'm going to cook when I put the key in the lock of my apartment door and find there is no resistance when I turn it. That's weird. I'm pretty sure I locked it when I left the house this morning. Or am I remembering yesterday?

A loud bang from inside the apartment makes me jump.

Oh Shit! Someone's in there! I'm being robbed! What do I do? I can't let someone take all of Derek's stuff that he's worked so hard for. Holding my breath, I reach for my phone as quietly as I can and call my best friend Becca.

"Becca, it's me. I got home early and there's someone in my apartment. I think I'm being robbed," I whisper.

I inch open the door and creep in, reaching for the first weapon-like item I can find when my fingers wrap around a curved handle. Looks like the cute ladybug umbrella I keep for rainy days is about to see a different kind of action. I suppose I could use one of the knives I'm already carrying, but like hell I'm going to get dirty burglar blood on one of my professional knives and risk it being locked up as evidence.

I couldn't afford to replace it if that happened. Working as a personal chef hasn't been as lucrative as I'd hoped, but it sure beats the long hours of grueling labor I'd have to put in working in some other chef's kitchen. When you're not partaking in illegal stimulants, kitchen hours are unmanageable and, unfortunately, I've always preferred coffee to cocaine.

"What? Did you call the police? Get out of there, you're going to get hurt. I'm serious. Don't do anything stupid."

"I'm fine," I whisper, hoisting up my umbrella. "I have a weapon."

"Like what? I know for a fact you won't dirty up one of your work knives, and those are the only things you'd have with you that could work." She knows me too well.

"I have an umbrella. I'll be fine, promise."

I hear another loud bang coming from somewhere in the back of the apartment, so I tiptoe in that direction.

"An umbrella? Have you lost your mind? Get out of there, Alex. I swear to god if you die trying to catch a burglar, I'm going to kill you!" Becca shrieks as she attempts to talk me out of what I'm about to do.

Also, threatening to kill me if I die? Not the smartest thing she's ever said. Of course, attempting to catch a burglar in the act instead of waiting for the police is far from the smartest thing I've ever done, so I'd say we're even.

"Shhhh, he'll hear you, and I need to catch this asshole intruder by surprise." Nobody messes with me and Derek and gets away with it. "This guy's going to feel my wrath and that of my ladybug umbrella."

I creep forward, choosing the placement of each foot carefully so I make the least amount of noise. A giggling sound stops me dead in my tracks. It's coming from further back in the apartment, like from the bedroom.

I groan inwardly and lower my umbrella. *Oh, come on, not again. I thought Derek was different. I mean, sure, he works a lot and barely has time for me and he thinks my cooking is a hobby, but still. He asked me to move in. I thought he was serious about me. Apparently, though, he's just like all the rest of them.*

My mind quickly races through all the boyfriends who've cheated on me. Which is all of them, in case you were wondering. I refuse to relive the shitty details, but yes, I caught most of them in the act, and yes, I ended it with all of them.

It's exactly as depressing as it sounds.

And now Derek is fucking someone in our bed when he's supposed to be at work. When we're both supposed to be at work.

"That motherfucker," I whisper yell into the phone. "Becca, come over, now."

"I'm already on my way. What is it? What's wrong? Are you hurt? Should I call 911?" Becca is freaking out. If she doesn't lower her voice, all the neighborhood dogs will come running. Actually, now that I think about it, that could benefit me. I've never had a pack of dogs attack a cheating boyfriend before. It might be fun to watch.

You might hear that and think I'm being callous and, well, you would be right. I am. I've been through this so many times now I almost find it enjoyable to find new and clever ways to get back at the cheaters once I've caught them. Not that I want it to keep happening for that reason, but you know what they say. When life hands you cheating lemons, beat the shit out of them until you get lemonade. Or something like that. I'm not great with sayings. The point is, putting my heart on the line for the chance of getting revenge isn't something that interests me. Sadly, I actually kind of like the guys before they end up cheating. But I suck at picking them.

Becca's car revs in the background. Good. If this is actually happening, I'm going to need backup. I creep up to the bedroom door and stop outside of it. I force myself to stop breathing and try to listen closely, my ear pressed to the door.

"You like that, huh? You like my cock in you, you dirty slut?"

Well, fuck. That's Derek, alright. He likes to talk dirty, even though I've never thought he's all that great at it. My body gets numb all over, and then a burning rage sears a hole in my chest. You think I'd be completely numb to this by now, but the betrayal always hurts at least a little.

"Becca? It's happening again."

"That asshole! I'm five minutes away, Alex. Make sure you save some for me. I'm going to take pleasure in beating his ass."

"He won't last another five minutes, Becca. I need to go in now. He doesn't have that kind of stamina. Believe me, my less-than-satisfying love life is proof of that."

She chuckles a little at my confession. Maybe she thinks I'm making a joke at Derek's expense, but I'm really not. He's not quite a two-pump chump, but he's pretty damn close.

"Yeah, Derek, harder, harder! It feels so good, your cock is so big," the dirty slut, his words, not mine, screams as I continue to listen at the door. Derek's dick is mediocre on a good day so either this chick has the tightest pussy on earth or she's lying.

I'm going with lying.

No one's pussy is *that* tight. Plus, I'm pretty sure I can hear a hint of sarcasm in her voice even from out here.

"Are you gonna come for me, baby?"

Shit, that's Derek's way of saying 'I'm coming soon and if you don't, that's your problem.' Ever the selfless lover, that Derek is. That means if I want to surprise him in the act, I need to get in there fast.

"Becca, are you almost here?"

"On my way up. Is the door unlocked?"

"Yup, come right in. I'll be the one in the bedroom swinging the umbrella."

I turn the doorknob to the bedroom, careful not to make any noise. It opens to the sound of moans and grunts. Fucking Derek and his grunting. He's facing away from the door, pumping into Miss dirty slut from behind, so I sneak up on him while raising my ladybug umbrella. From this angle, I can see his hairy balls flopping around. Gross. I can't believe I actually found him attractive. And that was this morning.

"It's happening baby, I'm gonna come now, it's happening... ungh, ungghhh," he groans obscenely.

I creep closer to the bed as Derek thrusts erratically and grunts some more. This angle is not exactly flattering and again I wonder what I ever saw in him. Whatever. That doesn't matter now. What matters is teaching him a lesson. I grip the top of the umbrella with both hands, step right into it, and swing that ladybug like I'm Babe Ruth, nearly breaking the handle off on Derek's cheating ass.

"And it's a home run! The crowd goes wild!" Becca yells from behind me. Looks like she got here right on time. She puts her hands up like a megaphone and imitates the sounds of a crowd cheering for me. Derek's screaming nearly drowns her out, though. He throws himself off the bed, leaving Miss dirty slut exposed. She's as scared as Derek is, but I'm guessing her reason differs from his.

Becca is in the room, still cheering as she pretends to run the bases while collecting the other woman's clothes from the floor.

"You have a girlfriend?" miss dirty slut screams at Derek. She frantically tries to cover herself with the sheet. "You fucker!"

"He *had* a girlfriend," I correct her, while Becca passes her clothes to her. "But good news. It looks like we broke up. He's yours if you want him. Though I have a feeling that you no longer do."

Derek's eyes are wide and he looks like a fish with the way he keeps opening and shutting his mouth. He's sitting on his hip on the floor while he rubs his umbrella-imprinted ass cheek gingerly, wincing every time his hand grazes the hook mark left by the handle. Good. I hope he can't sit for a month.

"I am *so* sorry," the girl says to me. Her eyes are wide and her lip quivers a little. "I didn't realize he had a girlfriend. This is what I get for day drinking to forget my problems, I guess."

"No worries," I tell her, heaving a sigh of relief. It's so much easier when the other woman feels bad about being the other woman. "I've been through this enough times that I know the side chick is rarely aware of the situation. I can't blame you for trying to have an orgasm with someone who told you he was available. All the blame lies with that asshole over there." I point the broken carcass of my umbrella, all bent metal and ripped canvas, at Derek. "Isn't that right, Dickhead?"

Derek flinches a little and scoots back while I point at him. He probably thinks I'm going to break the rest of this umbrella over him, which, I have to admit, he sorely deserves. The girl stands up, holding her clothes to cover her body as best she can.

"Um, so yeah. I think I'm going to get dressed in the hallway and go if that's cool with you?" She points to the door behind me and I nod. "So, I'll leave you and Derek to work this out." She looks over at Derek. "Don't call me," she says. "Ever."

She takes tiny shuffling steps past both me and Becca to get out the bedroom door. I hear her stop and get dressed in the hallway, and shortly after that, the door to the apartment opens and closes as she leaves.

"Alright, let's get to work, shall we?"

"You bet," says Becca, shooting a dirty look at Derek. "Be right back."

"Please don't hurt me Alex. I'm sorry, I love you. I'll never do it again. I didn't mean to do it. She meant nothing to me."

Tears fall down Derek's cheeks as he crawls around looking for his underwear while continuing to spew the typical cheater's bullshit apology: *I love you, I'm sorry, it was an accident; I tripped and landed dick-first in her vagina. Blah, blah, blah.* I've heard it all before. I kick his boxers over, not because I care about his dignity, but because I don't want to see his dick and balls flopping around anymore. I can't believe I ever thought he was cute.

Of course, crawling around on the floor while crying probably isn't a good look on anyone.

"Quit being a little bitch, Derek. I'm not going to hurt you more than I already have. Probably. One never really can tell what I'll do once I've discovered my boyfriend cheated on me. But then again, I've already ruined a perfectly good umbrella. I don't really feel the need to break anything else trying to teach you a lesson that I don't actually care if you learn. I'm sure you will cheat again, because once a cheater, always a cheater. But I can guarantee you won't ever cheat on me again. Want to know why?" I taunt him by spinning what's left of the umbrella around my wrist. "Because I won't give you that chance. Now get the fuck out, I have packing to do. I'll leave the keys with security."

All the boyfriends I've ever had may have cheated on me, but at least I'm smart enough to never give them a second chance.

Now, if I could figure out what it is about me that makes them cheat on me in the first place, I'd know what to avoid next time.

Derek begins to protest right as Becca returns with some boxes and a little something extra.

"Here slugger, catch." She winks and tosses me a baseball bat and I drop the umbrella to catch it. "You know, in case you're not done with batting practice."

I bounce the bat up and down, testing the weight of it, before making a practice swing. "Nice. Thanks."

That kicks Derek into high gear. He scrambles to pick up his clothes and keep an eye on me at the same before practically sprinting from the apartment in his boxers. "I'm going, I'm going," he's saying as the door closes behind him.

"I've got a few more boxes in my car. I'll grab them and make sure he leaves at the same time."

"Hey Becca?" I call out, causing her to turn around before she gets to the door. "Thanks."

"No problem, girl, that's what besties are for," she says with a sad smile.

I nod and turn away. I can't stand to see the pity in her eyes. Again.

I'm not sure why Becca had boxes in her car, but I'm thankful she did. I'll be able to pack and get out of here right now, and I'll never have to come back. I should have known Derek would cheat.

Because in my experience, all men do.

"Well, look on the bright side," Becca says, while packing my clothes into a box. "A few more shitty boyfriends and your batting skills will be good enough to join a major league baseball team." She can barely contain her laughter.

Becca's been my best friend ever since I moved to this city when I was sixteen, and she's been there to help me through my breakups with all my previous unfaithful boyfriends. Not to mention Connor, the boy I had to leave when we moved. My first boyfriend and first love. And the only man who never cheated on me. Despite how it ended, he's the only boyfriend I ever look back on fondly.

"I can't believe you broke an umbrella over his ass. That shit was hilarious. He's going to have a hook shaped mark on his cheeks for at least a month."

I snicker a little at that. "I feel kind of bad for the girl. I'm amazed she actually apologized. Usually they get embarrassed and run. She seemed pretty cool. I mean, it's not her fault Derek fucked her while he was still living with me, right?"

"Funny you should mention that. I ran into her outside when I went to grab more boxes from my car. She was waiting on her cab out front. She asked me to apologize to you again." Shit. That is cool. Under other, less adulterous, circumstances, she might be fun to hang out with. "And then Derek came over." I look over at her like she's about to tell me that miss dirty slut (yes, I know, it's not nice to call her that. Sue me, I found out my boyfriend was cheating. I can't help that I didn't get her name) had made up with him, but I see Becca struggling not to laugh. "And then she kicked him in balls and kneed him in the face!"

A snort of laughter escapes me, and I double over. Fucking Derek totally deserved that. That chick *is* so cool. Now I really regret not getting her name. I laugh until my stomach hurts before I get myself back under control.

"Okay," I say, pulling my long hair up into a messy bun on top of my head. "Let's get the rest of this shit packed up. You know the drill, all my kitchen shit, clothes, bathroom stuff, and recipe books."

"Got it, boss." Becca gives a salute while kicking her boots together, like some kind of army cadet. Not that she'd ever join the army. She's way too punk rock for that. I swear that girl has more ink than regular skin. When I met her, she was sixteen and already had two full sleeves and a chest piece. Now she's thirty-five , and most of the rest of her body is tattooed as well. I've noticed some scarring under the color, but I've never asked her about it. It's not my business unless she wants to tell me, so for now I admire the artwork and hope it's helping her.

Becca grabs a big box and takes it to the kitchen to get started on the pots and pans. I paid a shit ton of money for them and they come with me every time I move. I always work professional cookware into my contracts for working as a personal chef, too. It's hard to prepare food exactly the way I want it when I don't have the right tools. I could do it if I had to, but it's much more enjoyable with the right gear.

"So where are we moving this stuff to, anyway?" Not sure why Becca is asking. She already knows the answer to this question. "Want to be roomies again? I promise I won't cheat on you like all these dudes. Well, unless some sexy tattooed guy comes along and waves his big fat pierced cock in my face. No promises then." She waggles her eyebrows at me.

"I wouldn't blame you at that point. I might be tempted to cheat on myself if that happened to me." I laugh.

The rest of the packing goes quickly and I'm completely moved out of the apartment in less than an hour. We have an absurd amount of practice with moving me out of places, which is pretty sad, but it makes for much faster moves when the time comes. How I always get myself into these relationships is beyond me. I seem to attract all the assholes and then I move in with them. I guess I just love love and love really hates me.

"Let's go back to your place and chill for the rest of the day. You know, the usual breakup routine of bashing men, eating ice cream, drinking too much, and watching chick flicks." This is literally the last thing I want to be doing today, but it's become a sort of tradition. Becca has been with me through all my break-ups and if she wants to get shit-faced and eat ice cream with me, I won't argue.

Becca's phone rings from where she left it on the counter. Probably a client. She has her own photography business and makes most of her money shooting weddings, but occasionally she's booked for other things. She talks on the phone for a few minutes while I double check I have all my stuff. I refuse to see Derek ever again, so I don't plan on forgetting anything.

"Change of plans, Alex; no pity party today. I have to go shoot a promotional thing for the radio station tonight. Some local band is doing the last show of their tour and having a special meet and greet afterward. The station wants me to shoot the meets for people who won some call-in contest."

"Oh, no worries. I'm sure I can find something to do" I'm a little relieved. This has happened to me so many times now that I don't even care about the breakup ritual. It's like my heart doesn't break anymore, it's too strong. Either that or it's been broken since the first time and has stayed that way ever since.

She grins at me. "Actually, I convinced them I will need to bring extra equipment so they're giving me an extra press pass for my 'assistant'."

"But you don't have an assistant," I point out, confused.

"Congratulations," she says to me, throwing fake confetti. "You're hired. There is no pay, and the boss is a huge bitch. What do you think?"

I laugh, finally figuring out what the hell she's talking about. "That sounds like a much better breakup ritual. Thanks."

"No problem. Now let's get this shit back to our place and figure out a plan for after the show. Oooh, you can have hot rebound sex with someone in the band. I'm sure they fuck a lot, so it's possible they're awesome at it." She wiggles her eyebrows at me while walking backward toward her car. "Of course, it's also possible they're terrible and groupies are telling them what they want to hear. It could go either way."

"Ha, yeah right!" I flip her off as I get into my vehicle. "I'm not exactly rockstar girlfriend material."

"Who said anything about girlfriend? I said rebound sex. Get your mind *into* the gutter, girl," she yells from her open window while pulling out of the lot.

I shake my head and chuckle. She's such a bitch. That must be why I love her.

Hopefully, this band tonight is good. I might not be completely heartbroken, but I could use something to distract me from sitting around trying to figure out why I've been cheated on. Again.

2

Family is Overrated

Connor

"No, Mom, there won't be another show for a long time. We've been touring off and on for almost fifteen years and you haven't been to a single show. Tonight is the last night of the tour before we head back to the studio. Please come see me play." I pinch the bridge of my nose in exasperation. We have this conversation every time I ask her to come see me play. I've purchased plane tickets for her to come to other cities for fuck's sake, and she *still* hasn't bothered to show up.

I grab a smoke from the pack in my pocket and light it, taking a long drag. If I exhale with a little more force than necessary, that's my frustration manifesting as furious smoking.

"Connor, I don't think we'll be able to make it. I mean, I don't even have anything to wear." My mother is whining again, and I can tell she's angling for me to offer to buy clothes. And I'm a sucker, so of course I do. I've always done everything I can for my family, but I'm getting pretty fucking sick of it. It sucks doing shit for people who don't appreciate it, and my mother doesn't know how to show appreciation for anything.

"I'll call a shop I know and give them my credit card number. You go, bring your boyfriend, and Sadie and Amanda, and get something to wear. Hell, buy all new wardrobes if you want. I don't give a shit. I want you guys here tonight." Somehow she always gets something out of me just to perform what you would think is basic mothering. It's like I have to pay her to be a mom. She's lucky my band turned out to be so successful or she would have to actually work for a living instead of sponging off of me.

"Oh? Well, I guess it wouldn't hurt to have a look around. Ted needs some new clothes, too. He has nothing nice to wear when we go out to dinner and to the theater and such." Dinner and the theater on my dime, you mean, right Mom? Ugh, it pisses me off that I have to pay for that leech Ted, too, but Mom wouldn't come if I didn't include him. Him or whichever other "boyfriend" was currently mooching off her (and by her I mean me).

"Great. I'll leave your tickets and backstage passes at the box office. Get them and come down to the stage and Devon or one of the other security guys will show you where to meet me. I'm glad you'll finally be seeing me play. "In all the years I've been doing this my own mother hasn't been to a single show, but tomorrow she'll finally see what I've done with my life (and what affords her the lifestyle she currently lives). She may be a selfish bitch, but I still want her to acknowledge how far I've come.

"Alright, baby." Now she sounds happy, since she's gotten something else out of me. "We'll see you tonight. I can't wait for you to meet Ted. I think you're going to like him. He has some great ideas to discuss with you. Bye, Honey!" She hangs up before I can say anything else. I text her the address of the store I was talking about so she won't have an excuse to not show up.

"Fuck! Why must I have a family full of assholes?" I'm practically ripping my hair out as I throw the door open and charge back into the dressing room. I'm pissed off now. I should've known something else was up. She agreed to come because her new boyfriend 'has ideas to discuss' with me. He probably has a stupid business concept that he wants backing for. Not happening, I already give you enough money mom, no way 'Ted' is getting even more out of me.

"Ow, shit! Get off me." Ryder pushes the blonde's head out of his lap as I stride across the room to pour myself a drink. Looks like she was trying to get his zipper down and get her mouth onto his dick. I guess it's not every day that she gets her hands on the lead guitarist for one of the hottest bands in the country.

"Dude, what's your problem? You scared that chick so bad she nearly bit my dick off. Not cool bro, not cool." He's pouting now, and I can't help but snort out a laugh.

"Good. Someone needs to bite it off. Maybe then I wouldn't have to see it so much. I swear I see your dick more than I see my own." I laugh while he fakes like he's going to take his dick out again. I stab my cigarette out in the ashtray on the bar at the side of the room. All these venues are supposed to be nonsmoking, but no one has ever asked me to go outside yet. I normally don't even mind going outside, but there are too many groupies out there now. I don't need that hassle when I'm looking for a smoke.

"Oh, you love this cock. If you didn't, you wouldn't look at it so much." Oh shit, I was wrong. He wasn't faking. He's whipped his dick out again and is now waving it at every other person in this room, helicopter style. Crazy fucker has no shame. The collection of groupies someone let in here doesn't seem to mind, though. Every one of them is trying to catch his eye now that they've seen the size of his penis. The asshole is blessed in that department, even I can admit that.

Our manager, Denise, walks in at that moment. "Yes, Ryder, I believe that is a penis, albeit a little on the small side. I can get you a magnifying glass if you want to get a closer look to confirm it for yourself?" Ryder stares at her with his mouth hanging open like he's trying to catch flies. He's probably trying to determine exactly how big Denise's boyfriend's dick must be if she's saying his is small. The groupies look shocked that a woman would talk to him like that. Denise is always busting his balls and I, for one, love it. He always has it coming, and it's always hilarious.

"Now, it's time for you boys to head to the stage for sound checks. So take your dicks out of whatever wet holes you've got them in, put them back in your pants, and get moving." She turns on her heel, long black hair swinging out behind her, and opens the door while motioning to shoo us out. "Chop chop, gentlemen. The stage awaits. And you," she points to the half-naked groupies practically begging for our attention, "no sluts backstage today. The boys will find you if they want you." Denise might dislike the women who hang around us begging for any attention they can get, but she'd never break their hearts by crushing their hopes completely. They all rush out past her, giving us little waves while pushing their tits together, trying to get our attention one more time. They'll figure out soon enough that they won't be back again after the show.

Denise has been our manager since we started the band, and she's always been this way. Part sassy bitch, part mother, and part no-nonsense shark. There isn't a doubt in my mind that we wouldn't have made it this far if it weren't for her. She's never phased by any of our bullshit, including walking in on us with chicks in various positions, hence the 'dicks in wet holes' comment. As long as we wrap up, she doesn't care where our dicks go. Unless it's time to put them away and get on stage, that is.

Not that most of us have been partaking in the groupie scene much over the last couple of years. I can't remember the last time I did anything with an actual woman instead of my hand. Seems a lot safer when you consider most of these groupies will fuck anyone who gets on stage. Who'd have thought I'd have had enough of the rockstar lifestyle at the ripe old age of thirty-five , yet here we are. I started out with wanting to play music, and it seems like I'm right back where I started. This upcoming stint in the studio couldn't come at a better time. I miss hanging with the guys, writing and playing music.

"You okay, C?" Aiden stops in front of me as he heads out. "You seemed pretty pissed when you walked in here. Your mom cancel on you again?"

"She tried, but she'll be coming tonight, with her new boyfriend. And he apparently has 'ideas' to discuss with me." I roll my eyes. Aiden knows how my mom is, so he'll know that she and the boyfriend are after something. "I promised them all a new wardrobe to convince her to come before she sprung that on me."

"Shit dude, sorry. That's rough."

"Yeah, well, it is what it is. Everyone I know wants something from me, except you guys. You guys never ask me for anything." I slap him on the back as he walks past Denise. Aiden has his own demons with family, so I usually try to avoid complaining to him about mine. Having to buy stuff for my family is still better than hav*ing* no living family at all.

"That's not quite true." Travis gives me a shove on his way out the door. Good thing we're about to go on stage or I might have to punch him right back and start something. I'm pissed off enough that fighting him actually sounds pretty good right now. He's got a good four inches and forty pounds on me, but I think I could take him. All my time in the gym must be good for something.

"That's right." Travis' older brother, Johnny, stops in front of me as he walks by. "We ask you to sing like your life depends on it every night."

"Yeah," Ryder pokes his head back through the door with a mischievous grin. "And to shake your sexy ass so the ladies will come backstage and screw us all after the show."

"Fuck off, Ryder," Johnny yells after him. "He is such a dick-head." He grabs Travis by the back of the neck and they walk out the door. Having them both in the band can get complicated because of their brotherly dynamic. Not to mention, they are constantly arguing and fighting each other as only brothers who really love each other can.

Well, I guess it's time to head to the stage and get this over with. Mom's bullshit always puts me in a foul mood, but performing normally helps that all go away. I'll hit the gym and rid myself of this shitty mood after soundcheck so it won't affect my performance tonight. One quick look in the mirror to make sure I'm looking like a sexy lead singer and I'm out the door, too. I might not be interested in sleeping with the fans much anymore, but I gotta keep them thinking it could be possible, right? Gotta maintain the illusion of availability. At least that's what the label says.

"So Denise? What do you say?" I always ask her this before I go on stage. It's part of my "getting into rockstar mode" ritual. Over the last few years, it's started feeling more like an act, so I have to take a minute to get into character before performing.

"Time to fuck shit up, Connor" she replies with her usual answer while leading me towards the stage.

"Damn right," I mutter to myself as she walks away, leaving me with the guys. "Time to fuck shit up."

SOUND CHECK WAS GREAT, and now we've got a few hours to kill before we're needed again. I call up the shop where I sent mom and the girls to see if they made it there already, and they have. I guess they'll make it to the show after all. Mom has a habit of saying she'll do something and then not following through, though, so I won't get my hopes up yet. I give the shop my credit card number and confirm that my family can get whatever they need before hanging up. It feels like I'm buying their affection, but I don't know how else to get them here. My sisters would come, but even at eighteen and twenty-two years old, they still do whatever mom wants. Not that I can talk. I'm the one buying them all new wardrobes to get them to come to my show, after all.

With a few hours to kill before the show, I take a car service to the gym. I've been working harder on taking care of myself, though I have held on to a few bad habits. I have the occasional drink, but I rarely get wasted anymore. I still smoke, but a rock-star needs at least one vice, right? I'm off drugs and not sleeping with groupies, so smoking is it for me. Well, some might say my workouts are not the best for me either, but I need the release.

I usually go to whichever fight gym is closest to the venue, but since we're in my hometown, I go to my actual home gym. Not that I own it, I pay my fees like everyone else, but I am friends with the owner, Mike. The gym's a little older and doesn't get as many fighters as some of the bigger gyms in town, but I've been working out here since I moved to the city and I'm pretty attached to it.

"Hey Mike, you old bastard," I yell out to the old guy stand-ing near one of the heavy bags, surrounded by a bunch of what looks to be twelve-year-old girls. "I'm going to work out for a bit before the show tonight, cool?"

"Hey Connor! Didn't think I'd see you until after the show. Didn't think you'd want to get your pretty face messed up." Mike laughs at his own joke. He thinks he's pretty funny, so he's always cracking jokes and laughing at them himself. "There's a couple of guys in the back who might spar with you if you're up for it. But don't blame me if you're singing with a black eye tonight."

"Haha, funny Mike. You know I can hold my own with anyone you want to throw at me. Maybe I should quit the band and go pro?" I joke while he watches the girls throw combos at the bag. "Can I count on you to be in my corner?"

"Fuck that, Connor. You're too pretty to fight. Now piss off and get your workout in. I can tell you're cranky, and you're distracting my girls." It looks like a few of the girls have figured out who I am, despite my clever disguise. I guess maybe I'm finally getting too famous to wander around on my own, no matter what clothes I have on. Shit, there goes my independence. I may need to consider bringing Devon for security from now on.

Not that I really wear a disguise. I'm wearing a black ball cap over my dark brown, slightly curly hair, and a long sleeve moisture wicking shirt that covers my full sleeve tattoos. I've also got grey joggers over top of my workout shorts so I can come and go quickly without changing. I should shower before I leave, but I'd rather not confirm any suspicions about my identity, or have anyone take pictures of my junk, so it's easier to go back to the hotel to shower after a workout.

Despite my cockiness regarding fighting ability, I actually don't want to wind up with bruises of any type tonight, so I stick with jumping rope, shadow boxing, and a little pad work with Mike when he's done with the girls' training.

"So what's with the class of girls?" I ask when we're done with the pad work. "I didn't think you did classes here."

"Yeah, I didn't used to, but my friend's granddaughter got into a situation with a guy who didn't want to take no for an answer, so I thought I should show her some stuff. That turned into showing her friends stuff, and now I run free self-defense classes for middle and high school girls." Mike slouches a bit and rubs his hand over his head. "This girl got away from the asshole before he could do much, but I still feel better with showing these girls how to fight, in case one of them is ever in that situation again. I'd rather they not have to rely on luck, you know?"

"Oh shit, Mike. I'm sorry to hear that. Glad it wasn't as bad as it could've been. It's a great thing you're doing for these girls, though. If all girls had some fight training, maybe these little dickheads would finally get the message that they can't go around doing whatever they want. If you need money to hire trainers to help, let me know. I would love to get behind something like this." I've got two younger sisters and I wish they'd had an opportunity like this when they were younger. I can't help them now, but maybe I could fund some classes or something as a way to give back to the community. "We'll talk more about this. For now, I need to go get ready for tonight. You sure you don't want to come?" I wheedle. I ask him this every time we play nearby. He's been to one show, and he wasn't a big fan but at least he came.

"No thanks Connor, I need to keep what's left of my hearing intact. Plus, that shit you call music is straight up noise to me. Too much yelling, too much guitar." He grins at me as he says this, but I know he's telling the truth. He has also listened to a couple of our albums, so I know he's at least made a serious attempt. I doubt my mother has even bothered to do that.

I pull on my joggers and throw my hat back on. "Alright Mike, I'll check back in soon. Thanks for the workout." I give him a two finger wave as I walk out the door and get into the car that's waiting to take me back to the hotel. I should go to my house, but all my stuff is still at the hotel.. ne more show, and then I'll be back in my own home. This tour has taken a lot out of me and I can't wait tto e in my own space again.

3

The Only One

Alex

Sitting alone in Becca's apartment, the reality of my breakup with Derek really hits me. It's happening again. That's what I said to Becca on the phone. And she was ready to come running based on that alone. What is my life that I have my own emergency response team for being cheated on? How does this keep happening? What is it about me that makes every guy want to cheat?

I wouldn't consider myself the most attractive woman in the world, but I'm pretty enough, I think. Plus, being on my feet for fourteen hours a day keeps me in decent shape. I'm hilarious most of the time, and people seem to think I'm fun to hang out with. Becca is my best friend, but I have a lot of acquaintances and other friends that I spend time with occasionally. I wouldn't say I'm an especially needy girlfriend. I'm happy with doing regular activities and don't need someone romancing me constantly or always saying how much they love me. It's nice to have it every once in a while, but I don't need it every hour of every day. My past lovers have seemed satisfied, so I think I'm okay on that front.

I suppose I could be wrong about that, though. They did cheat, after all.

On paper, I'm a pretty stellar girlfriend. I guess that means there is something inherently wrong with me that I can't see, or that all men are cheaters. Either way, it's going to be much easier on me if I stay away from men for good. It will disappoint Becca that her little 'Alex fucks a rockstar' plan won't happen tonight, but that's probably for the best. I can't keep normal dudes interested, so there's no way a rockstar is even going to look my way.

Then again, I had a musician boyfriend once, a long ass time ago. "And he was the only one who didn't cheat on me," I add out loud.

"Who didn't cheat on you?"

"SHIT!" I practically jump out of my skin before spinning to see Becca standing behind me. "I didn't hear you come in. How long have you been there?"

"A few minutes." She shrugs. "I'm not surprised you didn't hear me; you looked pretty lost in thought. Who was the one who didn't cheat?" she asks, even though she should know the answer. When I first moved here after my parents died, it was her helping me through that and my breakup with Connor that bonded us. She was my lifeline during that time. I wouldn't have made any friends or done anything but mope around with teary, red-rimmed eyes if it hadn't been for her taking pity on me that first day of school.

"My first boyfriend, Connor. I was thinking to myself that, considering recent developments with Derek, I'm going to swear off men entirely. Then I thought of your plan for tonight and was telling myself that a rockstar would be the worst type of guy to get involved with since they're pretty much drowning in pussy and guaranteed to cheat. But then I remembered Connor was a musician, and he's the only boyfriend I had who didn't cheat. I suppose he might have without me knowing, though." I take a minute and think about that while I push my hair out of my face. I don't *think* he ever cheated. We never even slept together, so would it have even been cheating, anyway? "I creeped him online not that long ago, but couldn't find anything out. I wonder if he's still doing music? Man, I wish we had the same access to the internet back then as we do now. It would have been much harder for him to disappear off the face of the earth if I could have Googled him or added him on Facebook."

I always loved listening to Connor play for me, and his voice was amazing, too. I had a hard time convincing him to sing for me at first; he considered himself a guitarist, but when he finally did, I knew I was witnessing something special. I really hope he's made music a part of his life. It would be such a shame if he wasn't sharing that gift with the world.

"Oh yeah? What was his last name again? Maybe I can find something out. I'm basically a detective with searching for people online." Becca's already pulled out her phone to start her search.

"It's Connor Ferguson. You search while I get ready to go. I doubt you'll find him, though. It's been a few years since I've tried looking for him, but I don't think there'd be that much more information out there now." I grab a towel from the linen closet and my toiletry bag from one of my boxes and walk toward the bathroom. "If you find him, I want to know everything." I stop and think for a moment. "Unless it's bad, then don't tell me. I want to hold on to the belief that at least one of my guys didn't have a wandering penis."

She laughs. "You got it, girl. Good things only. Connor Ferguson is either a saint or he's dead to us."

I shake my head and close the bathroom door behind me. I let the shower warm up while I get undressed. A concert will be a fun distraction. Who knows? I might even like the music and get some new songs to add to one of my playlists. Speaking of playlists, I connect my phone to the bluetooth speaker in the bathroom and turn on my angry, rage music playlist and turn it up. Call me strange, but there's something about really hard rock that soothes me.

I use the music, my vanilla shampoo and body wash, and the hot shower to wash away all the bad feelings about Derek. I am upset, but the sad fact is I am used to it. It's not a thing that should happen so often a person can get used to it, but here we are. I know how to get back to normal relatively quickly, so by the time I'm walking out of the bathroom twenty minutes later, I'm feeling a little better about myself.

"So?" I say to Becca. "Any news on Connor?"

She turns off the screen on her phone, "Uh, nope, nothing to see here. No news whatsoever. My turn to shower."

"I guess he's dead to us then, huh? Probably a major dickhead, cheated on his wife, abandoned his kids, something like that?" I ask her. I changed my mind. I want to know even if it's bad.

"Yeah, something like that." She bolts to the bathroom like her ass is on fire and I hear the water running not ten seconds later. She's going to be pissed when she realizes she didn't bring a towel.

I decide to let it go and go find some clothes to get dressed in. Walking into my bedroom, I see the boxes that we've stacked there. Might as well unpack while I look for some clothes. I pull out the box that has most of my clothes and start going through it. I put my underwear into the top drawer of the dresser and set aside a black lace thong to wear tonight. Sexy underwear for a sexy lady, I think to myself with a chuckle as I pull them into place. "Good thing I had a wax recently, or I'd have bush hanging over the edges of this thing. That would not be comfortable at all." I mutter. I don't much care about pubic hair either way, but some underwear styles call for less hair than others. A little further down in the clothes box, I find my favourite skinny jeans, the ones with rips all up the fronts of the legs, and pull those on too.

"Hey Alex?" I hear Becca yell from the hallway. She must've finally realized she forgot her towel. "Can you pass me a towel?" Ha, called it.

"Yeah, hold on a sec," I yell back to her. "Be right there." Quickly digging through the box, I pull out an old Nirvana t-shirt that belonged to my dad, and throw it on before grabbing a towel from the hallway closet and bringing it to Becca. "I should let you suffer and drip dry for not telling me what you found out about Connor, but I can't do that to you. I'm the one who asked you not to tell me, after all."

"I have some news, but I don't want to tell you right now, not before the show. It's very interesting, though, and I think you're going to be surprised." She has a kind of mischievous look on her face, but that's not all that unusual for Becca. She always looks like she's up to something. I blame it on her perfectly shaped eyebrows. She draws them on in such a way that she always looks interested and slightly surprised. The effect is unnerving, like she's looked into your soul and seen your darkest secrets and finds them cute.

"Oh? Good news? He's not a dickhead?"

I'm adjusting my shirt in the hallway mirror. I cut the neck out ages ago, so now it's more of an off-the-shoulder top than the t-shirt they originally intended it to be. The opening exposes my left shoulder and shows off my half sleeve tattoo, dark pink peonies that creep up onto the back of my shoulder. I may not be as inked up as Becca, but I really love my peonies. I didn't put on a bra before I put the shirt on, but luckily (or unluckily I sometimes think) my boobs are nothing to write home about, so I've decided to go braless. The shirt was a little long when I stole it from Dad, so besides cutting the neck out, I also made it into a cropped shirt, a little shorter in the front than the back.

This makes wearing it braless a little more risky in the coverage department, but I'm looking for comfort tonight.

Making a mental note not to do any cartwheels at the show so I can avoid flashing my tits, I go back into my room to grab some shoes and to tie up my hair. I'm not even going to attempt drying it tonight, so I put it into a messy bun on top of my head and leave it at that. I quickly swipe on some black mascara and a little vanilla scented lip gloss, and that completes the look. High maintenance makeup queen, I am not, but I do tuck the lip gloss into my pocket in case I need to touch it up later. Most days I wear no makeup at all; it would melt off of me in a hot kitchen, anyway.

"I don't think he's a complete dickhead," comes the answer from Becca's room. She must be getting dressed now, too. "Decide that for yourself when I tell you. After the show."

"Ugh, fine. You suck." I pretend to be frustrated, but I understand. She wants us to have fun without me worrying about old boyfriends, whether that be Connor or Derek. "Can you tell me what kind of music this is, at least? How likely am I to get stomped on?"

"They're pretty hard rock so I wouldn't wear heels,"

I love how Becca knows exactly what I was getting at. We've been to enough local shows to know that mosh pits break out at most rock shows, and it's every girl for herself at that point. There are usually a bunch of big dudes around the outside of the pit who will help people who need it, though, so it's not really all that dangerous. We'll have Becca's camera equipment with us, so we probably won't get too close to that kind of action, but better to be safe than sorry.

"Gotcha. Trusty old Doc Martens it is." I pull my boots out of my box full of shoes and then find some socks so I can put them on. "I swear wearing these boots is better than going barefoot. It's like they're hugging me when I put them on."

"That's great," Becca says, coming out of her room. She's dressed in dark skinny jeans, a low cut, short-sleeved shirt with a picture of an anatomically correct heart on the front, and black Chuck Taylors. Her eyes are all lined in black and she's wearing blood red lipstick. "I won't remind you how long it took you to break them in, then. All the blisters and blood." She shivers at what must be the memory of me hobbling around with bloody feet for an entire month after I bought them.

"Totally worth it," I say back to her. "These boots are now a part of me after all that trouble."

"Not to mention chock full of your DNA." Becca laughs.

I grab my phone, cash, and ID and put them in my pocket with the lip gloss I stashed there earlier. "Are we all set? I want to grab a coffee at Bump & Grind before we get there. I've been up since four a.m. and I'm going to need some caffeine if I want to keep up with you tonight."

"Yup," she says, picking up her camera bag and checking to make sure she has everything she needs. "Let's get out of here and find some sexy rockstars."

"To take their pictures, remember? I'm not into the whole 'fuck a rockstar' plan."

"Oh yeah, totally," Becca says. "No rockstar fucking for you, gotcha. I might snag one for myself, though. It's been awhile."

She doesn't sound like she believes me, though. "I'm serious Becca. I'm not looking to hook up with a serial cheater. rockstars are basically cheating machines, and I am not down with that. Hard pass."

"Yeah, I hear you Alex. No worries. I will not try to hook you up with anyone. I got your back, girl."

For some reason, though, I don't believe her.

"Shit, this place is bigger than I thought. I can't remember the last time I came to a concert here. I thought we'd be going to a bar. Didn't you say these guys were local?" I was busy looking around the arena while Becca was getting her camera set up for taking shots of the show. They'd blocked off one end of the arena floor, and all the seats on that end as well, to make the stage for the bands to perform. "Who did you say was playing again?"

"Opening act is some band called 'Lives that Cared' and the headliner is 'Sleeping Dogs'. It's the last night of the tour for both bands. They're local because they live here, not because they're small." Becca seems proud of herself for fooling me. I was not expecting to go to an arena show. I was more geared up for a dive bar.

Not sure how she expected me to score a rockstar when the concert was at a place like this. A band that sells out a venue this size probably has women lined up for the chance to bang them. I guess it's a good thing I wasn't planning to go through with her idea, since there is no way it could have actually happened.

"What's the plan?" I ask. Becca is taking shots of the venue as it fills up. She has permission to shoot whatever she wants while she's here. Her job is to take a few photos of the meet and greet session after the show, but I know she loves to photograph all things music related so she won't pass up a chance to get some great shots of the show itself.

"We're going to stay up here and get some shots of the floor filling up, and then we'll go down to the floor. Press passes will get us backstage, and I'm hoping I know some of the security guys so they can get us right up in front of the stage so I can take a few shots of the bands performing. When Sleeping Dogs are nearly done, we'll go backstage to wherever they have the meet and greet set up, probably the dressing room, so I can get my head around the space. We'll take the pics I'm actually getting paid for, hopefully get a few good shots of the bands after the show, and then we'll go. You work early again tomorrow?" Becca lays down the plan for me while I drink my second coffee of the evening. They made me dump the last bit of my first coffee when we came in the building, but luckily I could buy another once we were in. It's not as good as the one I bought at Bump & Grind, but it's caffeinated, and that's all that matters.

"Not too early," I say. "The family is going out of town for the night and they won't be back until the afternoon. I don't need to be there until noon." Good thing, too. I'm going to need to sleep in after tonight. These coffees aren't doing it for me.

"Okay, that's good. I was thinking we could get into the after party and we can have some fun. Party it up, single girl style and whatnot." Becca lets a whoop and gives a little fist pump before she looks through her camera again.

"Sure, crazy girl. If we get an invite to the after party, we can go." I agree, because I seriously doubt we'll get the invite. We're dressed to blend into the background, not stand out and get the attention of rockstars. Not that I really want that attention, anyway. I'm off men for good this time.

4

Family Drama

Connor

"Dude! You almost ready? You already look prettier than any girl here tonight." Ryder is messing with me again, teasing me for taking so much time with my appearance. I may not be taking anyone home to fuck tonight, but they still need to look at me and think they have a chance. That whole *illusion of availability* thing, again.

"Fuck off, Ryder." I flip him off in the mirror while I debate wearing a shirt or not. Screw it, leave it on and rip it off later once I'm sweaty. That's a move that the crowd always loves. Of course, then I have to throw my shirt to the crowd, and I kind of like this one. It's an old Soundgarden shirt I stole from my first girlfriend about twenty years ago, so I don't really want to get rid of it. Maybe I can get away with throwing it at one of my sisters, to gross them out. That would be hilarious.

I stop messing around in the mirror and pull my phone out to text my mom. I haven't heard from them yet, but I know they went shopping for clothes. My credit card had a pretty big charge on it from the store I sent them to, so I'm sure they got quite a lot out of me.

Connor- You guys make it to the arena yet?

I put my phone back in my pocket, not expecting an immediate answer. They're probably still getting ready. I doubt they plan on being here for the opening act, anyway. Lives that Cared has some great music but none of it is really mom's or the girls' type of sound. Mom likes older stuff and the girls are all about pop music, and whatever they play at clubs right now. 'Something dance-y' they call it. Something shitty, more likely. I chuckle out loud, causing Ryder to give me a strange look.

"You feeling alright, Bro? Talking to yourself over there?" He raises an eyebrow at me, the left one with three piercings in it. I hate when he does that. So of course he does it all the time. Dick. Plus, who even has eyebrow piercings anymore?

"Yeah, I'm good. Just laughing at my sisters' musical tastes in my head. They're all about pop and dance music. Makes me wonder where I went wrong." You'd think having a brother who's a rockstar in a pretty famous band would give you better taste in music, but apparently, it doesn't make a difference at all.

"Not everyone can be cool like us, man." He says with a smirk. I've known Ryder since I was eighteen, and neither of us was very cool for most of that time. It's only since the band took off that women actually wanted to sleep with us. And they never really want us exactly, they want to sleep with a rockstar; who it is doesn't really matter.

I've had exactly one proper girlfriend in my life and I have a feeling it's going to stay that way, at least until I retire. There are too many gold diggers and chicks who want money vying for my attention out there. I won't even consider being serious about someone like that. I have a little more self respect.

The first few years after we made it big are a blur of sex, drugs, and rock and roll, as usually happens with young guys who gain too much fame and too much money far too quickly. But after a while I tired of casual sex with nameless strangers and decided that it was time to keep my dick in my pants and focus on the music. I was using all of that stuff to drown out the memories of my first love, anyway. I can admit that now.

It's been almost twenty years, and no one has come even close to meaning as much to me as Alex did. It was her belief in me that convinced me to pursue music. I remember playing my guitar for her for hours, the melodies and lyrics saying things I could never say to her with plain words. I don't think she ever knew that most of those songs I sang to her were ones I'd written for her specifically. She was my muse.

Hell, that girl inspired so much of my music that we really should pay her royalties from our first album. It was full of love songs, and even heartbreak songs, that I wrote about her. The way she loved to crank up angry music to calm herself down inspired even the angry music. For Alex, the more screaming there was in a song, the more it soothed her like a lullaby.

"Hello? Connor? You there? Did you hear what I said?" Denise is suddenly in front of me, waving her hands in front of my face. "We have a special meet and greet set up after the show tonight. Contest winners from a local radio station, a couple of kids from the children's hospital, and a few people who purchased special VIP packages. The radio station is sending a photographer to shoot the meet and greets, and she has permission to shoot the show and backstage areas, too. So you'll need to stick around after the show and be as charming as possible. Good press as you head into the studio will be important for future album sales."

"Jesus, Denise. Of course I'll be nice to everyone. Make sure you tell Ryder to avoid the groupies. No need to scar anyone with the sight of his tiny penis tonight, right?" My joke falls flat because Ryder isn't paying attention. "Plus my family is coming, so making the process quick and painless is in everyone's best interest."

Denise looks over at Ryder, a scowl on her face. "I've already spoken to Ryder. Apparently, he plans to behave himself tonight." She mutters something under her breath as she turns and walks out of the room.

I see Aiden and Travis sitting on a couple of overstuffed leather armchairs in the corner of the room and walk over to join them.

"Hey guys, Denise tell you about the meet and greet?"

Travis speaks up first. "Yeah, she said something about that. Are we really letting a photographer back here to shoot whatever she wants? Seems kind of risky."

"I think that's why Denise is saying that we need to be on our best behavior. Something about good press improving future album sales." I tell them both. "We need to make sure Ryder keeps his dick in his pants and that we're nice to the fans. The photographer can't shoot any crazy shit if there is no crazy shit, right?"

"That's true," Aiden bangs out a beat on his shoes while he talks. "I think all the crazy shit these last few years has come from Ryder, anyway. I don't know what his problem is. Denise is constantly cleaning up his messes; it's like he does stuff to piss her off."

I look over at Ryder, who seems to be busy doing something on his phone. Swiping through pictures from the look of it. "I think as long as we can keep him contained tonight, we will be fine. He can continue fucking up after the meet and greets are over, and the photographer is gone."

Denise pokes her head back in the door. "'Lives' is going on in fifteen minutes, guys. You've got probably a little over an hour before you hit the stage. Get yourselves presentable. The label is worried people will forget you when you head into the studio so they really want you to sell that "rockstar" image tonight."

I step away from Travis and Aiden and pull my phone out again. Mom still hasn't gotten back to me, so I send her another text.

> **Connor–** Hey, what's your ETA? We're going onstage in about an hour so you'll want to be here by then.

I barely get my phone back into my pocket before I get the ding that tells me I have a new text. Finally, they must be here already.

> **Mom–** Hi honey, we won't be coming after all. Thanks for all the clothes, though.

Wait, what?

> **Connor–** What do you mean you're not coming? Why not? And when were you planning on telling me?

> **Mom–** Well, Ted isn't feeling that well, so I decided we should skip the show this time. We'll come to the next one, though.

Connor– Leave Ted at home. You and the girls can still come. I don't even know the guy, so it's not a big deal if he can't make it. I want my mom and sisters to see me perform, not some random boyfriend I've never even met.

Mom– Connor, I won't have you talking about Ted that way. We won't go on a family outing if the entire family isn't there.

What the fuck? What the hell does she think I am, then?

Connor– What are you even talking about? You are my family. The girls are my family. Ted is not my family.

Mom– That's enough Connor. I won't allow you to treat me like this. Good night.

"I give up," I announce to the room while I slip my phone back into my pocket. "She'll never come to a show, no matter what I buy, or what I pay for. I'm done." I throw myself onto the big couch at the back of the room and Johnny comes over with a glass of whiskey he's poured for me. He must've sensed how angry I was getting as I texted my mom.

"Let's get through the show, man." He slaps me on the back before getting up and going to pour himself a drink.

He's right. We'll do the show and I'll worry about family drama tomorrow. Tonight I'm a rockstar. *Whatever the fuck that means.* I down my whiskey in one gulp. *Sorry, Denise, I* think to myself as I get up to pour another drink. *My best behavior might leave something to be desired tonight.*

5

Fuckboys and running away

Alex

WE'RE STILL IN THE upper levels of the arena when the opening band takes the stage, and I'm liking their sound. Becca gets some great shots of the crowd and the band from a distance, but now she wants to get closer, so we make our way down to the floor. It's tough to carry Becca's camera bag without slamming it into anyone, but people are so into the music that no one seems to notice if I bump them a little. I'm happy that I wore my Docs tonight, and I can see why Becca told me to avoid heels. I've been stepped on no less than five times already, and we haven't even made it to the floor level yet.

Becca stops in the back section of the arena where the concessions are and gets a new SD card out of her camera bag. She switches out cards and puts the old one back into the bag before turning to me.

"So, how are you liking the show so far?"

"It's great. The harder the rock, the calmer my soul, as I like to say." I shrug a little. I'm sure I'm yelling a little because my ears have that full, fuzzy feeling you get when you're suddenly taken out of a loud environment. "What are we doing now?"

"I want to go down to the front and get some closer shots of these guys before they're done with their set. We probably have half an hour still before Sleeping Dogs take the stage, so we need to hurry and get down there." She's already walking towards the stairs, leaving me scrambling to catch up. "No need to run," she tells me. "If we get separated, go to the security guys at the side of the stage. Show them your press pass and tell them you're with the photographer from the radio station. They'll show you to the meet and greet area and we'll catch up with each other there, okay?"

"Sounds good. I might go out into the crowd to soak in the concert atmosphere. It's been too long since I've been to a good rock show."

"But make sure you make it backstage before the Sleeping Dogs finish their set. You don't want to miss watching them come back." There she is, with that sneaky look again. The one she has when she's up to something. But what is it?

"Right, will do. But remember, we canceled operation 'fuck a rockstar'. I'm here to help you and enjoy some live music. That's it." It wouldn't surprise me if that's what she's planning. She's a big proponent of the adage 'the best way to get over an old flame is to get under a new one,' so I doubt she'll let up without a fight. "I can look for a rebound in a more realistic setting. rockstars aren't interested in anything I have to offer." I gesture to myself, and then to the crowd. "Have you seen the goodies on display here tonight? Those guys have their work cut out for them when they're picking out tonight's fuck buddies." From where I'm standing I can see at least a dozen women flashing the stage, and even more, are giving sex eyes to the dudes on stage. Blatantly obvious and aggressive sex eyes I can see at a distance. That's impressive. "You can smell the pussy buffet from here. I'm not interested in competing with that. Got it?"

She rolls her eyes at me. "Yes, Alex. I got it. Party pooper." She says something else, too, but the music is too loud to hear her. Hopefully, it's more agreements. "I'm heading up front now. Are you coming?"

"Not yet," I tell her. "I'm going to hang back a bit longer. Probably grab another coffee before I go to the floor." I'm already turning towards the concession.

"Okay, I'll catch up with you soon then." Becca grabs her camera bag from me. "And be backstage before the band comes back." With that, she walks away, leaving me to go back to the concession and grab a coffee. This night is already going to be too long. I think I should skip out on trying to go to the after-party. Nothing says you're getting old, like falling asleep in the middle of a loud party in a bar. I'd like to avoid that if possible.

THE OPENING ACT JUST left the stage and I'm still up on the second level. I haven't finished my coffee yet, but I should probably move down to the floor soon if I want to get a spot near the stage. People have cleared out a little now, going to get fresh drinks and hit the bathroom, so I should be able to get a decent spot before anyone gets back. I fight my way through the crowd, using my elbows to protect my coffee (I know my priorities, after all, coffee before personal safety). I'm the only one going toward the floor instead of the bathrooms, so there is a lot of crowd to fight through. People stream past me up the stairs while I hold on to a railing for dear life and protect my coffee as best I can. Somehow, I make it down with minimal spilling and no injuries, so I'd say that's a victory.

I see a clear spot off to the right on the floor, and I walk over that way. There are some extra security guards on this side, which I'm guessing means the entrance to backstage is over here somewhere. Meaning I should be able to get there fairly easily from this spot. I suck back the final dregs of my coffee—*yummy, coffee grinds*—and dispose of my cup.

While I'm waiting, I scan the crowd. I love people-watching and concerts always attract a diverse group. Right now, though, all I see are slutty groupies and fuckboys.

The groupies are refusing to give up their spots right at the front, which makes sense, I suppose. It's hard to get backstage with the band when you're too far away for them to notice you. They could always wait outside and try to catch them when they head back to their bus, but I don't think that would fulfill the whole 'he picked me out of the crowd and then we fell in love fantasy I'm sure a lot of these girls are entertaining. That's not very likely to happen, but best of luck to them.

The fuckboys are right there with the groupies, laying the groundwork. Not every groupie is going to make it backstage, and the fuckboys know that. Gotta hand it to these guys, that's not a bad plan. These chicks are hoping to sleep with a rockstar and if they don't get to, they might take a fuckboy as a con-solation prize. They're all attractive enough, and there's noth-ing wrong with consensual sex. As long as everyone involved is free and available, that is. Fucking Derek, that prick, obviously doesn't know that.

Even standing as far away as I am, somehow I draw the in-terest of a few fuckboys. Cute, tattooed, good hair. I'm not interested in meeting guys tonight, but it is flattering. I was serious, though, when I said I was off men, and it wasn't merely a way to get out of Becca's plans for me this evening. My heart may be made of stone now, but it still hurts a little when I'm never the one chosen for keeps. I'm still a little shaken up from walking in on Derek and that girl today. Every time I think of it, a little montage of all the cheaters I've had the displeasure of dealing with in my life runs through my mind. I'm sure these fuckboys who keep looking over at me aren't any better.

Speaking of fuckboys, here one comes to try his luck. I must need to work on my resting bitch face if this guy thinks my expression says, 'hey, come talk to me'.

"Hey baby," he says as he circles in behind me and rubs his fingers down my peony tattoo. "How did you know roses are my favorite flower?" Ugh, he doesn't even know what they are. Also, who the fuck said he could touch me? I'm not interested, but I decide to mess with him a little, to entertain myself.

"Just lucky, I guess." I turn around so I can see him better. He's not bad looking. Dark, messy fauxhawk, a pleasant smile, and he's wearing a tight shirt that shows off a decent amount of muscles. One problem though, he's looking at me with 'fuck me' eyes. "I'm here working though," I hold up my press pass for him to have a look, "so no time for a quick bang in the bathroom right now." His jaw drops, but I don't notice what he does next because the lights go down in the arena. "I guess I better move up and get started on my work. Nice meeting you." I throw back over my shoulder as I push through the crowd. I didn't want to be too close to the stage, but the front row seems devoid of fuckboys right now, so that is the spot for me.

I work my way through the crowd and end up right up by the fence, still a little off to the right. It's not completely dark and in the dim light, I can see the musicians coming out onto the stage. I can make out five people in total. One goes to sit behind a drum kit in the back, three more pick up what looks like guitars (but I'm sure at least one is a bass) two take up spots on the left and one on the right, and the last one steps up to the front of the stage where there is a microphone on a stand. It's kind of hard to tell, but they look to all be men. Slowly, a spotlight comes up on the drummer and he counts in the band's first song. The guitars and bass join in as they are gradually lit by their spotlights. They are all incredibly sexy. No wonder there are so many groupies.

Damn, I almost regret telling Becca not to try to hook me up with one of these guys. They are all so pretty. Even my thoughts are trying to get me under someone new. *Maybe I am not as off men as I thought.*

And then it happens. The last spotlight comes up, the rest of the stage is lit, and standing there, at the microphone, is the lead singer. Someone I had no hope of ever seeing again.

The day we met is ingrained in my memory, something I will never forget. I was walking home from school, passing by the park beside the Fallbridge library when I heard music coming from the direction of the slide. I couldn't stop myself from going over there, and to this day I couldn't tell you why. When I came around the slide, I saw him, just sitting at the bottom. Short, dark hair that looked like it hadn't seen a comb in days. His head was bouncing along as he strummed a guitar. His eyes were closed, and he seemed to be oblivious to his sur-roundings. He wasn't, though. He looked up at me, his huge chocolate-brown eyes staring directly into my soul, making my breath catch in my chest.

"If you're going to listen, you may as well come sit with me," he said, then he got up to sit at a nearby picnic table. He patted the space beside him, and I was powerless to resist. My feet were stepping before I decided that I was going to do it. I sat there listening to him play for hours.

And after that, there was no hope for me. Sometime between the first and last songs he played that day, I fell in love. We saw each other every day after that. Until I moved here to Westbor-ough when my parents died, that is. That was when I lost him.

But here he is, in front of me on this stage, larger than life.

All I can do is stare as I take in the only man who ever truly had my heart. He is hotter now than he was then. He looks out over the crowd, his eyes taking everyone in. Shit, that look must be what people mean when they say 'smolder'. I never got it before now. His dark hair hangs down over his eyes a little, and he runs a hand through it to push it back. Tattoos cover both of his arms and when he tilts his head back, I can see he has something with wings tattooed on the front of his neck. He's wearing a tight, vintage-looking, Soundgarden T-shirt with dark jeans that are a little tight, and burgundy doc martens boots. Looks like we have similar tastes in fashion. Actually, I used to have that exact shirt, if I remember correctly. He's wearing a lot more jewelry than I am, though. Most of his fingers have rings on them, and I can see a nose piercing.

I'm so busy taking a physical inventory of his entire body, I fail to notice when he turns and looks directly at me. I see his eyes widen slightly. His mouth opens a little like he's going to say something, and that's what brings me out of my trance.

"Well shit," I say out loud. "This is a surprise." Then, shocking even myself, I turn and run, pushing people out of my way, not stopping until I'm in the lobby. I need space to think about this development. I'm not sure I even want him to see me at all, let alone see me staring up at him from a sea of groupies. Because if there is one thing I'm not, it's a groupie. Not even for Connor. Not even if he is my first love.

6

More Family Drama

Connor

"ALRIGHT BOYS, THE OTHER guys are finishing up and you're on soon. Let's get moving." Denise comes in and starts herding us to the door. I stumble a little as I get up from my spot on the couch, possibly thanks to the drinks I've had since Mom told me they weren't coming. I don't know how she always takes me by surprise by not being there for me, but somehow she does. And I hate it.

"You alright Connor?" Denise looks concerned. "You haven't gone on stage anything but sober for years. Can you stand up alright? Or should we get you a stool to sit on?" She's kidding, of course. She knows that as long as I'm not blacking out, there is nothing that could stop me from putting on a great show.

"I'm great, dollface. But it's possible I had five or ten drinks to take the edge off my disappointment. Mom and the girls can't make it after all. 'Ted's not feeling well.'" I don't hide my disgust at the last part of that statement. I probably look like I'm going to be sick. No chance of that, though. I can handle my liquor.

"Who's Ted?" Denise says. She's missed the last half hour that I spent ranting about Mom's boyfriend to the guys. Can't say I blame her, really. I'm sure she's been taking care of shit involving the finer details of the show.

"Mom's new boyfriend." I wave my hand nonchalantly, cigarette dangling precariously from my fingers. "He's sick and they can't come to a family gathering without the entire family. BECAUSE I'M NOT FUCKING FAMILY AND HE IS APPARENTLY!" I yell, furious with my mother for putting me in this position again. Why can't she come to one fucking show? I do everything for her and that's the only thing I've ever asked for in return. Fuck. If I had more time, I'd go back to the gym to spar for a bit. It would be worth risking the bruises if it meant putting a stop to the way I'm feeling right now.

"Okay then, well, let's put a pin in that for now." Denise takes my cigarette and puts it out in the ashtray, grabbing my shoulders to lead me to the door. "Right now, you have a show to do. And you have meet and greets after the show. You promised you would be charming, remember? The photographer is out in front of the stage now to get a few shots of you performing. I'll ask her to come back and get set up after a couple of songs to make the meet and greets go faster. I'll take care of it. We'll make this the shortest meet and greet session in history and you'll be out of here before you know it." Denise sure knows how to put out fires. I haven't needed her help for something like this in years, but right now I appreciate her more than she'll ever know. "And Connor? Time to fuck shit up." She smiles and leads me out of the room.

Right. Time to fuck shit up.

Too bad I'm not actually feeling it.

7

Panic and Irish Coffee

Alex

I'M STANDING OUTSIDE THE arena, smoking a cigarette that I bummed off a biker-looking dude who's also hanging around outside smoking. He must've sensed I desperately needed one because he had no qualms about handing it over and giving me a light. I don't smoke very often, but there is nothing better than furiously smoking when you're upset. I'm taking deep, angry drags of my smoke, trying to decide whether I should even hang around to meet up with Connor, but before I can decide, Becca texts me.

Becca- Meet me backstage in the next ten minutes. The band's manager is putting a rush on the meet and greets, so I need to be ready to shoot as soon as they get back there.

Well, that settles it then. I text her right back.

Alex– Yeah, I'll be there in a few. We need to talk. You owe me an explanation.

Becca– Shit. You saw him, didn't you?

Alex– Yes. And I can't believe you didn't tell me. I'm on my way. Talk soon.

I'm already walking back in when I put my phone away. By the time I make it through security, buy myself another coffee, and walk down the length of the arena to the side of the stage, it's been twenty minutes. Becca is going through security at the side of the stage when I get there, so we follow a security guard to the back together.

"I'm not happy with you," I yell over the music. "How could you not tell me you found him? And how come *I* never managed to track him down?"

"I thought it would be a fun surprise. You said he's the only one who never cheated on you. I thought it might be nice to see someone who didn't throw you away. He goes by the last name Ashley now. That's probably why you couldn't find him. Plus, if you remember, internet searches weren't quite the same twenty years ago. People didn't put every minute of their lives on social media. By the time that happened you weren't searching all that hard."

Shit. She's right. Facebook was barely a thing when I first lost track of Connor. I didn't have many search options and by the time I did, he must've changed his name. Damn it. Becca wasn't trying to hurt me by not telling me she found him. I can tell she thought she was doing something nice. It's hard to stay mad at someone when they want you to be happy.

"Fine. I forgive you. But it's still a dumb idea." I'm speaking quietly now because I don't want the security guard to hear this. "He may not have cheated, but he still changed his phone number when I moved away. He might as well have cheated. It probably would have been easier than going from thinking we were fine to suddenly having no contact at all. And he's clearly popular now. He probably doesn't even remember me." Somehow, I've convinced myself that he didn't look directly at me a few minutes ago. There's no way he recognized me, right? That would be crazy. He was scanning the crowd.

"Not possible," Becca starts, "how could he not-"

"Shit, Becca, what if I go up to him and he doesn't remember me? That would be so humiliating. Tell me you haven't said anything. Please don't tell anyone." I am freaking out now, panicking that he's forgotten me completely. I've always remembered him so fondly, but what if he doesn't remember me at all? Maybe he looked at me because I am dressed so differently from what the women in the front normally dress like? I think that might break the last little piece of my heart that I've protected through all these terrible relationships. "Say nothing, Becca. We'll do what we're here to do, and then we'll go home. I wouldn't be able to deal with it if I try to talk to him and he doesn't even know who I am. I'll be your assistant and stay in the background, so I won't need to worry about it."

"Alex. Alex, relax. I promise I won't say anything." Becca strokes my back while I hyperventilate. "Let's go get set up. We'll be as quick as possible, which is what they want too, and then we're gone. No after-party, no messing around, nothing. We'll go home and that's it. okay?"

I take a deep breath. "Okay, let's go."

"Here we are, ladies," the security guard says, opening the door to a nicely furnished room. "And don't worry. Your secret's safe with me." He winks at me and stands off to the side to give us a little privacy. My jaw drops. He heard us. Please don't let him tell Connor.

"Shit shit shit," I'm pacing the floor now. "I can't do this. I'm freaking out. I should leave now, right? That would be better for everyone." My heart is racing and I feel like my breath can't catch up. "Is this what a heart attack feels like?"

Becca walks over to the bar at the side of the room and grabs a bottle of whiskey. Bringing the bottle over, she motions for me to give her my coffee cup. She opens it up and tops off my coffee with whiskey. When the lid is on the coffee, she gives it to me and takes the whiskey back to the bar.

"There, now you have an Irish Coffee. Drink that up and try to relax while I make sure I have everything ready. It could be an hour before they get back here, so there's plenty of time before you need to worry about anything. We can probably even sneak to the side of the stage to watch part of the show if you want. You know, watch him in action for a few minutes without the risk of him seeing you. Once I'm set up, we won't need to stay in here the whole time."

I can't even respond, so I focus on drinking my coffee. This is going to be a shit show.

8

Youthful Memories

Connor

As usual, I am the last to go onstage. The spotlights come up gradually, starting with Aiden, then on to Travis, Ryder, and Johnny, and finally, on to me. The sound coming from the crowd is deafening, and the excitement works its way through me. When my spotlight comes up, I squint out at the crowd and my eyes settle on someone standing near the stage. I must be drunker than I thought. Why would Alex be at our show?

She looks almost exactly like she did when I first saw her in the park all those years ago. We were fourteen, and when I saw her staring at me with her green eyes I was hooked. That was the day I fell in love for the first and only time in my life. It still hurts a little when I think that she just left Fallbridge, and me, without looking back. I wish I could say that she wasn't the reason I moved to Westborough when I turned eighteen, but I'd be lying. I always hoped I would find her somewhere, even if she ghosted me when she fled Fallbridge. She was grieving the loss of her parents, so it's not as though I blamed her for wanting to forget Fallbridge and everyone who lived there.

Shit still hurt, though.

I blink out of my memory and try to focus on her in the crowd, but the spotlight's up and I can't find anyone who looks like her. Must've been my imagination because all that's out there now is the usual, under-dressed, and overly made-up groupies who normally line the front row at our shows. Yeah. I was definitely seeing something that wasn't there.

I shake my head to get myself back in the game. We have a show to put on.

"Good Evening Westborough! We are Sleeping Dogs, and we are so happy to be here for this, the last night of our tour. You guys sure know how to welcome us home." The guys transition into the first song on our set list from the messing around they've been doing and we get the show underway. "This is Youthful Memories," I announce, forcing my band to switch gears. *This song* is always a crowd favorite. Nostalgic feelings with a hard rock vibe. I wrote it about Alex, after the sadness from our breakup lessened and I could face the memories and feel how big my love for her really was. It always hurt, but at some point, the memories became a buoyant force in my life and I celebrated what we had, instead of dwelling on what I lost.

It also wasn't the first song we had on the set list for tonight. We were going to play something from a more recent album, but after imagining Alex in the crowd, I somehow introduced Youthful Memories without even meaning to. Good thing the guys are professionals and can transition into any song. After my trip down memory lane, I have a feeling I'll be changing the set list more than once tonight.

9

Irish Coffee and Dirty Thoughts

Alex

"THAT'S ALL I NEED to do for now. Want to sneak out and catch a little more of the show?" Becca puts her camera bag down behind the bar and comes over to the big armchair I'm sitting in. "He won't be able to see us, and it could be fun to see him in action."

Truthfully, I'd spent far too many hours imagining what it would be like if we met again, but I never thought it would be backstage at his huge fucking rock concert. I assumed we'd be on more level ground. Now he's an enormous star and I cook food for moderately rich assholes. Not exactly what I'd call running in the same social circles.

But I suppose it can't hurt to look.

"Alright, let's go," I say, walking in the opposite direction, straight to the bar. "Let me top off my coffee again." I twist the top off the whiskey and fill up my cup. It has to be at least half whiskey by now, but I need the fortification. "Promise you won't let me do anything stupid tonight?"

Becca laughs. "Who are you calling stupid, babe? Connor?" Haha, she thinks she's so funny. Except that's probably partly what I meant. It's hard to tell with the amount of whiskey already running through my system. "I promise I will watch you as best I can while I'm working. That's the best I can do."

"Good enough." I'm already out the door. "Let's go find that cute boy."

Becca has her work cut out for her. I am halfway to drunk and full of stupid ideas now. Let's hope she is as good a friend as I think she is because I doubt I'll be able to keep my mouth shut for long once Connor and I are in the same room. My mouth *or* my legs.

Damn, that got dirty fast. I think I like this whiskey. Too bad I know it's not the whiskey talking. If I say or do anything stupid tonight, I'll have no one to blame but myself.

10

All I Ever Want

Alex

THE SET IS GOING surprisingly well, considering I've changed a bunch of stuff around on the guys. Ryder came up to me once and gave me a little shove to let me know he was tired of me fucking with the set list, but as long as the crowd doesn't notice that anything differs from what we'd planned, everything is fine. Looking out at them, all I see is a seething mass of movement. I don't think they've noticed anything is up, which is good. I can't even differentiate one body from the next. The front row is still all groupies, and I still have no interest in a single one of them.

I will go home alone again tonight. And not for the first time since she disappeared from my life, I'll be falling asleep thinking about Alex, thanks to the doppelgänger I saw on the floor at the start of the show.

Luckily the crowd is crazy enough to keep my attention for the moment. Nights like tonight are why I do this. Being in front of a crowd this size is a rush and that's what I love about performing. I'm taking charge of the stage, whipping the crowd into a frenzy. I close my eyes and let the music take over, moving to the beat while I sing what I think is one of my favorite songs that I've ever written.

I kill myself with alcohol,
And sex and drugs and rock-and-roll

But through it all I really want is you,
You left me here without a call
But screw it, all I ever want is you
You're all I ever want
(all I ever want)
But what I really want
(what I really want),
Is you
I try to numb the pain away,
With too many girls and too many drinks
It never works, all I really want is you
All I ever want, Is you
All I ever want, Is you
Is you

As I finish up the song, a flurry of movement off stage left catches my attention. I could swear that I saw Alex over there, spinning around and running off backstage.

That's not possible though, is it? I'm worked up from thinking I saw her earlier. The whiskey must be hitting different tonight, causing me to hallucinate Alex everywhere I look. All I see now when I look into the wings is a dark-haired woman with full-sleeve tattoos and a camera. It's not too hard to guess that she's the photographer Denise mentioned. It must be the combination of too many drinks, and the nostalgia brought on by adding the Alex-inspired songs into the setlist.

Of course, that doesn't explain the reason I added those songs in the first place; the Alex look-a-like that I saw in the crowd as the lights came up onstage.

Ahh, never mind. I'm sure it was the drinks.

There's no way Alex would be here tonight. Not after all these years.

11

Crazy Stalker Ex-Girlfriend

Alex

THE LYRICS OF THAT last song are reverberating through my head as I turn and run away from the stage. Becca tried to grab my arm as I turned around, but I couldn't stand there and listen anymore. That song feels too personal. I run down the back hallway, straight back into the room where Becca left her equipment, directly to the bar, where I grab the whiskey, open it up, and take a long drink right from the bottle.

"You like *All I Ever Want* that much, do ya?" It's the security guard from earlier, the one who showed us to this room. "It's so good you need to chug whiskey straight from the bottle. I'm sure it will please Connor that his words have affected someone like this." He's messing with me, I think. I can hear him chuckle under his breath, anyway.

"You followed me?" Shit, am I in danger here? Am I reading this situation all wrong? Is this guy going to do something? He's like six and a half feet tall and probably weighs around three hundred pounds, all of it is muscle. He even has a scary-looking tattoo on his shaved head. If he wants to hurt me, I'm sure there won't be much I can do about it, even with all the self-defense training my Pops has given me. And I'm sure the music from the stage is too loud for anyone to hear me if I scream back here.

Maybe running back here alone was a bad idea.

"Yeah, it's my job. Need to make sure you're not setting up hidden cameras or anything, you know?" He gestures around the room. "Sometimes crazy shit happens backstage and it would be bad for the band if that stuff got out to the press."

"Oh... shit." I put down the whiskey bottle. "Sorry, I didn't even think of that. I couldn't listen to any more of that song. I figured it would be easier to come back here than to go outside."

"Plus, the whiskey is here." He laughs. "It's fine. I figured I'd be back here tonight anyway since Denise said you guys would need to set up for the photo shoot. I didn't realize you'd get done so quickly, is all. And I really didn't expect you'd go out to watch some of the show and then run right back. Seemed a little suspicious."

"Sorry about making you chase me; I promise I have no ill intentions." I relax a little since it seems like he's not interested in hurting me. I walk to him and extend my hand. "I'm Alex. I'm not *actually* a photographer; I'm here helping my friend Becca, the real photographer." I laugh a little.

"Devon," he says, shaking my hand. "I am *actually* security, but I work for the band, not the venue."

"Alex, here you are. What happened? Did that song hit too close to home? Do you think it was about-"

"Becca, meet Devon. He works security for the band." I'm trying to tell her to shut up with my eyes. "Devon, this is my friend Becca, the actual photographer I was telling you about."

Devon politely reaches out and shakes hands with Becca.

"Hello, Becca."

"Hi," Becca says to Devon before turning to me. "So, are you okay?"

"Yes, Becca, I'm fine." I grab the whiskey from the bar again, throwing what I hope is a conspiratorial wink in Devon's direction. "I was thirsty." I punctuate that by taking a long swig from the bottle. "Good thing I'm not driving tonight." I laugh while I sway a little on my feet.

"And good thing I don't really need an assistant to help with taking photos, because you appear to be well on your way to shit-faced." Becca laughs at me and adds, "Is this taking your mind off the whole Derek thing?"

"Oh shit, is the boyfriend not happy you're hanging out backstage with rockstars? I wouldn't worry about that. The boys are pretty well-behaved these days, mostly. The only one you'll need to watch out for is Ryder. And honestly, you're a little too 'normal' for Ryder's tastes. He likes his women a little more, uh, 'available' looking." Devon looks a little uncomfortable telling us that last part. Poor guy.

I bark out a laugh. "You mean he likes them to look like they're giving it away?"

"Yes, exactly like that! Of course, with Ryder, they usually are giving it away. But your boyfriend has nothing to worry about. There are more than enough half-naked women waiting to throw themselves at Ryder after the show. I guarantee you'll be safe." Devon is trying to reassure me, but it's reminding me that Derek—and pretty much every other boyfriend I've ever had, let's not forget—chose someone over me. Now it seems like this Ryder guy wouldn't even look at me twice.

Maybe that's my problem? Am I not sexy enough? Or do I wear too many clothes? I pull out the neck of my shirt so I can look down the front of it. Doesn't look like too many clothes today, with the no bra thing. I chuckle a little, and Devon and Becca both give me strange looks.

"That's nice of you, Devon, but it's actually 'cheating ex-boyfriend' problems that Alex was having. But I think that's now been replaced by 'long lost first love' problems. Isn't that right, Alex?" I guess she didn't get the hint earlier that I didn't want her talking about this in front of Devon. You know, the hint where I flat out said I didn't want her to say anything.

"Shut up," I hiss at her. "You're going to give the band's security guy the idea that I'm some kind of crazy stalker."

Devon looks at me suspiciously, but then I see a look of comprehension cross his face. "So, Alex is a nice name," he says, the hint of a smile taking over his lips. "I've heard some stories of a girl named Alex. Something about meeting in a library park and convincing a certain lead singer to share his voice." He gives me a knowing smile. "What a strange coincidence that you share that name, don't you think?"

How long has Devon been working for these guys? I moved away from Connor twenty years ago. There's no way I was a topic in a recent conversation. I think I'm freaking out again. My heart is beating too fast and I'm having a hard time getting enough breath in my lungs. Maybe I'm dying? That might not be so bad. It would save me the trouble of dying from embarrassment later.

"I promise you, I didn't know he was here. I'm still not sure I'm sticking around here long enough to see him. I would die if he didn't recognize me and I can't take that chance." My words are coming out faster than I ever thought possible. "I promise I'm not some sort of crazy stalker ex-girlfriend."

Devon laughs, "Chill, girl. I know you're not nuts. You're too freaked out for that. Let's go catch the rest of the show and you can decide whether you're staying right before he comes off stage." He puts his arm around my shoulder and starts leading me away from the bar. "So tell me about this cheating ex. Do I need to go break someone's legs?"

Becca jumps in, "Ha! Alex has already taken care of it. You should have seen her break the umbrella over his ass. It was brilliant!" She laughs and pretends to swing a bat. Devon even chuckles. "Plus, you'd have to get in line. Her Pops has first dibs on any asshole that Alex doesn't take care of herself."

"Glad my terrible loss can bring you so much joy." I pretend like I'm about to cry and Becca stops laughing and looks guilty for half a second before I add, "That was my favorite umbrella." I break into laughter, too. It's probably more than a little fuelled by whiskey, but it feels good to laugh at the situation.

Devon laughs louder at this admission. "Must've been a great umbrella."

"Right? You get it." I stumble a little, bumping into Devon. "It was a ladybug. Red with black polka dots... well, you know what a ladybug looks like, I'm sure."

He laughs some more, and Becca is wiping tears from her eyes.

"Okay girls, let's get you back to the stage to watch some more of the guys' performance. And if I were you, Alex, I'd listen to the songs closely. I think you'll be surprised at what you hear."

Yeah, that's what I'm afraid of.

12

Naked Girls in the Bathroom and Finally Coming Home

Connor

"GREAT SHOW GUYS," I yell over the sounds of the crowd as we wait offstage. "Sorry I fucked with the set list so much. I guess I'm feeling off because I let myself get my hopes up about my family finally coming to a show." I don't really feel like telling them the real reason I changed things. Saying that I thought I saw Alex in the crowd sounds stupid even when I say it in my head.

"Yeah, that was pretty messed up, dude," Ryder says without even a hint of annoyance in his voice. "If I wasn't so amazing, it would have been hard to adjust. Good thing I'm the god of guitar that I am or—"

"Fuck off, Ryder," Johnny interrupts. "We all handled it fine. Plus, it was kind of fun to wing it. A little spontaneity for a change." He turns to look at me. "Don't worry about it Connor, we all have off days. It was an interesting way to finish the tour, at least."

We all take a moment to listen to the crowd's nearly deafening roar. I haven't been timing it, but it feels like it's been five minutes of cheering at least. At least they appreciate what I do, even if my mother has no interest in me.

Shit. Why'd I have to go back to that depressing line of thinking? I was feeling pretty good before I let that thought sneak in.

"Well? Should we go out and do a couple more songs?" Getting back out there should bring my good mood back, plus the crowd expects it. I don't know why every band runs offstage and pretends like they won't come back for a few more songs unless the crowd cheers loudly enough. They always do, and we always come back out. I suppose it's part of the whole show experience, though, and we want to give them their money's worth.

"Yes, definitely. But I'm picking the songs this time. And I'm not telling you what they are until we play. Let's go!" Ryder runs back onto the stage, leaving the rest of us standing there.

"Well, shit," Travis says. "I guess we'd better go out before he makes an ass of himself."

AFTER TWO ENCORES IT'S finally time to get these meet and greets over with, but first I need to take a piss. Too many drinks before the show, I guess. The guys go into the dressing room without me while I detour down the hall to the bathroom. I open the door, and I'm about to walk in when I see her. Fuck, how did she get in here?

"Hello sweetheart, what are you doing in here?"

"I was waiting for you, honey," she says, her eyes drinking me in while sending out over-the-top 'fuck me' vibes. She's standing there topless and pushing her obviously fake tits together, making a ridiculous pout with her inflated lips. A shudder runs up my spine. She's not unattractive, but she serves to remind me why I stopped hooking up with random women. At some point, they all look the same.

"Is that so?" She's completely drunk and not at all my type. Way too much makeup and way too few clothes. "And what's your name, sweetie?"

"It's Sasha, silly."

"Oh, yes, of course." There's something a little off about her, but it doesn't hurt me to be friendly right now. She lucked out and made it back here even though she shouldn't be. It's not her fault the guys and I don't really go for the groupie scene anymore. If we were another band, she'd be getting everything she wanted by now. "Devon?" I lean out the door and yell down the hall. Luckily, he was waiting outside the dressing room.

"Yeah, buddy?" he asks while jogging over. "You know I'm only security, right? It's not in my job description to hold it while you piss."

Hilarious.

"Yeah, good one," I deadpan. Opening the bathroom door the rest of the way, I motion for the already topless groupie to come out. "We appear to have a minor issue. Can you please escort the lovely Sasha here back to the lobby? She seems to have gotten lost backstage."

I grab a shirt from the bathroom counter, clearly hers, and slip it over her head. As she pushes her arms through, I take her hand and pass her to Devon.

From the look on her face, I don't think she expected that I would have her sent away from me before she got what she wanted. It's like these chicks haven't heard that I'm no longer in the groupie fucking game. Either that or they think they're going to change my mind and make me fall in love with them or something. I've seen way too many tits for that to work, doll.

"Oh, yeah. Sure thing, Connor." Devon smiles at the woman. After all, we still need to be polite to the fans, even if they have no sense of boundaries. "If you'll come with me, Sasha? I can have one of my team show you the way back to the lobby." He takes her elbow, firmly but gently, and leads her away from me.

"But, baby," she whines to me as Devon walks away with her. "When will I see you?"

"Make sure she makes it home alright, Devon. She seems a little out of it."

"You got it, man. And Connor?" Devon calls out to me. "Don't go into the dressing room until I get back, okay? I need to tell you about something first."

"Yeah, yeah," I call out as I'm closing the door. Will these people let me piss already?

After I'm done in the bathroom, I go into the dressing room without bothering to wait for Devon. I want to get the meet and greets over as quickly as possible. I'm sure whatever he needs to say can wait.

I keep my head down as I walk over to the bar, hoping to grab one more drink before I have to play the charming lead singer of Sleeping Dogs. All the people-pleasing and press shit is getting out of hand. And this event is being photographed candidly. I'll need at least one more drink to make it through with a smile on my face the whole time. I walk over to the bar and see that the whiskey isn't there.

"What the hell? Where's the whiskey?" I scan the room quickly to see where the whiskey got to. "You guys never drink whiskey, and it's not like I've had enough for you to hide the bottles on me now. Don't tell me this meet and greet is some kind of bullshit intervention."

"Oh shit, I'm so sorry," a voice comes from somewhere to my right as someone thrusts a whiskey bottle in my direction. "I was nervous, and I needed to fortify myself with many drinks. Um, here you go."

I reach out and grab the whiskey bottle, my fingers brushing against the fingers holding it out to me, and I feel a charge of tingly electricity shooting through my body, completely disorienting me. What the hell was that?

I look up to see who passed me the bottle and shocked me like that, only to have the air forced from my lungs as I look into the face of the most beautiful woman I've ever seen. Suddenly, my body jolts into the present and it feels like I've come home.

"Alex?"

13

I'm Totally Normal and Sane and—Wait. He's Wearing my Shirt?

Alex

"OH SHIT, I'M SO SORRY," I say to Connor, coming up to stand beside despite my earlier hesitation. I guess seeing him up close made my choice for me. How could I stay away when he's right here in front of me? I push the whiskey bottle toward his hand. "I was nervous, and I needed to fortify myself with many drinks. Um, here you go."

Shit. So much for staying out of the way and getting out of this unnoticed. Nice one, Alex.

Connor reaches out to grab the bottle before he even looks up. His fingers brush mine and I feel a tingling sensation that starts at my fingers and quickly travels throughout my entire body. He looks up into my eyes, and I feel like my soul slams back into my body. And here I didn't even know it was missing. Like I'd been wandering around lost and now I'm finally where I'm meant to be.

"Alex?" Connor looks at me like he's seen a ghost, almost as though he's not sure I'm real. I wonder if that's what I looked like in the crowd tonight when I first saw him. Before I ran away, that is. Damn, he's so much hotter than I remember. "Is it really you?"

"Um, so yeah. Funny story. I guess you go by Connor Ashley? Instead of Ferguson, I mean. I'm here with my friend Becca. That's her over there, the photographer." I gesture toward Becca as she points the camera at us, but I can't seem to stop talking. The words keep bubbling up and jumping out of my mouth before I can catch them. "Becca said you go by Connor Ashley now, and you don't use Ferguson at all. That's probably why I've never been able to find you online. Not that I've done that much creeping. Just like... a totally normal amount of creeping. Like the amount of creeping that a completely sane, totally normal person would do. Which I am. A totally normal, sane person, I mean. I'm sorry. I'm talking so much, I am a little drunk right now. How are you?" I don't even let him answer before I reach out and lift the front of his shirt, bringing my face down to inspect it more closely. Who is in control of this shit show? Because it sure isn't me right now. "Is that my shirt? It looks like my shirt." Shit. I do not sound like a totally normal, sane person right now. I sound completely insane. Fucking bonkers, actually, but I can't seem to stop. And also, I'm smelling his shirt like a crazy person. But Connor is smiling at me, so I can't be that bad, can I?

"And I think that's enough talking for you, Alex." Becca finally comes to my rescue, grabbing me shoulders and turning me away from Connor. "I need you to go into my bag and grab a new SD card, please. And take a second to calm the fuck down; you sound like a lunatic." She whispers that last part to me.

"I know I sound like a lunatic, thank you. Why didn't you stop me sooner? I smelled his shirt. God, he smells amazing. Shit. He's probably going to get Devon to throw me out of here for being such a weirdo." I feel like I'm whispering back to her, but from the looks I'm getting from everyone else in the room, I can tell they all heard me, too.

I stumble to Becca's bag and quickly find the new SD card she wanted, taking a couple of deep breaths before bringing it to her. I can feel Connor's eyes tracking me the entire time, almost like he's afraid to look away.

"It's okay Alex, I won't throw you out yet," Devon yells from across the room. "You convinced me earlier that you're a totally normal, completely sane person. Plus, I haven't cleared the room of rain protection and I can't take the risk that you'd come after me with an umbrella. I have a delicate heinie." And now Devon and Becca are both laughing at me again. Assholes.

Can't they see I'm having a crisis here?

"Alex." Connor has moved closer and practically breathes my name making my insides turn to goo. His gorgeous chocolate brown eyes are staring directly into my soul. Is it weird that I want to run my hands through his hair right now? Oh yeah, it's weird. Pay attention, Alex. Don't let his ridiculous good looks make you forget he ghosted you when you left. You need answers for that before you decide whether you can forgive him.

Connor leans in, reaching up with his hand to tuck away a strand of hair that's escaped from the loose bun I've tied on the top of my head. He leaves his hand where it is, cupping the side of my face, his thumb brushing my cheek, and I find myself leaning into his hand. The soft brush of his breath against my lips makes me shiver as he brings his mouth to my ear and whispers, "I can't believe you're actually here. I thought I imagined you. Did you like the show?"

Oh, holy hell. Talk about tingles. I can feel that right down in the lady parts. Did I say I wasn't going along with Becca's fuck a rockstar plan? Because that was a terrible decision.

I'm stunned stupid for a moment, unable to speak with him this close. I catch myself turning into his neck and inhaling his scent, right from the source this time. Fuck, he smells so good, like cedar and spices and sexy man. But then I remember we are in a room full of people and pull myself away.

"Oh yeah, what I saw and heard was great. But, um, I may have run away a little bit"—I pinch my fingers together and hold them up in front of his face—"when I saw it was you onstage." What the fuck, Alex, why did you say that? I am kicking my ass in my head. I need to get it together. But of course, instead of getting it together, I spew more unneeded information. "I was on the floor waiting for you guys to come out, but I didn't know it was actually you *you*, you know? And then I got chased right to the front by some fuckboy who wouldn't get the hint that I wasn't interested. I was stuck with a bunch of sexy looking chicks up there at the fence when I saw it was you. And then it seemed like you looked right at me and I panicked. So I turned, and I ran. I didn't want you to see me and think I was a crazy stalker groupie."

"You know what? I saw you, but then you were gone so fast I thought I was imagining you. And yet here you are, backstage, telling me how not crazy you are." His eyes are wide and his grin is threatening to take over. It almost seems like he's happy to see me.

It also feels like he might be poking fun at me. It's hard to tell because I'm pretty drunk and completely freaked out, so I look to Becca for confirmation. Yup, he's fucking with me, thank god.

"Yup." I nod enthusiastically, glad he finally understands. "Crazy stalker is one thing. Groupie is another animal entirely. I don't fuck dudes because they're famous." Shit, that was another dumb thing to say. Come on Alex, you're better than this. I'm usually witty and charming. Where is that Alex tonight?

Becca barks out a laugh. Looks like Devon is getting a chuckle out of it, too. And I hear more laughter from the other side of the room, as well. It's probably the rest of the band, but I'm not risking looking over there. I'm sure the alcohol and embarrassment have combined to turn me a lovely shade of red.

"Well, that's good to know. I guess it's safe to introduce you to my friends after all, now that I'm sure they're no competition for me," Connor tells me with a wink. He's so sexy I practically swoon right there. "Let me get this meet and greet over with, and then we can talk more. I think I need to know a little more about this umbrella story that Devon was talking about. Oh, and yes, this is your shirt."

Connor reaches over his head and pulls the shirt off in one smooth motion, handing it to me with another wink. He grabs a Sleeping Dogs shirt from a table full of merch and puts it on before heading over to join the rest of the band. I only had a second to look at his naked chest and back, but I know I need to see more. I'm not sure what exactly he does, but I can tell for sure that Connor works out. His lean body shows he has muscles in all the right places and I'm itching to run my hands all over them.

"Becca, what do I do now?" I whisper when I finally get my voice back. "Did you see that? How is he that hot? Shouldn't that be illegal? Is spontaneous combustion real? Because I'm pretty sure that's what's about to happen to me after seeing him shirtless a moment ago. Quick, get the fire extinguisher just in case."

Becca laughs at my rant. That's not helpful at all. Some best friend she is. Here I am, probably about to burst into flames, and she's laughing at me. That bitch. Good thing I love her.

"Hang out for a bit. It sounds like they want me to take some candid shots to help speed this along. And it seems Connor wants to 'talk' to you after this is all over." She uses air quotes for the word talk. "And lay off the whiskey. You sound un-hinged."

Yeah, I want to 'talk' to him too, my drunk, dirty mind says to me. Guess I found my way into the gutter after all.

No, Alex. You need to have a real talk with him about why he disconnected his phone and fell off the face of the earth as soon as you left town. Get out of the gutter!

"I won't desert you, though. But for god's sake, stop talking until you get a hold of yourself." Becca is talking to me but looking over at the band the entire time. Not that I blame her. They're all pretty attractive.

While I'm sitting, watching the band interact with their fans, I realize Connor looks so much more confident than he ever did when we were kids. He talks to everyone, takes selfies with them, signs whatever they want, and genuinely seems interested in their conversations. All the while, he continues to look over at me with a curious smile on his face. And every time he does, my heart speeds up and the butterflies in my stomach do a little dance.

14

Unfortunate Stories and More Running Away

Connor

WHEN THE MEET AND greet is over, I invite Alex and her friend to come with us to the bar for the after-party. I should have skipped it and taken Alex somewhere that it could be just the two of us, but I don't think she would have agreed to that. Not sure what I was doing back there when I let myself get close enough to kiss her, but I want to do it again, and I'd probably take it a lot farther if we were alone. I know that ripping off my shirt and giving it to her was probably a dirty trick, but I also know that she liked what she saw so I'm considering it to be one of those 'all's fair in love and war' sorts of things.

"So we finally get to meet the famous Alex. You guys dated when you were what? Fifteen ? sixteen ?" Ryder seems to be fascinated by my history with Alex. They all know that she is the girl behind most of my songs, the only one who's ever gotten close to me. It's kind of embarrassing to be thirty-five and have had one serious girlfriend. And for that to have been when we were kids. "Did you fuck?"

"None of your fucking business," I snap. "Like I told you before." Alex and I never slept together, but that's none of his concern. There's a reason I've never told them that, and that's because I could never break her trust that way. Even when I didn't think I'd ever see her again, I knew I couldn't betray her. "Now, can we move on to more important things? Like this umbrella thing Devon was talking about earlier? Why would he be concerned for the well-being of his delicate heinie?" I change the subject as the server drops off the drinks we ordered, pulling a few bills from my wallet and dropping them on her tray.

We're hanging out at Rough Mix, the bar we used to play in when we were starting out with Sleeping Dogs. We like to come back here when we're in town, and tonight's no exception. We owe a lot to Bill, the owner, and we do whatever we can to help him when we're here. Not that he wants to accept our help, we usually have to force it on him.

"Ha! I can tell you all about that." Alex's photographer friend jumps up from her spot beside Johnny. Becca reminds me a little of Johnny, actually. They have a similar vibe, with all the tattoos. Turns out what I'd thought was a design on her shirt earlier is actually a full chest piece. Johnny's upper body is completely covered in tattoos, although he's not currently showing it off.

"Becca, no!" Alex looks a little embarrassed.

"It's okay Alex, I'll be nice," Becca continues with the story. "So Alex's boyfriend—"

"Wait," I interrupt. "You have a boyfriend?" I look at Alex, but she's avoiding my gaze. She is clearly attracted to me. Does she feel guilty about that because of a boyfriend? I'd like to say I'll be an honorable guy and step back, but fuck that dude. Alex walked into my life again tonight, and I know I won't be able to watch her walk away again. She's mine now, whether or not she has a boyfriend.

Becca shushes me. "Quiet dude, it's story time." She goes on, "So anyway, Alex's boyfriend, Derek, was balls deep in some chick when Alex came home from work today. Of course, Alex didn't know this when she got there. She thought someone had broken in because the door wasn't locked, so she called me for backup and grabbed the umbrella to use as a weapon before investigating the apartment. Except while she was looking for the burglar, she realized what was actually happening."

I'm only half listening to the story because I'm too busy looking at Alex. She has the same dark blonde hair that I remember, and I bet if she let it down, it would go all the way down her back in soft waves. She's not overly made up at all. If I had to guess, I'd say she wasn't wearing make-up, but I saw her put something that smelled like vanilla on her lips. I'm playing with the loose little curls on the back of her neck and thinking about how I'd like to taste those vanilla lips when I feel her tense up suddenly. I drop my hand, thinking I'm the one making her uncomfortable until I turn my attention back to what Becca is saying and realize that's what has Alex freezing up.

"So Derek is doing this girl doggy style, pumping away, totally oblivious to anything around him." She humps the air, demonstrating the guy's erratic rhythm. "He's making some truly disturbing and horrible grunting noises, too. Not that there's anything wrong with being vocal during sex, but this guy sounded like he belonged on the farm, not in a bedroom."

No wonder Alex is tense. This is probably a really uncomfortable story to listen to, especially after having lived through it just today. And if Becca's reenactment is at all accurate, it's likely been a long time since Alex had any good sex. My mind flashes an image of how I plan to fix that as soon as possible, involving Alex with no pants and me using my mouth and hands to bring her to orgasm. My dick loves my plans so much that I have to rearrange myself in my pants. Good thing Alex's attention is on Becca.

"I get there right as Alex sneaks in and busts an umbrella, a cute little ladybug umbrella right off of Derek's ass, as he's coming in this strange chick!" Becca actually has tears in her eyes because she's laughing so hard. How can she be so callous about this? She's talking about Alex's boyfriend cheating on her, something that happened today. If she's her best friend, shouldn't she be more concerned? "Derek's all 'ugh oh yeah baby' obliviously thrusting away, and suddenly he's squealing on the floor."

Strangely enough, Alex is also laughing now. Why would she laugh at finding her boyfriend cheating on her, let alone finding out just this afternoon? I have a feeling there's a lot about Alex I don't know.

"So I start cheering, 'ahhhhhhh, ahhhhhh, ahhhhhhh'." She puts her hands up to her mouth as a makeshift megaphone and starts making crowd noises. "And then I'm like, 'it's a home run!' and start going around the room like I'm running bases, picking up the chick's clothes as I go." She finally sits down again; I guess she's done with the show-and-tell portion of the story. "The chick is trying to cover herself up while screaming at Derek. I guess she didn't know he had a girlfriend. Meanwhile, Derek's on the floor crying. He's babbling about how he's sorry and all that stuff. And get this, the chick actually stopped and apologized to Alex on her way out."

"But did she mean it?" Ryder is speaking up now. "She probably didn't want any of the slugger's wrath turned on her." He leans over the table and fist bumps Alex. Good, at least I know the guys understand this situation was all that tool's fault, and not Alex's. They seem pretty impressed she took revenge immediately like that. Fuck, I'm turned on at the thought of her showing that asshole Derek that she won't take shit from anyone.

"See, that's what I thought at first too, but then I watched her kick him in the balls and then knee him in the face when I went out to grab the boxes I brought to pack up Alex's stuff."

Becca throws her head back against her seat, she's rocking back and forth holding her stomach, her laughter reaching uncontrollable heights. Alex is next to me in the booth and when I look to my left, I see her head is down and her shoulders are shaking a little. Shit, is she crying? No, no, no. She's more upset about this than she lets on. How can I fix this? Right as I'm about to pick her up and carry her somewhere quiet so I can take care of her, a huge peal of laughter suddenly bursts out of her mouth, followed immediately by a huge gulp of air. As soon as she has enough air, she starts hysterically laughing, matching Becca for intensity and volume, if not physical movement. She's trapped in the booth by Aiden, but if she were on the end, it wouldn't surprise me if she fell onto the floor with how hard she's laughing.

Both girls laugh until they're clutching their stomachs, muttering complaints of not being able to breathe. The insanity lasts several minutes, during which the guys and I all look at each other, trying not to laugh too hard ourselves. It seems like Alex is really okay, but I don't want to seem insensitive by laughing too hard. She tensed up at the start of the story, after all. I'm sure it hurts more than she's willing to show.

"So, Alex." I turn and look at her while speaking. "You seem pretty okay for finding out about this today. Are you? Okay, I mean." Reaching out, I take her hand and lace her fingers with mine. Now that she's beside me, I can't stand not touching her. Hell, I don't even know if I'm going to let her go ever again. She's clearly attracted to me, too, but is that all it is for her?

She turns and opens her mouth to answer me, but Becca speaks loudly, getting everyone's attention again.

"Oh, she's totally used to this," Becca says, and I feel Alex freeze up again beside me. "This has happened to her before." Shit, Alex is nearly vibrating now. Her prior good humor has been replaced with what looks like rage. I can see the death glare she's shooting in Becca's direction. I don't blame her; it sounds like a pretty personal anecdote to be sharing with virtual strangers.

"I think that's probably enough of story time, Becca," Alex doesn't exactly sound angry, but her voice is a little too calm. "These guys don't need to hear this, you know?"

I was right. This information is not for the new friends' ears.

"Wait. This isn't the first time?" Johnny says this directly to Becca, obviously not picking up on how Alex is feeling about her personal life being discussed like this. I try to catch their eyes to tell them to shut up, but they've turned toward each other now, oblivious to the rest of us at the table. I wonder what that's all about.

"Not at all." Becca really needs to shut her mouth. I can feel Alex growing tenser by the second. She's practically frozen in her seat. "She's nearly into the double digits with cheating boyfriends." Becca waves her hand dismissively while taking a sip of her drink.

What the fuck? How is that even possible? I can't even hide the shock on my face. I can't believe one guy would ever cheat on Alex, let alone several. Where's she been all these years that these assholes keep finding her?

Alex springs into action, shoving Aiden out of the booth. "Okay cool, yeah. Thanks for the drink, Connor. It was really nice seeing you again. Nice to meet all of you." She gives the guys a brief wave as she slides over and gets up out of the booth. "I need to get going, though. I have work tomorrow. Maybe we can do it again sometime." And with that, she's disappearing into the crowd and moving toward the exit. I immediately get up to follow her, throwing a look of disbelief at Becca and Johnny.

No. No, no, no. I can't lose her again.

"What the fuck, guys?" I say over my shoulder.

I run to the door, but I don't see Alex anywhere. Becca talking about her past seemed to really upset her, more than the story about catching her boyfriend cheating today, and I need to see if she's alright. I can't let her go again. I didn't even talk to her much tonight, and since I first saw her after the show, that's all I've wanted to do. Becca chased her away before I even had time to get her number. I should have taken her somewhere private, after all.

Shit! I think that's her. I see her up the street, getting into a cab. I break into a run, but the cab pulls away from the curb before I can even get close.

FUCK! I lost her.

Becca has already left by the time I get back to our booth in the bar; she must've snuck past me as I was chasing the cab. The guys say she grabbed her stuff and left right after I ran after Alex, saying something about learning to keep her big mouth shut. And to make matters worse, Johnny didn't get Becca's number. I assumed he would have, since they seemed to hit it off. I guess she'd run out just as fast as Alex, so he didn't get the chance, either.

Now I have no way of finding Alex.

It's like we're sixteen, and I've lost her all over again. This time, though, I'm going to find her. I have to. Because seeing her tonight has made me happier than I've been in years, and I refuse to let that go without a fight.

15

Hangovers, Pops, and Pizza

Alex

I wake up the next morning to the sound of someone try-ing to knock down my door. Wait, no, that's the banging in my head. Shit, I am way too old to be drinking the way I did last night. I got home and had downed another four shots of whiskey before Becca walked in not fifteen minutes after me. We had a good talk. She apologized for getting carried away, and for not listening when I told her to stop talking about my past, and we're all good now. Being best friends for twenty years trumps being a dick for five minutes.

But she better not do it again.

Now if the marching band that's taken up residence in my head could fuck off, I'd be golden.

"Hey girl, sorry to wake you, but I thought you said you have to go to work today?" Becca pokes her head in the door, looking like she's still feeling sheepish about blabbing my business to the guys last night.

Huh. Looks like someone was trying to knock down my door after all. Okay, she was probably knocking normally, but my hungover ass experienced it as a loud banging.

The guys. That's another problem. I wanted to talk to Con-nor more, but I left in such a hurry I didn't get that chance. Af-ter hearing about my track record, he probably wasn't feeling it anymore, anyway. Hell, I was probably drunkenly hallucinating the flirting he was doing at the meet and greet. It was only his rockstar persona coming out. But then why did he invite you out? Ugh, shut up brain. I can't deal with you right now.

"Yeah." Holy shit, my mouth is dry. I smack my lips and wiggle my tongue in my mouth to get some saliva moving, immediately repulsed by the taste of my breath. "I have to work at noon. Why? What time is it now?" I need water and medication. And maybe a bucket.

Scratch that.

Definitely a bucket.

I jackknife out of bed, ignoring the increased pounding in my head, and do and stumble to the bathroom as fast as my wobbly legs will take me. I barely make it to the toilet before I'm puking up everything I drank last night. And everything I've ever eaten in my life from the looks of it.

"Ew, gross. Let me grab you some water." Becca runs to the kitchen to grab a bottle of cold water from the fridge. The angel also brings me some Tylenol while she's at it. "Here, take these, too. And make sure you drink the entire bottle of water. It will help."

"Oh my god, thank you so much." I lean back against the nice cool bathtub and take the pills and water bottle from her hands. "So, what time is it?"

"Yeah, about that. It's already eleven-forty-five. You are going to be so late if you don't start running, like, right now." Becca looks amused at the thought of me running right now, and rightfully so, considering I can't stand up at the moment. I may even have to crawl my ass back to bed after I' finish puking. "Can I do anything to help?"

"Shit. Can you grab my phone, maybe? I'm calling in sick. They can order food today. I'm sure they'll survive." It's probably not the best idea, considering they already don't like me, but there's no way I can even look at food right now, let alone prepare it. Even thinking of having to touch raw meat has me throwing up again. Oh, look. I have some food left to puke up, after all. I weakly stretch up and flush, grabbing some toilet paper to wipe my mouth while I'm at it.

"Oh, sweetie." She frowns at me. "I'll get your phone and leave it here on the counter for when you're ready. I'd call soon, though. It's pretty much noon now." Becca goes to my room and grabs my phone for me. I pick it up and dial my client right away.

"Alex." She picks up on the first ring. "Why aren't you here yet? We're having people over this afternoon and you need to prepare the food."

"That's actually why I called, Mrs. Johnson. I'm very sick today and I won't be able to make it in. I'm sorry for the late notice. I wish I'd known in advance that you were having company though, I would've begun preparing everything yesterday." Of course they would plan a party and expect me to cater without telling me first. Too bad the thought of preparing food throws me into another round of loud retching.

There is good news, though. There's no way there's anything left in my stomach now. From the looks of what's in the toilet bowl, I'm going to need to take some new Tylenol, though. The last ones didn't even get the chance to dissolve.

"This is completely unprofessional and totally unacceptable, Alex. I will consider this your resignation. Your last check will be mailed to you. Do not come back." And she hung up on me. Okay, then. I guess I also need to find a new job now.

"Awesome news, Becca," I yell out. Huh, when I yell into the toilet, it makes an echo. "Hello, -lo, -lo, -lo." I laugh at the echo that greets me from the porcelain bowl.

"What the fuck are you doing?" Becca is back in the doorway now, looking at me funny. That's fair. I am yelling 'hello' into the toilet and laughing after all.

"The bowl makes my voice echo," I explain, even though it should be obvious. "But I have good news. I don't have to work today after all. Turns out I'm fired." I chuckle about that. Maybe I'm still drunk? That could explain why everything is so funny. "So my calendar opened up. What are we doing today?"

"Oh Alex, that sucks. But I gotta say, you don't seem very broken up about it." She laughs and cocks an eyebrow.

"You know I hated that family. The husband was a dirty old pervert who 'accidentally' brushed against me too many times. I wouldn't have lasted too much longer, anyway. At least being fired now means I won't have any assault charges to look forward to." I've never actually been charged with anything, but I have used violence to solve problems before and it's really only a matter of time. I turn and use the side of the bathtub to help push myself off the floor. If I keep my head tilted a little, it doesn't pound as hard. That's a pleasant discovery. "So, should we go out and celebrate?"

"Raincheck?" Becca asks. "I have a wedding to shoot today, and they want me there for the entire day. I have to stay and shoot the entire reception, too. It's a big paycheck, and the couple is very well-connected in Westborough society. If I play my cards right, I could shoot every major wedding in the city next summer."

"Oh yeah, totally. That's no problem." I can't help but feel a little bummed. We sorted out our issue last night, but I wanted to talk some more about what happened—or more precisely, didn't happen—with Connor. But I suppose we can do that later. "I guess I can get started on my job hunt, then. Set up some interviews and stuff."

"Okay, awesome." Becca is checking all her camera bags. I didn't even notice that she was wearing one of her tailored suits already. This one is a medium grey color with a bit of a sheen to it, and she's paired it with a pastel pink shirt. The wedding must start soon if she's already dressed. "I need to be going now if I'm going to make it in time. I can text you later if I think I'll be home early enough to do something tonight, okay?" She doesn't even wait for my answer before walking out the door. She must really be in a hurry.

Guess I'll go see Pops later, then. But first I'm going back to bed. Thanks to my bitch of an ex-boss, I get some time to sleep off my hangover. This day is turning out to be not so bad after all.

WHEN I FINALLY GET up around dinnertime, my hangover is gone. In its place is that kind of ravenous hunger that can only follow a period of being violently ill. My stomach is growling so loudly I might scare the neighbors, so I go down to the pizza place on the next block and grab myself my favorite pizza (all the vegetables please, and yes, that includes broccoli, don't judge me). I also grab some ginger ale in case my stomach rebels again after the pizza. It's so hard to tell sometimes whether a hangover is truly gone. Better to be safe and have some ginger ale on hand.

Becca's neighborhood and I guess my neighborhood again now, too, is not as nice as the one I lived in with Derek. There's lots of graffiti, a little crime, and not a lot of green space. It's your basic big city block. Our apartment is in a well-maintained, small, four-story building in between a locksmith shop and an old boxing gym.

That gym belongs to my Pops. Pops is the person who showed me the miracle that is 'all the vegetables' pizza ('it's basically health food, Lexi Girl' he'd always say). He even had Tino, the owner of the pizza place, name it after me, which he was more than happy to do since he didn't want to be associated with creating what he considers a monstrosity.

After grabbing the pizza, I stop in at the gym to see if Pops is there and wants to share with me. Not that I really expect that he won't be there. He loves that place and is there from sunup to sundown every chance he gets.

When I came to live with him when my parents died, I spent a lot of time here, too. I graduated from high school by studying for all my tests in his office. I haven't been here much in recent years because the hours in my line of work are ridiculous and I haven't had a lot of time. It will always feel like home, though.

Nothing like the smell of sweaty fighters and heavy bags to bring on those feelings of nostalgia.

"Hey Pops," I yell as soon as I open the door, "You in here?"

"Lexi Girl," comes the gravelly reply from the ring set up in the far corner of the large gym space. "Give me five minutes and I'll be right there to squeeze you."

Pops branched out a few years back. Boxing was declining in popularity, and mixed martial arts was skyrocketing. Pops got in early, remodeled the gym, hired some MMA trainers to offer training in the fighting styles he wasn't familiar with, and has held his own against the bigger fight gyms that have opened up in the city. He's a savvy business owner underneath his gruff old man exterior, and he's probably my favorite person in the world.

I go sit up in the office on the second level. It's not really an office, more of a platform with a fence around it that allows him to keep watch over the entire gym, but it has a desk and a couple of chairs, so it's the best place to eat this pizza. Plus, there's no chance a fighter will walk by and drip sweat onto me or the pie. Win-win.

Pops takes exactly five minutes and then he's up in the office, lifting me out of my chair and squeezing the life out of me. For a seventy-five-year-old man, he still has a lot of squeezing power.

When I was a kid, he'd hug me so tight that I'd be forced to choke out, 'Pops, you're squeezing too hard,' before he'd let go. That's why we call them squeezes instead of hugs now. Every time he hugs me, he squeezes like he hasn't seen me in years, and it's one reason I love him so much. He's never let a minute go by without letting me know how much he loves me. Pops is my inspiration for how I want a man to treat me, but somehow I never find a man like him. Instead, I keep getting losers like Derek.

"Lexi Girl," he says, putting me back on the floor and taking a seat in a chair opposite me. He opens the pizza box and grabs a slice. "What brings you down to see your old Pops today?"

"Do I really need a reason to come see you, Pops?" I ask, grabbing a slice of pizza for myself. "I missed you. Oh, and I am living in the neighbourhood again..." I leave that hanging in the air, knowing he will pick up on it.

"Oh fuck, what did that little fucker Derek do?" Pops has always been very perceptive. Nothing gets by him.

"Oh, you know me, Pops." I try to make light of the situation because I know his heart is still soft and hurts for me every time a guy lets me down. "I can't be tied down to one guy. You know I gotta play the field. Living that ho life."

"So he cheated, huh?" He cocks an eyebrow and puts his pizza directly down on his desk before brushing the crumbs from his fingers. "Did you take care of it? Or do you want me to deliver a message?"

Leave it to my Pops to threaten violence against a man half his age. The funny thing is that he would actually do it, and he would come out on top of that encounter. Not that Derek was a complete wimp, but that Pops is still tough at his age. He's been training fighters for over forty years, and that has kept him in shape too.

"Nah, I'm good, Pops," I say around a mouthful of pizza. "I sort of caught him in the, uh, act, and may have destroyed my favourite umbrella when I found him. Side note: my batting skills are improving. Becca says I have a shot at the majors."

"Ha! Classic! That's good, kid. I'm proud of you." He pats me on the knee. "I don't know how a sweet girl like you keeps getting caught up with these jerks, but I'm so impressed that you don't put up with it. You deserve so much better. Speaking of—"

"No, Pops." I shut that down quickly. "I do not want you to set me up with one of your fighters."

"I wouldn't set you up with a fighter, Lexi Girl." Pops picks up his pizza and grabs a big bite. "Their cauliflower ears would make it too hard for them to hear you. But I have a nice kid in mind. He works out here when he's in town. He probably could be a fighter if he were serious, but I have a feeling he likes his job too much for that."

"Oh shit, that reminds me." I brace myself to tell him about losing my job today. "That grabby asshole's wife fired me today. I can't say I'm sad about it, but I will need a new job, so if you have any leads on anyone looking for a chef, put in a good word for me, would you? I can do excellent work with bulking or cutting plans for fighters."

"I'm not sad about it either." Of course he's not sad, he told me to quit ages ago. "You should've let me deliver a message to him when he grabbed you the first time. One of these days, I am going to deliver a message to someone who wrongs you. It's my right as your grandfather. It's completely unfair that you've denied me all these years." He actually pouts a little. Ever seen a seventy-five-year-old man pout? It's hilarious.

"I promise to come to you next time, Pops." Because let's be real. Something is bound to happen, especially if I ever let myself get involved with someone again. "Clients will always be off limits, but the next boyfriend who hurts me is all yours to do with as you will." I heave a sigh. "For now, though, I should get home to begin my search for new clients. Hopefully, I can find one that will need me all the time. I really don't want to juggle schedules again. And I really don't want to go back into restaurant work."

"Mike, you old bastard," someone yells from the front door. "I need to work out some frustration. Got time for some training?"

"You bet, kid," Pops yells back. "Go get warmed up and I'll be there in a minute."

We both stand to go and Pops picks me up in a giant squeeze again. "Come see me again soon, Lexi Girl. Let me know if you need anything while you look for clients. And I'll let you know if I hear of anyone looking, okay?"

"Alright Pops, will do." I turn and open the office door. "Love you," I say to him, before I turn and run down the stairs.

"Love you, Lexi Girl," he yells out as I push open the gym door and go outside.

I love visiting Pops. He always has my back. And now I have my confidence back. Time to make my computer my bitch. Searching for clients, here I come. Because finding another job is a problem I can solver, whereas finding Connor? Yeah, that one probably won't be so simple.

16

Close Calls and Beating Up Old Guys

Connor

"MIKE, YOU OLD BASTARD," I yell before the door is even closed behind me. "I need to work out some frustration. Got time for some training?"

"You bet, kid," he yells from somewhere in the distance. It takes a minute, but finally, I see him through the fence of the raised platform he calls his office. "Go get warmed up and I'll be there in a minute."

Going over to the ring in the corner, I strip down to my shorts and grab a weighted jump rope from the wall. Sweat is pouring off me before I allow myself to stop. Grabbing a seat on a bench, I wrap up my hands while I wait for Mike. The least I can do is protect my hands while I hit stuff today. I may not always play my guitar during shows, but I play when I'm writing new music. And now that the tour's over, and we're working on a new album, I will do a lot more writing.

"Alright son, you ready?" Mike is walking over to where I'm finishing wrapping up and he takes over for me. He grabs my gloves from my bag and helps me into them, fastening them for me. "So, you wanna tell me why you're all worked up and looking to fight?" he asks, while inspecting my gloved hands.

"You're usually a little more cheerful when you come in to train."

"Girl troubles, Mike. You know how it is." I try to sound lighthearted, but I fail miserably.

"Ha. Good one kid. I don't have any clue about the girl troubles a musician has. Too many to choose from? Crazy ones following you around? Got a kid somewhere you're just finding out about?" He shakes his head while laughing. "I don't think I would be much help with those. I only ever loved one girl in my life, and I married her as soon as she would have me. When she passed, I put that part of my life away. Until my granddaughter came to live with me, all I had was this gym. So yeah, girl troubles are not my area of expertise."

"It's actually none of those issues, Mike. I recently found my first girlfriend again and lost her before we really reconnected. And now I have no way of finding her. I don't know where she works or anything." I punch my fists together. "But enough about that. Let's get to training."

"You got it, kid." Mike gets up and goes to grab some pads. "And hey, if you decide you want to meet a good girl and settle down, let me know. My granddaughter keeps getting caught up with shitty guys and could stand to date a nice one for once."

"Good one, Mike." I chuckle a little. "She must date real assholes if I'm your idea of a good guy." I grin and start throwing punches in the air. First Alex, and now Mike's granddaughter. There must be a lot of assholes in this city if two nice girls like them keep getting caught up with them.

"Yeah, well, it's possible my standards are a little low." He barks out a laugh and holds up the pads. "Now get over here and let some of that frustration out. You'll feel better once you've beat up an old man for a while."

Fucking Mike. He always knows how to make me laugh. I knew it was a good idea to come to the gym today. "Alright, gramps, get ready. I won't take it easy on you. I don't care how old you are."

17

New Jobs and New Beginnings

Alex

MY JOB PROSPECTS ARE looking slimmer than I expected, as few people are looking for a personal chef right now. I was able to set up one interview, through a former client that I've remained friendly with. It's for a six-month contract, round-the-clock hours, seven days a week. I would have to live onsite for the duration. It sounds pretty intense, but the money is worth it. I need to make it through this interview and convince this woman that she wants to hire me. Because if I don't get this job, I'll need to go back to a restaurant kitchen. I'd rather go back to the handsy old guy with the past-her-prime trophy wife than that.

The address the woman gave me is in the nicest part of Westborough and as soon as I pull up to the house, it's clear I'm out of my element. I've worked in the homes of more affluent people before, but this one far surpasses any of them. It's beautifully designed modern architecture, with stark, sharp angles and enormous windows that I'm thankful I won't have to wash. It looks to be three stories high, surrounded by rock gardens with minimal flowers here and there. A place this nice no doubt has a pool around the back.

Now I *really* want this job.

"Hello. Alex Wilson?" The woman standing at the front door looks to be about my age, but she's so much more put together than I am. Long, straight, black hair frames her beautifully made-up face. She's wearing a vintage Guns n' Roses tee shirt with a leather pencil skirt, and she's topped the look off with bright yellow peep toe booties with a high platform wedge heel. Geez, can I be like her when I grow up? I look down at my cuffed, distressed boyfriend jeans, loose, white, v-neck t-shirt, long grey cardigan, and low-top black converse sneakers. If I didn't have my hair styled and a little makeup on, I'd look like I just rolled out of bed. She did say with was a casual meeting, right? Or was I hearing things?

"Hi. Yes, I'm Alex." I have to physically shake myself to get back to the present. "Are you Denise Lathan?"

"Sure am. Come on in and let's get started. This shouldn't take too long. It's more of a formality than anything. I've already contacted your list of former clients and looked over your qualifications, so I want to get to know you a little before I make my decision." She turns and gestures for me to follow her inside. "Let me show you the kitchen, since that is where you would do most of your actual work."

"Sounds good to me. I assume you already saw my list of kitchen requirements? Those items would be available if you offered me the position?" I mean, I can cook with pretty much anything, but I have preferences for cooking utensils and supplies. "I bring my knives with me, but the client usually provides everything else."

"Yes, that would be no problem," Denise tells me. "You'll find that the kitchen is very well appointed already. The last chef we employed was also very particular about equipment, and most of it is still here. You will also have a company credit card for grocery purchases and you could use that for any other equipment you might need."

"Alright. So what should we talk about? What would you like to know about me?" Usually, the client wants to discuss my requirements because it can be an enormous expense to buy all of that equipment at once, but she seems to have no issue with the expense. And since she said she already knew enough about me professionally, I'm a little confused about what this meeting is for.

"I need to get a feel for you and tell you some of the more sensitive aspects of the position. If we decide to go ahead, there will be some extra paperwork you would need to sign in order to protect my clients." Oh, she's hiring me on behalf of someone, not for herself, after all. Interesting. Now I'm even more curious about this job. "So how about for now you tell me a little about yourself."

"Um, yeah, okay. Sure. I grew up in a little town a few hours away from here, but when my parents died, I moved here to live with my grandpa. I was fifteen when they passed in a car accident and grandpa was the only relative who could take me in. He owns a gym on the other side of town, and that's where I spent most of my time until I graduated high school and moved out with my best friend. I decided on culinary school because I like to cook and I like to feed people, so it seemed like a perfect fit. So far, it's been great. I've had a lot of kitchen jobs as I was coming up in the industry, working my way up to running my own kitchen as head chef, but I was burning out, so I decided to move in a different direction."

"About five years ago, I transitioned to starting my business as a personal chef. I've had some great clients and some not-so-great clients, as with any other job, I guess, and now I am here." I smile to let her know that I'm done with my brief speech. "Is that kind of what you were looking for?"

"Mostly, yes. I can't really ask personal questions, legally, but is a live-in position something you could manage in relation to family and such? You wouldn't have to leave anyone behind in order to stay here for the duration of the contract? Your partner or spouse wouldn't be allowed to move in, unfortunately. We've found that people who are, uh, unattached have better luck with working out the length of the contract. We prefer not to have to find someone else in the middle of the time frame, but please don't assume you can't date. For security reasons, your dates couldn't come here, but you'll have a little time off to pursue your own interests elsewhere." Ahh, so this is more what she was looking for. She wants to know if I have a spouse or significant other, I would miss too much to live here.

"I only have my grandfather and my best friend, and I am more than able to live away from them. I also broke up with my ex because I caught him cheating, so there is no boyfriend in the picture either. And there is no possibility of reconciliation, just so you know. I would be fine to live here for six months and since I'm living with my best friend temporarily I could move in and start right away." Denise seems almost relieved to hear that I don't have a boyfriend which is a little strange I suppose but who am I to say?

"Great, that's great. A previous chef had to leave us when her boyfriend found out who my client and their friends were. He was jealous and couldn't handle having her around them."

Okay, now I'm really curious. Who is this client? Probably a famous movie star. Or a reality TV star. I hope it's not a politician. Not that I would turn the job down if it were. Even having a politician for a boss would be better than going back to a restaurant.

"You have officially piqued my curiosity, but I'm going to go out on a limb here and say that you can't tell me who this person is?" I'm impressed with myself for figuring this out. "Confidentiality and all that?"

"Yes," she laughs. "You're the first person who's figured that out before I got to this next part. In order to work here, you would be required to sign an NDA. Do you know what that is?"

"I think so," I say. I watch enough TV to know a little, at least. "Basically, it's a contract that says I have to keep my mouth shut if I don't want you to sue the pants off me?"

Denise chuckles. "That's the gist of it, yes. Because of the identity of my client, and the business that they do here, you may become privy to information that might harm my client's career or public image should it go public. The NDA says that you will not divulge information regarding anything you see and do here as it pertains to my client's private interests and activities." She is serious now. The ease with which she says this tells me she's had this conversation a lot, or she's a lawyer. Or both. Either way, it's obvious she's comfortable being in charge. "The identity of the client also cannot be divulged until you've signed the NDA and we complete a background check."

"Oh." Not knowing who I'm working for makes this decision more difficult. "Is there anything you can tell me about the environment, without telling me who this is, that can help me decide? I understand the need for privacy, but I don't want to agree without some notion of what my time here would be like."

"Of course." She seems pleased that I won't jump in with no knowledge. "I suppose you can guess that my client is very famous. They keep odd hours, so most of your work would happen later in the evening, or even in the middle of the night. They have occasional parties. They do work here, so the client's coworkers would be in and out at all hours as well. Often you would need to prepare food for them as well. If they know they will work extra long hours, they will let you know and are happy to eat food that you have prepared in advance. Aside from the fame, they are fairly laid back, as are the friends, so you wouldn't need to worry about any drama queen-type tantrums you hear about in gossip magazines. Does that help you?"

I smile widely, nodding. Whoever this person is, I think I need to take the job just to satisfy my curiosity. If it turns out Denise is downplaying how horrible they are, well, it's only six months. I'm pretty sure I can handle almost anything for six months. "That eases my concerns. If you are still interested, I would be happy to come on board."

"Perfect." Denise claps her hands together. "I will get the paperwork for you to fill out right now, and then you can go pack. We'll plan for you to move in this weekend. Barring any problems with the background check, you will start Monday."

She gets up and leaves me alone in the room. I guess I really do work here now.

I get up and start familiarizing myself with the kitchen while I wait for Denise to come back. I wonder what my room looks like. Might as well get right to the important stuff. I send a text to Becca.

Alex-I got the job. I'm moving out this weekend. Can you help? I'll supply the pizza and beer.

Becca- *I can't say no to that. At least this time the move is planned in advance lol.*

Alex- Bitch <3

18

Writing and Whining

Connor

"Denise called. The new chef doesn't start until Monday, which means we're on our own for food for the weekend. You guys want to order in? Or actually go to a restaurant or some shit?" I'm fucking around with one of the guitars I keep in my home studio, trying to work out a melody that's been stuck in my head. "I don't feel like going anywhere, so I say we send Devon out to pick up sushi."

"Fuck that," Ryder complains. "I am not eating raw fucking fish tonight. I want some proper food. Burgers and fries, pasta, a whole turkey dinner. Hell, I'd even eat sandwiches over sushi. I need something filling. I'm hungover, and I'm pretty sure I'm also starving to death."

"You're always hungover, dude," Aiden jokes from behind his drum kit before playing himself a little sting (ba-dum-tiss) to cap off the insult.

"You can fuck off, too," Ryder shoots back. He can't deny it, though. Out of all of us, he is the one who still does a lot of partying. He's all business when it comes time to write and perform, though. As long as he keeps his antics to his personal time, the rest of us don't interfere with it. When it becomes a problem for the band, we might have to talk to him, but for now, he has it handled. I worry about him sometimes, though. The rest of us seem to have grown up in the last twenty years, but he's stuck, and I don't know why.

"Okay, no sushi then," I concede. "What about pizza? I'll send Devon over to this locally owned place near my gym. It doesn't even have a name. The sign just says 'PIZZA' and it's this little hole-in-the-wall place. I finally tried it last time we were home, and it's the best pizza I've ever had."

"Sold!" yells Ryder. "Get me one with all the meat." He thinks for a second, then adds, "And another one with ham and pineapple. For dessert." Gross. I don't care what anyone says. Pineapple does not belong on pizza.

The other guys chime in with what they want and I call in the order before sending Devon out the door. He grumbles a little about being an errand boy, but we enjoy having him around so we find things for him to do even when we don't need security. He's our friend, and we'd have let him in the band if he'd had even a little musical talent. But he didn't, so we made him our security guy.

19

Bitches and Beer

Alex

"WELL, I GUESS THAT'S it for packing, then." I look around the room I've been living in for the last week. "Well, I guess it's a good thing I have only unpacked some clothes and toiletries. I probably could have moved into the other place right away and gotten out of your hair sooner."

I don't think Becca could roll her eyes any harder if she tried. "Oh yeah, it's been totally rough having a professional chef cooking for me. I can't wait for you to leave me to my disgusting frozen pizzas and old Chinese takeout. Now that's food."

"You know sarcasm is the lowest form of humor, right? So not only are you being kind of a bitch right now, but you are also not funny," I deadpan.

"Ha! I know my being a bitch is one of the main reasons you love me so much. And it doesn't matter if you think I'm funny. *I* think I'm funny and I laugh at my own jokes so..." She trails off and sticks her tongue out at me.

I'll give her that. She does laugh at her own jokes, a lot. Sometimes I laugh more at her laughing than I do at the joke itself. "You're right, you're not a bitch, Becca. You are selectively bitchy, and you've used it for my benefit when I'm around. It's kind of like a superpower that you use for the good of the people you care about."

"I knew you loved me." She throws her arms around me in a hug. "Now bring on the pizza and beer. You promised to feed me for my help with packing. It's not my fault you packed already."

"Nuh uh, I said pizza and beer to help me move. That has yet to happen. But..." I add slowly, "Since I have zero interest in cooking tonight, I will grab pizza for us. You go grab the beer since it's in the other direction and then we'll meet back here to feast. Deal?"

She sighs while pulling on her sneakers. "You drive a hard bargain, girl. But since I don't trust your taste in beer, I will agree to your terms. See you shortly."

"Bye," I say to the door as it closes behind her. I call down to PIZZA and place my order. Of course, I get the all-vegetable Lexi Girl, but I also get Becca's usual chicken with hot peppers, since she refuses to eat any of my pizza. She says that most of the vegetables I get don't belong on a pizza. She doesn't know what she's talking about, though. After all, who's the chef around here?

THE BELL ABOVE THE door jingles and draws my attention to a giant of a man who just walked into the pizza place where I'm currently waiting for my pizzas. What the hell?

"Devon?" Shit, maybe I can ask if Connor wants to see me without being too obvious. Of course, I put little stock in how smooth I can be. I've ended up with my foot in my mouth enough times to know I am not a smooth person.

"Alex." He comes over and stands next to me. "What's up? What a crazy coincidence. What are you doing here?"

"Oh, you know," I lean back on my stool a bit, "Chillin' like a villain." Fuck, that sounded dumber than I intended. I didn't quite put my foot in my mouth; instead, I made myself sound like an idiot. Stupid Alex. Get it together.

"Ha! Yeah, I guess that was a dumb question, hey?" Lucky for me, he thinks I was calling him out on asking why I'm at a pizza place instead of being a dumbass. "I guess you're here for pizza, considering this is a pizza place. At least that's what I assume from the sign out front that says 'PIZZA' in three-foot-tall letters."

I chuckle. "I'm here picking up an order for me and Becca. She was helping me pack because I'm moving this weekend. As is customary, I promised pizza and beer for her help." I explain before jerking my thumb over my shoulder. "She's down the street grabbing the beer because I have terrible taste. At least that's what she thinks." I make a face and roll my eyes a little, letting him know that she's wrong about that.

"Well, from what I recall," he says, nudging me with his elbow, "you're a little more partial to whiskey, anyway." He laughs a little when I groan.

"Ugh, don't remind me. I have never been more hungover." Maybe now's my chance to sneakily work Connor into the conversation without sounding like a stalker. "You missed it, but after you left, I hung out with the guys at the after-party for a bit and had another drink. Then I went home and drank all the whiskey in my apartment." I leave out all the embarrassing bits, like the stories Becca was telling about everyone cheating on me.

He barks out a loud laugh. "Yeah, that'll do it. I'm sad I missed it. I had to go help my best friend's little sister with a problem she was having."

"It gets worse," I add. "I was so sick when I woke up that I had to call in sick to work. For the first time ever, I might add.

And they fired me." I snicker. I didn't know how ridiculous it sounded until I said it out loud. "Luckily, I hated that job. I needed to find something different, anyway. Getting fired gave me the push I needed to do it sooner."

"Oh shit," he laughs. "So I guess you could say that this was one of those rare times that getting a hangover was a good thing?"

"Yeah." I chuckle. "I hadn't thought of it like that, but it did me a favor for sure. I already have a new job lined up. That's why I'm moving this weekend. Who'd have thought a hangover could be a blessing?" He looks toward the counter where the owner, Tino, has put a stack of pizza boxes all marked 'Devon'. He must be picking up for all the guys. I count ten pizzas, and with the way Tino loads them, each pizza feeds at least three people. I wonder if they know what they're getting themselves into.

"Looks like those are mine," he says, looking back at me. "It was nice to see you again."

"Yeah, you too." I'm a little disappointed that I didn't get any hints that Connor wants to see me, but I still have a great idea for Devon. "Hey, want to try the best pizza this place has? It's named after me."

"Oh, yeah?" He raises an eyebrow in interest. "I don't have much time, though. I really ought to get back."

I look over at the counter where Tino has put my pizzas. Both say 'Lexi Girl.' "You're in luck," I say. "Mine is ready now, too. Take it. I'll get Tino to make me a new one. I practically live next door, so I can run back and grab it after I bring Becca her pie."

"I couldn't take your pizza. Are you sure?"

"Positive," I say, while grabbing one of my pizza boxes and checking to see if it's the right one. "Tino, can you make another Lexi Girl, please? I'm giving mine to my friend here." I place the box on top of Devon's stack and grab half. "Let me help you bring these out so you don't lose any."

"Hey thanks," Devon says. "The guys would be so pissed if I dropped a pizza. They each like something different, and they're not good at sharing." He laughs. We carry our boxes outside and walk to where he parked his truck. He opens the back door and motions for me to put my stack down first.

"That's funny." I set the stack of boxes on the seat of his truck and then he puts his stack down next to it. "Well, tell everyone I say hi." That's as close as I get to Connor, I guess. Fuck. I should ask about him. It's easy. Just open my mouth and say, 'can you give Connor my number?'. Nothing to it. But I can't make my mouth say the words. I'm still stuck thinking that he probably doesn't want to see me.

"Okay, I'll do that." He gets into his truck and starts it up. As he's about to pull away, he rolls down the window and yells at me as I'm going back in, "We'll let you know how the Lexi Girl pizza is." Then he drives away with a wave.

Yeah, sure. Let me know. How are you going to do that? None of you have my number. And I'm the idiot who just missed my last chance to give it to you. I sigh. It was nice while it lasted; I guess I might as well go back to swearing off men. Clearly, I was misreading the Connor situation. He is a rockstar, after all. Flirting is basically his job.

20

Weird Pizza and Amateur Stalking

Connor

"Pizza!" Devon pokes his head into the studio, letting us know he's back with food.

I don't allow food in the studio, so we all get up and go to the kitchen to eat. Devon has already opened up all the boxes and taken plates out of the cupboard. Everyone takes a plate and then we all start grabbing slices.

"What. The fuck. Is this?" Travis is looking into one box with disgust on his face. "Is that... broccoli? And cauliflower? What the hell is this pizza?"

Devon laughs. "Oh yeah, that's called the Lexi Girl. It's apparently an 'all the vegetables' pizza. If you look closer, it also has cabbage and green beans on it. It's pretty messed up, right?"

"Uh yeah, you could say that," Johnny says, grabbing a piece of said messed-up pizza, anyway. "But I'm not afraid. I'll try anything once."

"Why would you get that pizza, anyway? Pretty sure that wasn't in our original order." I decide I'll try it too. Can't let Johnny take all the risk.

"Keep that shit away from me," Ryder says around a mouthful of his meat pizza. "I'm allergic to vegetables when I'm hungover. They're not greasy enough." He laughs with his mouth still full of food. See? He still hasn't grown up.

Devon places a slice of the Lexi Girl pizza beside the variety of other pieces he has stacked up on his plate. The dude is enormous and eats like it. He comes over and sits at the table with the rest of us and immediately bites into the vegetable pizza.

"Shit, that is weird. But it's good." He says and takes another bite. When he's done that bite, he drops a bomb. "That Alex girl from the show the other night, the one who beat her ex with an umbrella? She told me to get it. She said it's her favorite. Apparently, it's named after her and everything." He takes another huge bite, completely oblivious to the fact that the rest of us are staring at him.

"What?" he asks when he finally notices our eyes glued to him. "What did I say?"

"Alex?" Ryder yells. "The Alex that Connor has been brooding about since she ran away after the concert, leaving him with no way to find her? Friends with the photographer chick? That Alex?"

"Um, yes?" Devon seems confused. "I haven't seen you since the meet and greet. And from the way Connor and Alex were eye-fucking each other, it looked like everything was good."

"That's what I thought too," I say. "But then Becca started telling some bullshit stories, and then Alex got up and left in a huge hurry. I tried to chase her down, but I got there as she was getting into a cab. She idn't even leave her number." I sit down and put my head in my hands.

"The story about her cheating ex, Derek? I heard that story. Apparently, Alex is quite the little slugger." Devon laughs. "She broke her favorite umbrella, though. That's shitty."

"Yeah, that's not the only story that Becca told, though," I sigh, still facing the floor. "She talked about other boyfriends having cheated, saying that almost ten of them have, and that's when Alex got up and left. She ran out of there like she was on fire. I chased after her right away, but I didn't find her until it was too late."

"Yeah, and Becca got up right after Connor did," Johnny adds. "I think she realized she was saying something she shouldn't be. She was cool, too. I was going to ask for her number, but I didn't get the chance after all that."

"Uh, well. I guess it doesn't help at all that she told me to tell you guys hi?" Devon shrugs. "I told her we'd let her know how the pizza was. How was I supposed to know that we didn't actually have any way to contact her?"

"What if we call the pizza place? Maybe they can tell us something?" I sound desperate, but I can't bring myself to care. I found Alex, and I lost her again. That makes me desperate. I can almost hear Ryder laughing at me in his head. Fucker.

"Nah, that won't work. She knows the guy by name. I think he'd be too protective of—" Devon stops in the middle of his sentence. "OH SHIT!" he yells. "Why didn't I think of this before? She actually gave me her pizza and got the owner to make her another one."

"You took her pizza?" I lift my head from my hands and look at him. "That seems like a dick move."

"Whatever, she insisted." Devon stares right at me, looking excited. "But forget that. She told me she lives pretty much next door, so it would be easy for her to come back and grab it."

"What?" This is amazing news. I can go over there and wait for her to show up. I can use the pizza place as an excuse, so I don't look too crazy. Or even the gym. It's a little further away, but it's pretty close. Close enough to use as a reason to be there, anyway.

"Oh, fuck." Devon looks disappointed now. "She was getting pizza because she and Becca were packing. She's moving. This weekend."

"No." Ryder dramatically falls to his knees and shakes his fists in the air. "Now we'll have to listen to Connor whine for months about not being able to find her."

"Fuck you, dude." I throw my pizza crust at him. "I can't explain, but I feel like I need her. I need to find her."

"Well," Travis finally joins in the conversation. "We have a big SUV with tinted windows parked right outside. Who's up for a teenage crush drive-by?"

"Haha, Travis. That's not funny."

"I'm serious," he says. "We're not getting any work done in the studio, anyway. It's already Friday. If she's moving this weekend, then we should be able to catch the moving truck and see where she lives right now. And if she's moving herself, we will see her making trips with boxes and stuff. It's really your last chance. Once she moves, who knows if you'll be able to find her again?"

He really is serious. He thinks we should act like teenagers and drive by my crush's house like we're trying to get a glimpse of her. And I'm just crazy enough that I'm leaning toward doing it. It's really the best option I have besides hiring a private investigator to track her down, and I don't think I'm there yet.

"If she sees us all driving by, she's going to know something is up." Aiden is the voice of reason, as usual. He's the oldest of us and usually keeps us all in line. "What if we do it in shifts?" Scratch that. He's as crazy as the rest of them.

"What the fuck, guys? We can't stalk Alex."

"You're no fun," Ryder, of course. "We're not stalking. We're merely looking for her during the only time available to us to do so, at the only location we know of that we could possibly find her. Do you really want to give up now and let her move away forever?"

Fuck. When Ryder starts making sense, I know my head is messed up. But I already lost her once because she had to move away when her parents died. Alex was supposed to call me when she got to her grandfather's place and give me her new number and address, but she didn't. I can't blame her for that, though. Her parents had just died. She had more important things to think about. I can't let something like that happen again, though. It nearly killed me the first time.

"So." I look around at the guys, my mind made up. "Who wants to go for a drive?"

21

Missed Opportunities and Misunderstandings

Alex

EVEN AFTER WAITING FOR my second Lexi Girl pizza, Becca and I meet up at the door to the building at the same time and she has only to glance at me to see that something's wrong. I've been told I have a very expressive face. Do you know how some people wear their hearts on their sleeves? Well, I wear mine on my face. That's how Becca knows something is up before I even say it.

"Hey Girl, I got this new"—She stops right in her tracks, a look of concern painting her features—"What happened?" She asks. "You look like someone kicked your puppy."

"I don't have a puppy," I say, earning an eye roll from her. "I ran into that security guy Devon at the pizza place."

"Alex, that's awesome! Are you going to call Connor as soon as we get upstairs?" She is so excited for me she's already side-hugging with the arm that isn't holding our beer.

"Not exactly." I open the door to the building and hold it for her to go through first before following behind her. "I didn't get his number from Devon. Or give Devon mine."

"What? Why not? He wouldn't give it to you? That dick!" Becca is always quick to jump to my defense. Too bad in this case it's totally unwarranted since there's no one to blame but myself.

"Because I didn't ask him for it," I groan, banging my fist against my forehead. "I didn't want to seem like a stalker. I sort of hinted around, asking about the guys, hoping Devon would say that Connor has been looking for me, too." We're up the stairs and at our apartment door. This time, Becca opens it and holds it for me. "It clearly didn't work, though. I even gave him my pizza and told him to tell the guys hello. As he was driving away, he said they'd let me know what they thought about the pizza, which I found a little weird. I didn't give any of them my phone number, so how would they do that?"

"That does seem strange." She drops the beers on the counter before opening one and handing it to me. "Was he acting friendly? He wasn't brushing you off, was he?"

"I don't think he was." I go over the entire encounter in my head. "He seemed genuinely happy to see me. We joked a little about whiskey. I told him about my new job. It was like talking to a friend. It didn't seem like he was trying to brush me off at all."

We both grab plates and a couple of slices of pizza and sit down on the couch to eat. She looks like she's really trying to figure this out. From what she saw, and what I've told her about how Connor interacted with me, she is sure that he was interested.

"Did you see Devon at the after-party at all?" she asks before taking a big sip of her beer. It's some sort of craft brew from a local brewery. Becca is a bit of a beer snob. That's why she never lets me go get the beer. I grab whatever looks good because it all tastes the same to me, anyhow.

"No, the last time I saw him that night was at the meet and greet. He helped escort all the fans out, and then I didn't see him after that. He told me today that he'd gone to help his best friend's sister with something. Why?" I'm not sure where she's going with this.

"Well. The last Devon saw, you and Connor were making eyes at each other at the meet and greet, right?" She continues before I can answer. "Maybe he doesn't know that you guys don't have each other's information? If I didn't know you and saw you guys at the meet and greet, I would have said for sure you'd get each other's numbers. Or skip that part and go home together."

"You think?" Had I read him properly? "That would make sense if Connor was actually interested. What if he was doing the flirty rockstar thing?"

"He was only flirting with you, though. There were attractive female fans at the meet and greet. Plus, I overheard Devon telling the band's manager that he had to get rid of a groupie who'd snuck into a bathroom and surprised Connor before the meet and greets. He made it sound like Connor was sick of groupies getting past security. If he wanted to play the flirty rockstar, you'd think he'd want more groupies around, not less."

Becca is making sense. Well, she is saying the things I wanted to hear, anyway. I want to believe that Connor was actually interested in me. The problem is that I'll never be able to find out for sure.

"That is fine, Becca." I try to talk some sense into her, but mostly into myself. "But there's no way for me to find out for sure. I don't have a way to contact him, remember?"

"That's true, for now," she says. "Give me some time to get in touch with some people at the radio station. Maybe we can get in contact with a PR person or something like that. There has to be a way for you to track him down. And you never know, maybe he's even looking for you."

I want to believe that is true too, but what are the odds that a famous rockstar is looking for me?

I'm the girl that constantly gets cheated on by mediocre boyfriends, not the girl that super hot, successful, rockstars track down after talking for a few minutes one night. Even if we had a connection before, he's the one who cut off all contact when I left. He might not have cheated, but it was a betrayal. We'd planned on trying the long-distance thing and instead of that, he changed his phone number and I never heard from him again. Maybe I don't really want to find him as much as I thought. I should stay away from all men as I planned.

Because if there's one thing I know for sure, it's that my heart can't take any more breaking.

22

Unsuccessful Searching and Sleeping On It

Connor

"ALEX TOLD YOU SHE lived next door? That doesn't make sense. There's a pawn shop next door, and it doesn't even have an apartment over it." I'm looking at the buildings as Devon drives us all in the Escalade that we use when we need to fit the whole band in one vehicle. The other guys are in the back seats, looking out their respective windows. Other than Ryder, of course, who is looking down at his phone, texting.

"She said she *practically* lived next door. As in, almost, but not quite, next door. Besides, as far as I could tell, she was on foot, so she can't live too far." Devon is driving as slowly as he can without being too suspicious. This isn't the worst neighborhood, but it's not the best either. We don't want anyone to get the wrong idea.

"Well, there is only one apartment building on this block, but it's right next door to my gym. I'm sure I would have seen her at some point if she lived that close. When we're not touring, I come and work out pretty much every day." Could she really have been that close all this time? I didn't even ask her where she's been living all these years. It would be so crazy if she's been here since her parents died. Maybe she's lived here with her grandfather all these years. Older people don't normally move around a lot. And would I really have seen her? I keep my head down so no one recognizes me and I never look at people's faces because that makes it harder for them to see mine.

"But remember, she recently broke up with a boyfriend. What if they were living together, and she just moved here? Maybe she's crashing with a friend until she moves?" Fucking Ryder, always butting in with the bad news. "Not only that, but when you go out in public, you pull your hat down and refuse to look anyone in the eye. She could have walked right past you and you would never even have noticed."

"Fuck off, Ryder," I say, without turning to look at him, pissed off that he's probably right. It's hard to recognize people when you keep a low profile and don't look at anyone's face. "You're not helping right now." Plus, the thought of her living with someone else has jealousy bubbling up in my gut. That, and the hate I feel for this Derek dude for hurting Alex the way he did, makes me want to cause him some serious pain.

"What if someone around here knows her?" Travis asks from the very back of the SUV. "If she lives in the neighborhood, that must mean she frequents some of these places, right? Do you think anyone at the gym would know who she is? What about the old guy who owns the place? He has to have been around for a long time. He's probably familiar with the people in this area."

"He might be, but I don't think Alex would hang around a boxing gym. She always hated violence of any kind." Alex was always so sweet and innocent when we were kids. She'd be the one running in the opposite direction if someone started fighting. There was no way she was hanging around to watch. "She got in one fight when some drunk chick at a party tried to crawl up on me to kiss me. It wasn't much of a fight, though. Alex grabbed the chick by the hair, threw her on the ground, kicked her in the ass, and told her to fuck off. It was awesome, but then she cried about it for three days. She even tried tracking the girl down to send her an apology note."

"Yeah, okay," Devon says with a chuckle. "It doesn't seem likely that a boxing gym would be her favorite hangout then. Are there any coffee shops or bars on this street that you think we should check out?"

"This is stupid." I blow out a breath in frustration. "Let's go back to the house. She probably went home to keep packing, anyway. I doubt we'll see her anywhere tonight."

"I was kind of thinking the same thing. She said that Becca was grabbing beer, and it didn't really sound like they were heading out again tonight." Devon tells me while turning the Escalade around so we can drive the block one more time on the way home. "Sorry, man. I feel terrible for not getting her number for you. I honestly thought you had it already."

"It's fine," I say. "You didn't know how we left it that night. If you'd asked me at the meet and greet if I'd be seeing her again, I'd have said yes, absolutely. How was I to know the after-party would turn out the way it did?"

"Right?" It's Ryder again. "I was there and I still don't really believe that it turned out that way. I saw the way you guys were looking at each other, man. There was something there."

"Thanks, Ryder," I say without turning around. "I felt something as soon as she gave me the whiskey bottle back at the venue. Like an electric current or something. It felt like I was finally home. Or whole. Or... fuck, I don't know. It feels like a part of me I didn't even know was missing is finally back where it belongs. Does that even make sense?"

"I don't know anything about that, dude. But what I *do* know is that you're making me want to puke." Ryder laughs. "Fucking singers, man. Y'all have so many feelings. Seems to me you're complicating things. You should have taken her into the bathroom and fucked her. I'm sure you'd feel pretty good after that. I know I would."

Aiden reaches over and punches Ryder for me. "Shut the fuck up, Ryder. Don't think I don't know that you've been trying to fuck your feelings away. Don't forget, I'm pretty fucking observant."

Ryder looks a little surprised. Aiden rarely calls anyone out, so for him to get involved this way is serious.

"You're right, man." Ryder looks at me. "Sorry, Connor. I didn't mean anything by it. You know I'm an asshole."

"You're not wrong about that," I say. "It's fine. Don't do it again, though, or you and I will have words. Somehow I am going to make sure Alex is in my life, and I don't want anyone making her feel uncomfortable."

"You got it, buddy. You'll see nothing but the utmost respect from me from now on." Ryder actually looks like he feels bad. Good. Alex is too important to me to let him run his mouth about her. "Well, regarding Alex, anyway. Other chicks are still fair game." And he's back. Ryder can't stop being Ryder for long.

I'm a little surprised when I look up to see that we are already almost at my place. I guess Devon has been driving the entire time, and I didn't notice. We pull up to the garage and wait for the door to open so Devon can pull the Escalade in. Once we're all in, we head back to the kitchen and start eating the pizza that we left out. Stalking is hungry work, I guess.

"You guys hanging out or heading home tonight? Your rooms are ready to go if you're staying. I'm fucking beat though, so I'm probably going to crash right after this." I'm already yawning and stretching while eating a piece of the Lexi Girl pizza. It's fucking weird, but it tastes okay. And knowing it came directly from Alex makes it the best pizza I've ever had.

I am completely exhausted. After a tour ends, I usually want to sleep for about a week straight. The label has given us a tight deadline for this next album, though, so the guys and I all figured we should get started right away.

Not that we've gotten much done this week. We were all a little out of sorts, but I was the worst. I'm all twisted up over Alex, and I don't know how I can fix it. Tomorrow I'll go to the gym early and see if Mike knows anything. He's been in that neighborhood for so long that if anyone knows anything, it's him. After that, who knows? Hire a private investigator? Maybe I should start by waiting around to see a moving truck. It might be my last chance to find Alex before she moves away for good. If I can't find her before Monday, then I'll call in the professionals. Because I'm not willing to lose her again. Not before using all the tools at my disposal.

23

Packing and Planning

Alex

"So who will you be working for, anyway? The contract sounds pretty intense. It must be someone important for them to require a background check and an NDA." Becca is finishing up her third beer while we relax on the couch and watch a movie.

"I'm not sure yet. The woman was supposed to tell me after I passed the background check and signed the NDA. I guess she forgot about that part though because her text said that I passed the check and could move in tomorrow. I still need to let her know what time I'm going to be there."

"I vote for the afternoon." Becca hates mornings. She would sleep until noon every day if she could. Unfortunately for her, the wedding business usually requires her to spend her mornings in meetings or behind the camera. "Then you can make me a delicious breakfast before we go and you disappear from my life for six months."

"Haha, hilarious," I deadpan. "I'll still be able to see you. I'm going to work, not prison."

"Wait, how is me helping you move in going to work, anyway? Am I allowed to be there? I haven't signed any agreements." Becca sits up quickly, concerned that she won't be able to help me after all. She really is a good friend. "I'll die if I don't find out firsthand who you're working for. This is the biggest thing to happen to us all year." Scratch that. She's not that good a friend, she's curious.

"I will move into the pool house and the clients will remain in the main house for the duration of the move. It's already been all arranged. That's why I have to let Denise know what time I'll be coming. She will have to arrange to 'have all concerned parties in the appropriate locations' or something like that." I had thought of that too, so I asked about it when my background check came in clear. "But that means that we will go in the morning. Pops wants to help too, and he is willing to step away from the gym in the morning tomorrow. He doesn't have any clients booked early, and he's fully staffed with other trainers."

"Aw, man. That sucks," Becca whines. "But I suppose if it means I get to see Pops outside of the gym, I can get up early. I can't remember the last time he was even out of that building. Sometimes I think maybe he's a ghost who haunts that place." She's joking. Pops goes home every night to sleep. But he spends every waking minute at the gym.

"Right?" I can't believe that he's leaving his gym to help me move, either. "I'm pretty sure it's less about helping and more about making sure I'm going to be safe. He'll probably wander off to the main house and try to get a peek at who I'm going to be working for. He's a little worried I will be stuck with a dirty politician, and I can't lie. I'm a little worried about that too. That's the worst of all the possibilities I've gone through in my head."

"I'm thinking it's some famous movie star. You said the chick who interviewed you was wearing a leather skirt and a G n' R shirt. People who work with politicians usually wear something a lot more conservative." Becca seems pretty sure of this. She has a point. I have never seen a businessperson of any sort, let alone a politician, wearing a leather skirt. Even those on the more

Liberal end of the spectrum tend to dress pretty conservatively. Except for social media moguls, who can get away with tee shirts and hoodies as business attire. "I'm a little sad that I won't get to find out, though. A pool party sounds amazing. Now that I know you're living in the pool house, that is. I don't exactly get a lot of opportunities to lounge around at pools. There's too many people staring at me when I go to public pools."

"Hey, Becca?" I broach this subject carefully. "One day, will you tell me what all your tattoos are covering? Only if you want to, of course. I've loved you for this long without knowing, and if you don't want to tell me, it won't change anything. Just... if you ever want someone to talk to, you know?"

"I will, one day." She chews her bottom lip and avoids making eye contact with me. "Very few people know what happened, and I haven't talked about it in years. It's not a pleasant story. But I bet all the therapists I've seen would agree it's healthy for me to talk about it with my best friend."

"Okay, well, know that I'm here. And I love you." I go over and give her a hug, then joke, "Even if you are a bitch some-times."

"Haha, you're hilarious," she says through an enormous yawn. "But I better get to bed now. Apparently, I have to help some asshole move early tomorrow morning." With that, she gives me a little side hug and gets up to go to bed. "Wake me up with coffee when you're ready to get going. I can guarantee I won't do a thing without at least two cups in me first." She turns and goes into her bedroom without waiting for an answer.

I wonder how early I can get away with waking her up?

I clean up the pizza boxes and beer bottles and set my alarm for seven before going to bed myself. That will give me time to get over to Bump & Grind for some fancy coffees, pick up Pops at the gym, and get back here by eight to wake up Becca. I text Denise to tell her we'll be there at nine. Since I have almost nothing to move, it shouldn't take long at all. Pops will be back at the gym by lunch and I will be settled in and unpacked by mid-afternoon. I'll have one whole day to get used to my new digs, and then the next chapter of my life starts on Monday.

Man, I really hope that the clients are nice. I can't deal with another dickhead for six months.

24

Even More Family Drama

Connor

THIS MORNING MY ALARM went off at six. I was intending to get up and go to the gym, but fuck, six is too damn early, so I set it again for seven and slept in a little longer.

When I finally drag my ass out of bed, I go to the kitchen to grab some coffee and make myself an omelet. I can't wait for my new chef to start. I'm tired of omelets and takeout as my only food options. I suppose I could learn how to cook, but I know I could never make the kinds of things a professionally trained chef can. And since I make enough money to hire one to do the cooking for me, I may as well do that. Only a couple more days of fending for myself and then I can eat some proper food again. Not that we ask the chef for anything extravagant. They're probably itching for a challenge again after they finish the contract with us.

As I'm about to sit down to eat, I hear my phone ding. A quick look at the screen tells me it's my mother. Great.

Mom- Hi honey

Connor- Hey mom, what's up? Is Ted Feeling better now?

Mom- Yes, he is, thanks for asking. It's the funniest thing. He was better almost immediately that same night. Oh, I need to ask you something. I was wondering if you were still going to send money for your sister's tuition. The payment is due soon and I haven't seen anything from you.

Of course. She's texting me because she needs something. Too bad I already figured out her little game and paid the school directly. I even prepaid for all of Sadie's books, her meal plan, and her dorm for the entire school year. And since I paid for them all to get a new wardrobe when I thought they were coming to my show, there's really nothing left she needs money for.

Connor-I've already paid for it. Sadie is set to go. Books, dorm, meals. She doesn't need to do anything else but show up.

Mom- oh, good. Well, Amanda is also going to need some stuff

for school. It's her senior
year. The prom is coming up.

Connor-Cool, yeah. I've talked
to her about this already. We're
going to go shopping in the next
week or two. I'll even pay for
her hair appointment.

Connor- Gotta go now, Mom, I'm
off to the gym. Talk to you
later.

Before she responds, I put my phone away. I'll read her messages later. She probably needs some time to think of another way to get something out of me, anyway.

It's not like I mind paying for stuff for my sisters. I have the money, and I don't want them to miss out on college or school activities because our mother is useless. They're both a lot younger than me, and I've always felt more than a little responsible for them. None of our fathers stuck around, but I've tried to stay present in their lives as much as possible.

There is something I don't like about financing my mother's life, though. I've never been able to put my finger on it. The closest I can figure is that the way she feels entitled to my money bothers me. That, and I can never be sure what she's using the money for.

Shit. After all that, my food is cold. So instead of eating, I light a smoke and go out to the deck off the kitchen to finish my coffee. I enjoy sitting out here because the deck overlooks the pool and the yard. Not that there's not a lot going on back there. I bought a house with an enormous yard full of trees so I could have some privacy. The pool house is also back here, but I use it more like a staff house most of the time.

My new chef will live there. It seems to be easier to get someone to commit to a round-the-clock contract if they are at least guaranteed their own separate space. I rarely avail myself of the all-hours aspect of the contract, but I keep later hours than most people. It's nice to have the chef here to cook meals later in the day than normal or to get stuff ready in advance if I know we'll be working late in the studio.

After I finish my smoke and my cup of coffee, I decide it's time to finally head on over to the gym to see if Mike knows of Alex. If I get lucky, maybe I'll even see a moving truck. It's only eight-thirty now, so if she's moving today, she might still be packing up the truck. I'm not sure where she's moving to, but I know I won't let that stop me from seeing where this can go. I can't forget the way she made me feel the other night. Actually, I haven't been able to think of anything but her for this entire week. Hopefully, I find her and she feels the same.

25

Moving In and Mystery Clients

Alex

BY THE TIME I grab the coffee and pick up Pops, Becca is dressed and ready to go. We get to work right away and get all the boxes loaded into our two vehicles by eight-thirty. Once that is done, we drive straight over to the new place to meet Denise.

I pull into the driveway and go right around to the back of the main house where Denise said the pool house is located. As soon as I pull up, I see her standing beside the pool house door, waiting for me.

"Hi, Denise, how are you?" I say, getting out of my car. "Are we all set with everything for today?"

"Hey, Alex. It's nice to see you again," Denise says while walking over to me. "I'm so sorry to do this to you, but I have a meeting with a client in a few minutes, so I have to get going. It's sort of an emergency. I was hoping to go through the pool house and all the security codes and such with you, but I'm going to have to give you this instead." She passes me a large envelope and a set of keys. "This key is for the pool house, and this one is for the main house. The codes for the alarm panels are in the envelope, as are your copies of the contracts and forms. Oh, and I also put some blank background checks and NDA forms in there for you. I'm sure you'll want to have someone visit you at some point, so I will need those filled out and back to me ASAP. I know you will have someone helping you move today, but as long as you don't invite them to the main house, it will be fine. None of the guys are around, but I have instructed them not to bother you until Monday." She looks around, like she's trying to remember something. "That should be everything, but if you have questions, please call or text at any time. And again, I'm so sorry to be running out on you like this. If it wasn't an emergency, I would be here to help get you settled."

She waves at me as she gets into her car and immediately drives away. I didn't hear it, but I'm pretty sure it was running the entire time. Oh crap, I still don't know who the client is. At least I have forms for Becca to sign so that she'll be able to come visit. That should make her happy, especially since this pool is amazing. And my place is only a few steps away.

Grabbing my new keys and getting the alarm codes out of the envelope, I walk over to my new place. After opening the door and disarming the alarm, I go inside to have a look around. Looks like a nice enough place. Smallish kitchen, but it has a gas range, and it looks like the appliances are newer. The kitchen is on the left of the entryway and it opens up into a large combination of living and dining space. Modern-looking furniture is spaced throughout, large enough for comfort but not so large that it overwhelms the space. The far side of the living room holds a set of French doors that open onto a small deck overlooking a large yard with a forested area at the edges of it. It's hard to even tell we're in the city anymore.

I can't believe I get to live here for the next six months. I guess that hangover really was a blessing in disguise.

Going back in, I notice that behind the living room area, on the other side of the kitchen, is a set of stairs. Following them up, I find the master bedroom with a king-size bed and a huge ensuite bathroom complete with a soaker tub and separate glass-enclosed shower with a two-headed waterfall shower head. I could get used to this. Across the hall from the master is another slightly smaller bedroom, also with an ensuite, but this one is a lot less extravagant. Still a pleasant room, though. It will be a good place for Becca to sleep if she comes to a pool party and drinks a little too much.

After I'm done looking around upstairs, I go back to the main floor and out to my car. As I'm pulling out the first box, Becca drives in and parks beside me. She insisted on taking Pops with her and they both get out of the car now.

"Well shit, Lexi Girl." Pops whistles as he looks around. "This place is nice."

"And look at that pool," Becca says longingly. "Let's get in our suits and lounge around it for the rest of the day."

"Here." Pops hands me a fresh coffee. "We stopped for some more coffee. I wasn't sure what the coffee machine situation would be like. That Xena girl at the coffee shop sure is a pistol. I called her 'warrior princess' and she pulled a sword on me." He laughs as he relays the story. Xena is the owner of Bump & Grind and rumor has it she hates to be reminded of the character who shares her name. She has a sword she threatens people with when they forget and call her 'warrior princess'.

"Thanks, Pops. I hear you're not the first person Xena has threatened with that sword. I'm pretty sure it's not real, though. Anyway, you guys go on in the pool house and have a look around. I'll be right behind you." I pass my coffee back to Pops to bring inside for me.

I bring in a few boxes while they take themselves on the tour. When I'm dropping off boxes, I can hear both of them marveling at the master bath. I'm outside grabbing another box when I turn around and find them both coming out to join me.

"Did you see the view off the deck in the back?" Pops asks. "It's like a private retreat. You can't even see the main house from there. You'll have your own little oasis."

"Yeah, it's nice, isn't it? I think I really lucked out with this job. The accommodations are beautiful."

"Okay, yeah, but what about the client? Who is it? I'm right, aren't I? It's definitely a movie star." Becca is positive she's right.

"I actually still don't know," I tell her. "Denise had a client emergency she had to attend to. She was only here long enough to give me the keys and alarm codes. Oh, and she left forms if you want to fill out a background check and NDA, so you can come over and hang out by the pool." I have a gigantic smile on my face while I give Becca a brief nod in the envelope's direction.

"Yeah!" Becca cheers. "It's pool party time, bitches!"

"You don't know who you're working for yet?" Concerns colors Pops' voice. "It must be someone horrible if they're hiding it for this long."

"I don't think so, Pops. I honestly think it slipped her mind. She seems pretty busy." I talk as I unpack a box of books onto a shelf in the living room. I may only be here for six months, but I will need some reading material.

"Well, I don't like it," he grumbles on his way out the door. "She's hiding something."

"Meh, I think it's fine," Becca says to me, following Pops. "I have a good feeling about this one. I think this job will bring nothing but good things."

Pops and Becca go out to grab the last couple of boxes while I bring all my clothes upstairs. I really don't have that much stuff to unpack. This place is fully furnished. I even noticed my preferred kitchen utensils when I was looking in the cupboards and drawers. All I really need for cooking is my knives, which is perfect.

I'm with Becca on this one. I think this job is going to be great. For now, though, I'm going to finish unpacking, and then I think I might go for a swim.

26

Finding Fans but Not Finding Alex

Connor

"Hey, is Mike around?"

I can count on one hand the number of times I've been here when Mike wasn't. The guy rarely leaves. Of course the one day that I' really need him to be here is the day that he takes some time off.

"No, sorry, dude." The guy says, then looks up at me. "Oh shit, are you Connor Ashley?"

Shit, I forgot my hat and my long sleeve shirt. When was the last time that happened? I take a deep breath and reach out a hand. "Yeah, that's me. How are ya? What's your name?" Gotta be polite to the fans, right? Especially here. Mike would rip me a new one if I were an asshole to one of his employees. He doesn't care how famous I am.

"Great, man, this is awesome. I'm Ryan. I was at your show last week, man. It was amazing. You guys were great!" If the way he's pumping my hand is any indication, this guy is really excited to meet me. "What do you need Mike for? Can I help you train or do anything for you? My girlfriend would probably die if I told her I was training with you today."

"That's a nice offer, Ryan, thanks. I'll take you up on that next time. But I really need to ask Mike a question. Or maybe you know? Do you know of a woman named Alex that lives nearby here?"

"Oh no, sorry, I don't," he says. "I'm pretty new here at the gym and I live on the other side of town."

"Okay, no worries. Could you let him know I stopped by?" I'm already on my way out the door. "It was nice meeting you, Ryan. I'm sure I'll see you around the gym sometime. Maybe next time I'll take you up on that workout offer." I'm out the door before he can start asking for selfies or autographs or anything. Normally I don't mind talking to Sleeping Dogs fans, but today I have one thing on my mind: find Alex.

Since I'm not able to talk to Mike, I decide to try my luck with walking down the street and stopping in at a couple of businesses to ask around for Alex. Maybe if someone recognizes me, it will get them to trust me enough to tell me where she lives. And if not, maybe I'll see the moving truck. It's not here right now, and it's still early enough that I doubt she's done moving already. It would take longer than this to move a single piece of furniture. Moving your whole life would take longer, I think.

I spend the next while walking up and down the four blocks surrounding the gym. I've decided that is the distance that I would walk with pizza, so I don't explore any further than that. The pizza place isn't open this early, so I can't ask there. I keep an eye out for moving trucks while I'm walking, but I don't see one at all. After about an hour and a half with no leads, I realize it's time to call it. There's nothing to see. I'll call the pizza place later and see what they say. I'll call Mike too, to check in with him. He has been in the neighborhood for a long time and I am sure he knows something.

As I get back into my car, my phone dings with a notification. There's a text from Denise.

Denise- Hey Connor, I've had
to go take care of something
with Ryder. The idiot got too
drunk last night and got himself arrested. Your new chef is
moving in today. She's been told
not to bring anyone to the main
house, but she may come in on
her own to familiarize herself
with the kitchen. Don't you guys
dare ask her for anything. She
doesn't start until Monday. You
can fend for yourself for a
little longer.

Okay, well, at least that part of my life is going as planned. I only hope this chef isn't as obsessed with the band as the last one. We told people that her boyfriend made her quit because he was jealous, but I actually needed to have her fired. She kept showing up naked in our beds. And since I'm the one at the house the most, she was always in my bed. It was getting so annoying to get her out that I finally had to have Denise fire her. I want the chef to cook for us, not warm my bed at night.

As I finish reading Denise's message, another one comes through from my mom.

Mom- Well honey, they are going to need spending money for
incidentals and whatnot. You
transfer it to my account and
I'll give it to them.

I suppose this is as good a time as any to confront what's going on with her. In the past, she's been more interested in getting me to buy her things, but lately, it seems there's been a heavy focus on getting actual cash from me. It has me worried. The last time this happened, it was because she was using. Something that she promised me would never happen again.

> **Connor-** What's going on, mom? You seem to be pretty intent on having me send you cash. I remember what was going on the last time this happened.

Since I know I won't get a straight answer from her, I also text both of my sisters. They were a lot younger last time mom was using, but now that they're older they probably can recognize what's going on.

> **Connor-** hey Sadie, hey Amanda. Is everything okay with mom? I told her I've already paid for all your school and stuff, and she's pushing for me to send money for you guys. Is there anything you two need? Let me know and I'll buy it for you. I want to make sure you have what you need.

Sadie gets back to me immediately.

Sadie- no, I'm good. I have everything I need. Thank you again, so much, for paying for school and everything. I can't wait to get out of here.

I wait around for ten minutes, but mom and Amanda don't get back to me. After taking another look around for moving trucks on this street, I decide to leave. Guess I'll go home for now and this afternoon I'll give Mike and the pizza place a call. I'll call Devon later too, to see if he's had any luck tracking Alex down. If none of these things pan out, I'm not sure what I can do.

27

Solo Pool Party and Preparation

Alex

AN HOUR LATER, BECCA, Pops, and I have everything un-packed and I officially live in the pool house of my mystery client. The first order of business, once everything is inside, is unpacking my coffee maker and brewing a pot for the three of us. Once that's done, we take our cups out onto the small back deck to drink while we enjoy the quiet.

"I can't believe how quiet it is out here. We're still in the city, right? We didn't somehow drive further than we thought?" Becca says from the comfort of a wooden porch swing that's hanging from the roof over the deck. Pops is sitting opposite her on an old-fashioned rocking chair, holding his cup in his lap while his eyes slowly drift closed.

"It is peaceful, isn't it? I think I'm going to like it here." I'm curled up on a well-padded loveseat. "Don't you love how you can hear the leaves in the trees rustling in the wind? I'm going to need to turn the volume on my phone way up because I'm going to be napping out here a lot. I'd hate to miss the client's calls because I'm asleep on the deck of the house they're letting me live in."

"Yeah, that might be an awkward conversation. 'Sorry I didn't come to cook for you. I was napping at the beautiful house you've allowed me to live in for the sole purpose of my being available to cook for you as required. My bad.'" Becca laughs. "That might breach the terms of the contract or something."

"Yeah, I wouldn't want to do that. This seems like the perfect position for me. I'm going to be sad to have to find something else after the six months is up."

"As long as you don't rush into anything that your heart isn't really in. You'll make enough money from this contract to take your time deciding what you really want to do."

"Yeah, you're right. Plus, I've got six months here to figure out my next move, right? So I will do some soul searching and see what really lights me up."

"That's all I ask." Becca stands up. "On that note, I think it's time to get Pops back to the gym. I can drive him, you know, to give you more time to get settled in. Make sure you get my forms to your lady so that I can come hang out soon. I need to get a swim in that pool." She smiles as she leans over to tap on Pops' shoulder. "Time to go, Pops. Can't leave those meatheads in charge of the gym too long. Never know what they'll do to the place if you're not there to keep them in line."

"What?" Pops grumbles a bit while he wakes up. "Oh yeah, right. Better get back then." He turns and gives me a huge squeeze. "Love you, Lexi Girl. Call me when you find out who you're working for, so I know if I need to deliver a warning message." I shake my head and squeeze him back.

"No messages necessary, Pops. I'm sure everything will be fine."

Becca grabs up all the boxes that we unpacked, probably to store them until the next time I need them, and then waves goodbye again as she walks out to her car with Pops. I stand at the door, waving until they drive back around the main house and out of sight.

Well, now that I'm alone in my new place, what should I do?

After very little deliberation, I go back inside and up to my bedroom to change and grab a towel. It's pool time.

I swim laps for a bit, then I get out to lie on one of the deck chairs. Swimming is a good workout, but if you're not actively swimming, then hanging out at a pool is pretty boring all alone. After a few minutes of lounging, I go back inside and grab a book. While I'm in there, I also grab my phone and headphones and start one of my Spotify playlists. I'm sure there's a sound system out there somewhere, but I don't want to disturb anyone in the main house, so my headphones will be fine. I grab myself a drink and go back out to my lounge chair. Now I'm ready to spend the afternoon relaxing. Unfortunately, I relax a little too hard. It takes less than fifteen minutes to fall asleep, and that's where I stay for the next three hours.

WHEN I WAKE UP, I'm disoriented until I remember that I'm laying by the pool at my new place. Thank god I had the sense to lie in the shade or my not-so-brief nap would have turned into a really nasty sunburn. I gather up my things and go back into the pool house. Stripping out of my suit as I walk through my place, I go jump in the shower to wash off the pool smell. I love swimming, but I do not love the smell of the chemicals used to keep the pool clean.

I put on denim shorts and a loose white tank top over panties and a strappy blue yoga bra. I leave my hair down today, to give it a chance to air dry, the loose dark blonde waves reaching down past my bra line and soaking the back of my tank.

My stomach surprises me with a loud growl, reminding me I haven't eaten lunch. And then I remember I have no groceries. I guess now is as good a time as any to go shopping. I make a list, even though there's no actual need for one. There's literally nothing in here besides coffee, so it's a pretty quick list. I don't really need to write 'everything' after all.

I suppose while I'm at it, I can do the shopping for the main house too, so I look in the envelope Denise left me. There's a list of requested meals and favorite foods in there. Whoever these people are, they don't eat very fancy, so I should be able to get most of the ingredients I'll need at a regular grocery store. That's nice. Cooking gourmet meals all the time can be exhausting. It's one reason I don't enjoy working in restaurants anymore. I guess I should go to the main house to check on what will need to be stocked, though. That way I can do all the shopping at the same time.

After slipping on a pair of pink Chucks, I grab the keys, the alarm code to the main house, and my phone, and slip the company credit card into my wallet. I set the alarm when I leave my place and walk over to the main house. The entrance at the side of the house should lead directly to the kitchen, if I remember correctly. There is another entrance at the back, but it's a walkout basement and I haven't been to that part of the house, so I stay away. I don't want to walk into a stranger's bedroom or something.

The house is still empty, so I use my key and disarm the alarm at the side door. I was right. This door does lead to the kitchen. I put my phone, wallet, and keys onto the bar-height counter and start looking around the kitchen. After checking out the fridge and pantry, I notice this house is going to need almost a complete restock as well. It makes more sense to make a list of what we already have as opposed to what I will need to buy. The easiest way to do this is to take pictures of what's here already, so I go back to the counter and grab my phone.

With my phone in my hand, I begin by taking pictures of each shelf in the pantry. These people don't even have most of the staples, which makes me wonder if maybe this is a vacation house for them. It would make sense to clear most items out before closing up the house for half the year. Because even if the last chef they hired was mediocre, she should have at least had things like flour and rice on hand.

Once I'm done in the pantry, I move on to the rest of the kitchen cupboards. May as well make sure I have all the kitchen gadgets I need while I'm going shopping, too. So far, so good in that regard. I will only need to buy a garlic press and a handheld lemon juicer, which is nice. This kitchen is much nicer than any other home kitchen I've worked in. It even has stainless steel work surfaces, so it's clear that they made it for actual cooking, not merely looking nice.

I've just turned and opened the fridge, ready to take pictures of its contents, when I hear voices coming from the front of the house. I guess now is as good a time as any to meet the people I'm actually working for. I'm not exactly professionally dressed, but I also don't really start until the day after tomorrow, so hopefully, they don't mind. Plus, it's not like they provided a uniform, so I think I can wear whatever I want.

"Hi," I call out before anyone walks into the kitchen. "I'm Alex, the new chef. I'm in the kitchen making a list before I go to buy supplies, so don't be surprised when you walk in and see a stranger standing here."

28

Sketchy Surveillance and Amazing Coincidences

Connor

I MEET DEVON AT my front door when he arrives. He has some contacts from before his security days that might be able to help me track down Alex. I'm not sure if it's exactly legal, or if I even feel comfortable tracking her down like this, but I would like to consider all my options. First, though, he wants to hear about my morning of checking out her neighborhood.

"Mike wasn't even at the gym when I went this morning. Which is just my luck. This is the first time I've been there specifically to ask him something, and also the first time I haven't seen him there. Seriously, every single time I've been there in the last eighteen years, he has been there. The guy never leaves." I'm complaining to Devon, because he'll listen. He's my friend first and my employee second.

"Shit, man," He says, "What about the pizza place? What did they say when you called?"

"Even better," I laugh humorlessly. "He says he knows who she is, even has her phone number, but won't give it to me. Not for any amount of money. He thinks of her as a favorite niece and isn't about to give a 'sketchy fuck' like me access to her without her permission. So I trusted him with my number to give to her next time he sees her."

Devon bursts out laughing. "Well, it's nice to know someone is looking out for her. I mean, you are a sketchy fuck, but how could he tell that over the phone?"

"Apparently, he saw me wandering up and down the street this morning. Just because he's not open doesn't mean he's not there." At least now I know why their pizza is so good. "Did you know he starts his day at four a.m.? He makes the dough fresh every day and buys and preps fresh ingredients every morning. He's a bit of an ass, but I will for sure order from him again."

At that exact moment, we hear a feminine voice come from the kitchen. "Hi, I'm Alex, the new chef. I'm in the kitchen making a list before I go to buy supplies, so you're not surprised when you walk in and see a stranger standing here."

I stop dead and look at Devon. "What are the odds my new chef is a completely separate woman who is also named Alex and sounds exactly like her?"

"That would be a fucking crazy coincidence, man, but you'd have to be the luckiest asshole alive for it to actually be her," he says as he starts walking again. "I'll check it out first."

He gets a little further down the hall and stops dead in his tracks when he can see into the kitchen. Then he laughs. "Time to buy some fucking lottery tickets, dude." He yells at me.

"Devon?" she sounds so confused. "What are you doing here?"

Holy shit! It *is* her.

I follow Devon as he walks further into the kitchen and watch as he picks up Alex in an enormous bear hug, spins her around, and sets her down with her back facing me. He's giving me a chance to surprise her. That sneaky bastard. He must be a romantic at heart.

"Shit, girl. This is your new job? You're a chef?"

"Yeah," she says. "Didn't I mention that at the pizza place? Guess not, since you're asking. I officially start on Monday, but

I finished moving in early and got bored sitting around the pool house. I need to stock up my kitchen anyway, so I figured I'd come get a head start here, too. Both kitchens are pretty much empty. I need everything. I'm going to have to make multiple trips to get it all in here. I'm not sure my ego could take it." She laughs at her joke, but I see my chance to get her attention.

"You know, you're going to have to try a lot harder if you want me to believe that you're not a stalker. Showing up in my kitchen without me even knowing about it isn't really helping you prove your case." She spins around, and I can't help but laugh at the look on her face when she finally sees me. Her eyes are open almost as wide as her mouth. "But if you want help, I could always come shopping with you and bring it in when we get back here. I can even help put everything away when I'm done. You'll have to tell me where you want it to go, though. This might be my kitchen, but I honestly have no idea where anything goes."

I can see Devon snickering a little behind her back. Alex hasn't gotten past the surprise of seeing Devon to really think about why he's here. The band pays him well, but not quite enough to buy this house.

"Wait. What?" she yells.

Yeah, she's feeling surprised, alright. I mean, so am I, but I'm trying to play it cool because it's more fun to mess with her a little. Alex always was easy to surprise.

"This is your house? I'm working for you?"

"Mostly for me, I guess, but also kind of for the band. We'll be working at the studio here in the house often, and we all tire of takeout. That Lexi Girl pizza was pretty good, by the way. A little weird at first, but good."

She seems to be in some kind of shock; her mouth is moving, but she's not really saying words of any kind. Devon pulls out one of the bar stools and leads her over to sit down, then gets her a bottle of water from the fridge.

"Have a drink, darlin'. It'll make you feel better." Devon gives her the bottle after taking the cap off.

"Did you know about this?" she asks Devon, after taking a long drink of the water. "Did you guys know yesterday, with the pizza?"

"Not even a little bit," I say. "I didn't know who the new chef was until five seconds ago when walked into the kitchen and saw you standing here. Denise hired you, but she's been a little distracted lately and didn't get around to telling me who you were. I knew the new chef would move in today, but that's all I knew."

"Yeah." Alex seems to relax a little. I see her shoulders drop and she lets out a breath. "She pretty much only had time to hand me keys and codes before she had to run off and deal with some emergency this morning. She told me I could come in and familiarize myself with the kitchen, though. I hope I'm not in the way or anything. I can come back later, if you want."

"Oh shit, no, don't think that." I finally move a little further into the kitchen, closer to where she's sitting. "We were only surprised to find *you* standing here in the kitchen. You are more than welcome to be here any time you want."

Devon plays with the keys that he's pulled from his pocket. After thinking for a second, he tosses them over to me. "Why don't you guys take the Escalade and go to the store to get everything Alex needs? I can stay and hang out and wait for the rest of the guys. I wanted to look at the security system here in the main house, anyway. And maybe later when you're back I can look at the system in the pool house too? I've been thinking about adding a few upgrades while we're in town. I have a feeling Connor won't mind me updating security now that you'll be living in the pool house."

I shoot him a look of thanks. I know he's trying to get me a little time alone with Alex before the guys get here. And hopefully, he fills them all in so they don't say anything stupid when they see her. This is the only thing I've been able to talk about all week, so the chances are good that one of them will say something on their way in that I might not want Alex to hear. At least not before I talk to her, anyway.

"That sounds good to me," I say. "Let me get changed and then we can go, if you're okay with that, Alex?"

She looks at Devon, and then at me, and nods wordlessly. I hope that's the good kind of speechless and not the bad kind. I guess we'll find out in a few minutes.

"I'll be right back." I turn and hurry down the hall to change.

I rush through throwing on a long sleeve shirt and hat before heading back to the kitchen. I can't her a chance to change her mind and decide to go alone. I've been searching for this woman for a week and now she shows up in my house? Yeah, this really is fate or something.

New Job, Old Love

Alex

"THIS IS SO FUCKING wild!" Devon's excitement is almost pulling me from the stupor I'm in. What is happening in my life right now? This can't be real. "I can't believe you are the new chef. When you said you were moving, I thought you meant leaving town. Not moving into Connor's pool house." He's laughing and shaking his head a little. I'm not sure why. I'm the one over here losing my mind.

I really want to text Becca, but I can't. Stupid NDA. As soon as her background check is complete, we will discuss this at length. I rub a hand over a pain in the middle of my chest. My heart is pounding so hard it feels like it wants to climb up and jump out of my throat.

"I am so confused," I finally say. "Was Denise at the show last week? I didn't recognize her when I interviewed for this job."

"She was, but I don't recall if she was in the room when you were. Even if she was, she would have been preoccupied with making sure the guys behaved. She might have seen you but not recognized you after the fact." He's so nice. I knew I liked Devon for a reason. "You know Connor has been trying to get in touch with you all week? He didn't get your number before you left the after party, and he's been driving us all crazy since then. That they hired you to be his chef is some next level cosmic shit."

"Really?" It seems strange that Connor would look for me, but before I can ask Devon more about it, Connor is back. He's wearing a long-sleeved shirt and a ball cap now. He looks like any regular guy who just came from a gym. A smoking hot guy with a sexy body, but a regular guy all the same.

"Really what?" Connor asks, walking over to us.

"Reeeaaally, are you going to wait until I'm back to check the security system in the pool house?" I quickly cover. Smooth, Alex. Not suspicious at all. "You can go ahead inside while I'm gone if you like, Devon. I have nothing to hide."

"Oh, okay," Devon answers. "I didn't want to invade your privacy. I'll try to stay out of your underwear drawer. Unless you want me to double check security in there too? Set up some booby traps for your booby traps?" He winks obviously, laughing at his dumb joke.

"Yeah, I'm pretty sure it's secure enough for my needs. Thanks, though." I feel my face burning a little as I blush at Devon's joke, but I laugh anyway. Booby traps for my booby traps? Hilarious. I turn and look at Connor. "Shall we then?"

Connor is still laughing, probably at my red face. "Sure, babe. Let's grocery shop." He leans over and whispers in my ear, his voice sending tingles through my body. "I might need you to hold my hand, though. I haven't done my own grocery shopping in years. I might get scared."

I didn't think it was possible for my face to get redder, but the way Connor looks at me says differently. I grab my wallet and keys, shoving them into my pockets, and gesture for Connor to lead the way. "You lead. I don't know where you're parked." I say. "See you later," I shout behind me to Devon. "If any of my underwear goes missing, I'll be checking with you first."

Devon and Connor both start laughing as Connor grabs my hand, sending a rush of butterflies to my stomach, and starts walking me to the front door. "Don't encourage him," he says to me. "He'll hide them all over your place to get a reaction out of you. It'll be like an Easter egg hunt, but for panties."

"That fucker," I say with a laugh. "He better not. I don't know what I'll do for revenge, but it'll be bad." That actually sounds kind of funny, though. I almost hope he does it, if only so I can think of something horrible to do back to him. There's nothing wrong with a good prank now and again, right?

The grocery store we go to is about ten minutes away, and Connor drives the Escalade. We don't talk for the entire drive, except for me telling Connor where to go, with both of us looking straight ahead at the road. It feels strangely natural that he holds my hand for the entire drive. When we pull into the lot, Connor parks far away from the store.

We both get out and he comes around the vehicle and immediately grabs my hand, lacing his fingers with mine. Fucking butterflies again.

"So, did Devon tell you I've been looking for you since I saw you last week?" He asks me, while looking at me out of the corner of his eye.

"Um, yeah," I say. "He sort of mentioned it."

"I didn't get your number that night, and I was sort of worrying that I wouldn't see you again. That it would be like when we were kids, and we didn't see each other for twenty years." He is looking down at the ground when he says this last part. Which is weird, since he was the one who changed his number at the time. What does he have to be upset about? I was the one who got dumped.

I stop and look at him, shaking my hand free of his. "I tried to call. Why'd you change your number, Connor? If you'd wanted to break up, you could have done it before I left instead of telling me to call you when I knew my new phone number. Not only was I grieving the loss of my parents, I also had to grieve the loss of you." Oh, shit. I'm going to cry right here in the grocery store parking lot. Looks like I'm not as over this as I thought.

30

Mother's Betrayal and the Hits Keep Coming

Connor

"WHAT DO YOU MEAN? My mom said she had our calls forwarded when she had to change the number? You should have still been able to get through." I had found it weird that the number needed to be changed at exactly that time, but I didn't doubt my mom's reasons. She said she was avoiding an ex-boyfriend.

But thinking back on it now, wouldn't having calls forwarded have done the same for his phone calls? I can't remember how it worked back then, but somehow I don't think picking and choosing which numbers were forwarded was something they could do.

How could I have been so stupid? "Shit!" I yell, possibly a little too loudly for a grocery store parking lot. "She fucking lied to me. That bitch!"

"What?" Alex asks. "What do you mean, she lied?"

"She told me she changed the number to avoid calls from an ex-boyfriend, but she also said that she had calls from the old number forwarded so that you'd be able to get through." I take off my hat and run my hand through my hair, letting out an exasperated breath. "I didn't doubt it at the time, but now I realize she didn't actually forward calls. Why forward calls when you're avoiding calls from someone? Fuck, I was so stupid. How could I have thought that made sense?"

"So, she changed numbers, and what?" Alex shrugs and raises her eyebrows. I never told her the extent of how horrible my mother is, so I'm sure this is confusing for her. "Figured me leaving forever and never being able to contact you again wouldn't matter?"

"I know it's hard to believe, Alex, but that is exactly something my mother would do. She is a terrible person. If something doesn't affect her directly, then it doesn't matter to her." I almost can't believe it either. I'm so angry I'm almost vibrating. My priority now is making Alex believe me, though. My mom is a problem for another day. "I tried to get her to come to the show last week. She's never been to one of my shows. Ever."

"Really? Ever? That's horrible." At least she seems a little sympathetic. I still see some mistrust in Alex's eyes, but she seems to want to believe me.

"Yeah, it is. She even had me buy entire wardrobes for her, her boyfriend that I've never met, and my two sisters. Because she had nothing to wear to the show, she said. And then when I finally tracked her down right before the show, to see when they would arrive, she said that the boyfriend was sick and they wouldn't do a family activity if everyone in the family couldn't attend." I sigh. It sounds worse saying it out loud to someone else.

"But you've never even met that guy? And what about you? Why aren't you family?" Alex is raising her voice now, getting angry on my behalf. "Your mom's a piece of work. No offense."

We've started walking toward the store again. Alex hasn't dropped my hand yet, so I think I'm still doing okay with her.

"Yeah, she is. I never realized how long she's been like this until you told me about the phone number just now. I'm so sorry Alex, I didn't know she did that. I was so dumb to believe what she said about forwarding calls. Thinking about it now it makes no sense." I stop again and pull her into a hug, resting my head on top of hers. "I was so upset when you didn't call. I thought you'd gotten to your new life and decided you didn't want any reminders of the old days. I couldn't be mad at that, considering you'd lost your parents, but I was upset at losing you."

Alex wraps her arms around me and leans into the hug. "I thought you wanted to cut the little orphan girl out of your life. Too much baggage for someone so young to handle." I can feel her tears soaking into my shirt, even though she was clearly trying not to cry.

"Oh no, babe. No." I lean back and use my thumbs to wipe the tears from her cheeks. "I never thought that, not even for one second. If I'd known where your grandfather lived, I would have come to you and demanded to know why you cut me out of your life. There would have been no stopping me. I'd have run right through gramps to get to you."

She laughs at that a little. "That would have been funny to see. Twenty years ago Pops was fifty-five, and in great shape. He would have beat your ass for trying it. Even now he likes to say he has seventy-five years of fight experience, even though he's seventy-five years old." She laughs a little harder, wiping the rest of the tears from her eyes. "And he's lived in this city for his entire life. He's been running the same gym for over forty years."

"No shit?" I ask, surprised. I'm not sure what I expected her grandfather would do for a living, but running a gym wasn't one of them. "What kind of gym? I'm pretty attached to the one I go to currently, but I'd love to come and meet your Pops. Maybe he can give me some pointers so I can finally tag the old bastard I train with. He's twice my age but runs circles around me." I'm not ashamed to admit I'm not the best fighter, plus

Mike is one tough dude. Maybe we can set up a fight between him and Alex's Pops? See who the better old man is?

"Yeah, it's actually a block from the pizza place where Devon got those pizzas from the other night. It's called Westborough Boxing. It's pretty old school, but he's kept up with modern fight trends and does lots of MMA training. If he doesn't know how to do it himself, he hires a trainer who does." She looks so proud when she talks about her Pops and his gym.

I'm staring at her with my mouth open, looking like a dumbass. Because I think she's telling me I've been training with her Pops all these years. And if that's true, I am a dumbass.

"What?" she says, looking at me. "You go to one of those fancy new gyms downtown? You won't find a better trainer than my Pops, no matter where you go in town."

Holy shit. This is fucking unbelievable.

I grab her hand again and start walking into the store. "Come on," I say. "We'll talk about this while we shop or we're never going to get out of here." I grab a shopping cart from inside the doors and continue on inside. "So tell me more about this gym. How much time did you spend there?"

31

Years of Near Misses and a Sweet Kiss

Alex

IT FEELS NICE TO have Connor holding my hand, like I was missing it all these years and didn't even know it. It's hard to believe that someone's mother would do something as underhanded as change their phone number and tell lies about it, but Connor seemed so sincere in his anger and surprise that I can't help but believe him.

"I pretty much lived there when I first moved here. I spent every day after school there, and most of every weekend. Pops didn't have as many trainers working for him then, so I had to be there if I didn't want to be at home alone. As I got a little older, I started spending more time with Becca on the weekends. And then right before I turned twenty, I moved out and started culinary school."

"So you're saying that you basically lived there until you were twenty? Every day?" Connor asks with a lift of his eyebrow. "After that, you weren't around as often?"

"Yeah," I say. "I don't know how to fight very well, though. I'm not bloodthirsty enough for it or something." I laugh. "Why?"

"Call me curious." Connor stops pushing the cart and looks at me. "Did your Pops help you move this morning?"

"Yeah, he did." I say. "He insisted on it, actually. Pops said he wanted to come and make sure I wasn't working for some dirty politician. He probably won't be much more approving of a famous rockstar, though." I flash a teasing grin. I get the feeling that he doesn't enjoy being called a rockstar by his friends.

"Oh, I think he may be cooler with it than you think." He looks at me with a knowing glance. "Have you told him yet that it's me?"

"Not yet. I wasn't sure if I could since he hasn't filled out the NDA. I haven't told Becca yet either, because her background check hasn't come back yet. Well, those reasons and I haven't exactly had time to talk to either of them since I found out. We left the house to come here as soon as I found out, remember?"

"You should call him. Wouldn't want to keep him waiting. He's worried about you. Plus, I have a feeling we won't need to worry about him going to the tabloids with any insider information on me." He gestures to my phone. "Go ahead, I can wait."

"Okay," I drawl. "Pops will appreciate the call, I'm sure. Thanks." I pull up my contacts and call the gym.

"Westborough Boxing. Ryan speaking," says the voice on the phone.

"Hello Ryan, can I talk to Mike, please?"

"Sure thing. Hold on a sec." I hear the hold music come on for about ten seconds before Pops picks up.

"Mike here."

"Hey Pops, it's me. I found out who I'm working for and wanted to let you know so you can stop worrying. It's not a dirty politician. It's actually someone I knew before I moved in with you."

"Oh yeah," comes Pops' reply. *"Who's that?"*

"It's actually that boyfriend I had before I moved here. Do you remember me telling you about Connor Ferguson?" I give him the name Ferguson because I know he'll remember that. Pops never downplayed my heartache from Connor simply because I was also mourning my parents. He hugged me and listened to me cry. I will forever be grateful to him for somehow knowing how hard it was to be a teenage girl. It's not often that a man, let alone an old one, can empathize with a fifteen-year-old girl. "But he goes by Connor Ashley now. He's in a band."

Pops laughs so loud that I have to pull my phone away from my ear. I'm even more surprised when Connor laughs just as loudly and hysterically beside me in the store. This day keeps getting weirder and weirder.

"Pops? You okay over there?" Connor calms down a little beside me, likes he's waiting on Pops' reply as much as I am.

"Just… just… just fine, honey," comes the answer, followed by more hysterical laughter from both Pops and Connor.

"What the hell is going on?" I say to Pops and Connor, hoping one of them can calm down enough to answer me. This is turning out to be the strangest day.

Connor calms himself a little and reaches over. "Pass me the phone a sec?" he asks.

"Mike, you old bastard. You still there?" is what he says into the phone, followed by a little snickering.

"You little fucker!" is all I hear Pops say before he breaks into more peals of laughter. He's so loud that I can hear him, even though I'm not holding the phone. *"Put my granddaughter back on the phone."*

Connor laughs even more and passes my phone back.

"What is happening right now? Do you guys know each other, Pops?" I ask when I get the phone back.

"Yeah, we do, Lexi Girl. Connor has been working out at the gym for going on eighteen years now." I look over at Connor and mouth eighteen years? And he nods his head. *"And that's the reason I haven't said anything yet about how he ditched you when*

your parents passed away and you moved here. I'll beat his ass next time he comes to see me."

"Actually, Pops, I don't think I can let you do that." I tell him. "Apparently, there were extenuating circumstances involving a shitty parent, so I can't blame him anymore."

"*Oh yeah? Well then, maybe only a mild beating.*" Pops chuckles. "*Listen, kiddo, I gotta go. I have a client waiting for me. Call me tomorrow maybe and tell me more about the new job, now that you know who you're working for, okay?*"

"Okay, Pops. Love you. Talk to you tomorrow. Bye."

"*Love you, Lexi Girl. Bye.*" Pops says and then he hangs up.

"You asshole," I say, turning and slapping Connor on the arm. "You set me up. When did you figure out that it was the same gym you go to?"

"Not until you mentioned it was close to the pizza place. Speaking of," he says, looking a little concerned. "We may need to call that guy Tino and tell him I'm not a sketchy fuck. He is not my biggest fan."

"Oh? What did you do to him? He's the nicest guy."

"Nothing, really. I called him trying to find you. I knew they named the pizza after you, and we figured you lived nearby because you were on foot when you saw Devon there. Apparently, it's weird for a man to call a pizza place and ask for a customer's phone number." He shrugs, but I can tell he's being sarcastic. He knows it's weird. "Tino may have also seen me walking around the neighbourhood looking for anyone who might know you," he says, hiding his mouth behind his hand a little.

I bark out a laugh. "Yeah, I could see Tino calling your a sketchy fuck for that. You have to admit, it is a little weird."

"Hey," he says, pulling me into a hug. "I was desperate. I finally found you again, and then immediately lost you. I thought you were leaving town and my only chance to find you was by wandering around the neighbourhood I thought you lived in, hoping to stumble on you accidentally."

"Yeah, that is a terrible plan." I laugh. "I really should have talked to Devon when I saw him at Tino's. But I wasn't sure you'd even want to see me. I was scared of being rejected, I guess."

"That is not something you ever have to worry about," he says. "I will always want you to find me." He kisses me on the top of the head and lets me go. "Now, what do we need?"

I pull up the grocery list on my phone. "Yeah, we probably should get moving here. These groceries won't find themselves."

Connor pushes the cart to the first aisle.

"I can't believe you called Tino." I say, shaking my head. "And here I was worried you'd think I was a stalker for being at your concert. You actually did some real stalking, you sketchy fuck."

"Haha, very funny," Connor deadpans, before plastering a big smile on his face. "If I'd known you were moving in with me right away, I would have saved myself the embarrassment. I don't even know if I can go back to the gym now. That entire neighbourhood has probably heard about my stalking and sketchiness. First your Pops is going to beat my ass and then the other townsfolk will chase me away with torches and pitchforks like I'm Frankenstein's monster."

"Whoa, whoa, whoa. I didn't exactly move in with you. I moved into staff accommodations on your property. Not the same thing. You're right about one thing, though. People tend to stick together on that side of town. I didn't put it together, but Tino called me to say someone was trying to convince him to give out my number. If I'd known it was you, I would have told him to go ahead."

Connor smiles, "Yeah?"

"Yeah."

He passes me his phone. "Better give it to me now so I don't have to do anymore stalking. I am terrible at it."

"You really are." I take his phone and send myself a text. "There. I messaged myself, so I have your number too. Don't worry, I promise I won't sell it," I joke. "By the way, I like your disguise."

"Ha, thanks. I usually can get away with people not recognizing me if they can't see my tattoos, and if I wear a hat to hide most of my face. I have a feeling that won't be the case for much longer, though. Some little girls your Pops was training at the gym last week recognized me even wearing this. I don't think I'm ready for that yet."

"Don't worry, Connor. I'll be your fame beard for now. No one would suspect a famous rockstar to be grocery shopping, let alone with a woman as plain as me." I smile at him and put my arm in his.

"Oh Alex, you are not plain. Not at all." He says to me and then leans down and kisses me softly on the lips. "And you're going to be so much more than a fame beard." His voice deepens.

Damn it, those butterflies are back again.

32

Managing Expectations and Fixing Reputations

Connor

THE REST OF OUR shopping excursion passes without incident. Alex was right when she said she'd need to make more than one trip to get it all into the house. We had to grab a second shopping cart to put all of our items in, and even that wasn't really enough. We loaded both carts right to the top, and then some.

We had a bit of a disagreement over who was going to pay for everything until she points out that using the company credit card ensures my accountant can keep track of the grocery expenses properly. I agree to using the company card but insist that she pay for her groceries for the pool house on the same bill. She is, of course, always welcome to whatever I have in the main house where she will do most of the cooking, but I understand the need for her own space with her own favorite items on hand.

And of course, keeping myself distracted with thoughts of groceries and who's paying for them is helping me not freak out over the only thing I really care about right now. How am I going to keep Alex in my life now that she's back?

As we're loading the groceries into the truck, I broach the topic of having the guys at the house. "Did Denise tell you that the guys will be at the house most of the time, too? They all have rooms there, but they also have their own homes. Once we really get into writing and recording, they will probably spend the night more. We try to not to treat the chef like a short-order cook though, so you won't need to worry about cooking five or six different things at a time."

"She mentioned something about it, but she wasn't able to go into too much detail during the interview because of confidentiality concerns. I thought it might be easiest if I made you a menu of meals I've planned for the week? And then I can give you a list of things that I will always keep on hand to cook on short notice, since your food preferences seem to be pretty basic. I'll save the fancier stuff for the main weekly menu, and then if you guys need something different, it will be easy enough to throw something together. My contract has me available to cook twenty-four hours a day, after all."

We finish loading the groceries, and I close the hatch, turning to give her a look. "That part is still in there? I honestly hate that part of the contract. It doesn't seem fair to make someone be available around the clock because we sometimes keep late hours." I especially don't like it now that I know Alex is the one we've hired. "What if, instead of having you available at all hours, you make up something that we can grab from the fridge if you're not available? We can work out some hours that will coincide with when we do most of our work, so it wouldn't be a typical nine-to-five day, but it would be a little more regular for you, so you can still have a bit of a life?"

"That's unnecessary, Connor," she tells me. "I'm being well compensated with the expectation of being available all the time."

"Yeah, it seems like you are, but I've always considered it to be too low. I'm going to talk to Denise about it, anyway. She can straighten it out with you later. I don't want you to feel like I'm giving you preferential treatment or anything, though. This is actually something I've been considering for a long time, for all the staff we hire at the house." And it is. I make a little money now, and I want to make sure that I take care of the people I hire to make my life easier. If I'm pushing to make it happen now because Alex is the chef, well... Too bad.

"Let's head get back, shall we?"

I can tell this is making her uncomfortable, so I drop it.

"Good idea. Since you don't start until Monday, should we order pizza and pick it up before we go back? You know, and maybe you can tell Tino I'm a good guy at the same time?"

She chuckles. "Let's go back. We have a truck full of groceries and I'm a professional chef. I'll make something instead. I've been dying to cook in that kitchen since I first saw it. Maybe lasagna? Let me get some use out of that kitchen of yours."

She seems excited at the thought of cooking in my kitchen, but not nearly as excited as I am at the thought of having her there.

"Deal." We both walk to the front of the Escalade and get in. "You still have to call Tino, though." I tell her seriously.

She laughs. "You really can't handle him thinking poorly of you, can you?"

"No, I can't. I can tell that he cares about you, that you're important to him. I want him to know that I am worthy of your time. And the first step is you telling him I'm not a sketchy fuck." She looks slightly surprised at my serious tone. "The rest I'll have to do on my own."

After watching me drive for a few minutes, Alex grabs her phone from the center console. She does something on the screen and puts the phone up to her ear.

"Hey, Tino?" she says, glancing over at me. "It's Alex. Got a sec?"

I smile to myself but say nothing. Now I only need to figure out how to show her I'm serious without scaring her away.

SECOND CHANCE

33

Settling In and Making Friends

Alex

I FINISH UP MY phone call with Tino as we pull into the garage at the house. He is going to be a little more trusting of Connor but is still leaning towards thinking he's sketchy. When I tell Connor this, he laughs.

"At least you tried, babe. I'm going to have to work hard to earn his trust. He did see me running all over your neighbourhood asking everyone about you, after all," he says. "Now let's get this stuff inside and we can start on the lasagna. I'm starving."

When I head around to the back of the vehicle, he waves me off, telling me he's got it. Really, what he does is grab one bag and walk into the kitchen with me on his heels. Sitting on the bar stools and at the table, I can see Devon, Travis, Johnny, Aiden, and Ryder. Devon gives me a brief wave, and Ryder jumps out of his seat.

"You really found her?" he yells, before running over to hug me. "I'm so glad you're here. Now he can stop his moping." He laughs over at Connor.

"And that's why you get to carry all of Alex's personal bags to the pool house. They're in the back of the Escalade. Everything comes in here first, so we can sort out what belongs in this kitchen." Connor points to the door that we came in and all the guys, except Devon, get up to help. Since that part is taken care of, I go over and turn on the oven to preheat.

"I didn't tell them about you when they got here. I told them that Connor went to the gym and would be back soon. When they realize you are the new chef, they're going to lose it. Connor wanted me to prepare them so they wouldn't say anything stupid, but I knew they'd be fine." Devon is giggling to himself a bit as the guys to file in, each with a few bags in their hands. They put the bags onto the counter and turn around to grab the rest from the truck.

"Okay, girlie," Ryder asks when he's barely even back in the room. He crosses his arms over his chest. "It just hit me that Connor said your stuff is going out to the pool house. Why is that?"

"Fuck off, Ryder," Connor says, laughing. "You'll find out soon enough."

"Actually," I explain, giving Connor a dirty look. He's trying to stir up trouble for no reason. "I am a professional chef, and Denise hired me to work here for six months. So I guess we'll all be seeing a lot more of each other."

The other guys all express their surprise at this turn of events, and Johny asks, "Will Becca be coming over too?"

"Once all the paperwork is approved, she wants to come and hang by the pool. She doesn't like swimming in public spaces."

I busy myself with separating my few bags out from the main pile on the counter and leaving them by the side door.

"What an amazing coincidence, right?" Connor says, his voice taking on a higher pitch. "I was doing everything I could to track her down and today, when I walked in here with Devon to figure out my next move, I found her standing in the kitchen, taking pictures of the cupboards." He walks over and kisses me on the temple while giving me a little side hug. That gets some strange looks from the rest of the guys.

"So, you two are a thing now?" It's Aiden this time. He's already started unloading some groceries into the fridge.

I feel my face heat as I think about that. He's been very touchy with me, even kissed me a couple of times, but there's been no actual conversation about it. All I've learned is that he didn't ghost me like I thought he did, and that's been enough to take in for now. "And on that note. Ryder? Grab the bags, please. I'll come with you to my place. I need to grab my knife roll to start dinner."

Ryder runs over and picks up all the bags I've set at the door and follows me out to the pool house. It's not that far across the yard, but those bags are pretty heavy, and by the time we reach my door, Ryder looks like he's regretting his decision to carry all the bags at once.

"What the hell did you buy?" he asks me. "And why does it weigh so much?"

"I had to stock the entire kitchen in here. Lots and lots of spices and other staples are in those bags." I pull items from the grocery bags and putting them into the small pantry. "Can you put the cold stuff into the fridge for me?"

He puts things in the fridge but apparently decides that now is also a good time to ask me a bunch of questions. "So," he says. "You and Connor, hey? You've known each other for a while."

"Sort of." Voicing some of my concerns to another one of Connor's friends seems like it might be a bad idea, but I do it anyway. "We knew each other a long time ago, and now it seems we have a chance to get to know each other again. A person can change a lot in twenty years. He might be very different from what I remember." I'm worried he'll be that rockstar stereotype instead of the sweet guy I knew, but I'm not about to tell Ryder that part. From what I hear, Ryder is the most 'rockstar' of the whole band.

"I've known Connor for a long time, babe." Ryder turns to look straight at me while he's talking. "I'd even heard about you long before last week. Our entire first album is how he dealt with losing you when you guys were kids. I think you should listen to it."

"I don't know if I can," I tell him. "We figured out today that we had different experiences of what happened when I had to move. He thought I didn't call because I wanted nothing more to do with him because he lived in a town that reminded me of my parents. I called and the phone number was disconnected, so I thought he'd decided that dealing with my grief from losing my parents was too much trouble. I'm sure there's a lot of anger on that album that I'm not quite prepared to hear."

"Yeah, there is some anger. That's what helped launch us onto the hard rock charts. But there is also a lot of hurt, loss, love, and awe, along with that anger." He looks at me with a little sadness in his eyes. "I think that listening to it might give you a little more insight into where he's coming from. But not until you're ready, of course." He tosses me a smile. I can see that he is a heartbreaker. He's got dark hair and dark eyes and definitely has a 'dangerous man' vibe going on. He raises a pierced eyebrow at me. "Are you ready to go back to the house? I don't want Connor to think I'm making moves on you. He may think I'm a slut, but I know where to draw the line." He punctuates 'slut' with an eye roll.

I think over that last comment as we put away the last few items and start walking back to the house. I don't know what exactly it was about the way he said it, but the eye roll makes it seem like he's hurt by being called a slut? Or by having his friends think he's a slut? There's a story there for sure. I'm in no place to get that story, though. I just met the guy. I am a helper by nature, though, so I reach up and touch his arm to stop him before we get to the house.

"Hey, Ryder," I breathe. "I'm a complete stranger to you, and please tell me to fuck off if I'm overstepping, but if you ever need a friend with a sympathetic ear, I'm your gal, okay?"

He looks at me like he can't figure me out. He thinks for a minute before holding his hand out. "Give me your phone for a sec." Then he takes my phone and types something before giving it back. "My phone is in the house, so I sent myself a text. Now I have your number and you have mine. I might take you up on that offer, Alex. Making new friends in this business is tough. And my old friends... Well, let's say I'm fucking that up pretty well on my own." He slips his arm over my shoulder and starts walking again. "Now let's get in there, pal, and see what those assholes are up to. I'll even help you cook. As you can see, I'm wasting away here." He laughs and pats his abs as though he has a belly.

"Alright, friend." I laugh with him. "How good are you at grating cheese?"

34

We're All Sketchy Fucks

Connor

"So you just walked in and she was here?" Aiden has grabbed himself a beer from the fridge and is sitting at the counter next to Devon. "Wasn't that a little weird? Did it occur to you that maybe she's a stalker, and she broke in?"

"Not even for a second," I say. "But I joked about it when we walked in, because she was so concerned about it at the meet and greet. I'm not sure she thought it was funny. She was a little shocked to see us though, so that could have been it, too."

"Did you confirm with Denise? I mean, it's not outside the realm of possibility that she could have broken in here and is pretending to be a chef." That's Aiden for you, always looking at the worst-case scenario.

"That doesn't even make sense, dude." Devon answers him. "She has the keys and the alarm codes. Plus, how would she have even known we were hiring a chef, or that one was expected to be coming today?"

"Yeah, I suppose that's true." Aiden admits.

"But I confirmed it with Denise anyway, more to marvel at how she hired the exact person Connor has been searching for than to make sure she wasn't a crazy stalker." Devon says. "So you can rest easy."

Travis and Johnny have been sitting over at the table this whole time, whispering to each other. They seem to be debating something when Alex and Ryder come back inside. I'm glad Alex missed the whole stalker conversation. Joking about it is one thing, but Aiden having actual concerns might have upset her. I want everything to go smoothly until we get the chance to have a serious talk about where we can go with this. It might seem like I'm moving fast, but I've been waiting my entire life for her to come back into it. I can't lose her again. The first time broke my heart, I know another time would break me altogether.

"So, Alex." It's Travis who starts talking first, "Are you working yet or are we ordering takeout again? Either way is fine with me. I only want to know how long it's going to be because I'm starving."

"I'm technically not working until Monday," Alex answers while walking into the main part of the kitchen. "But Connor and I decided I would make lasagna tonight instead of ordering takeout. We thought about ordering that pizza you guys had last night, but Tino still thinks that Connor is a sketchy fuck, so it might be safer if I make dinner here." She looks at me when she calls me a sketchy fuck, and then she and Devon both burst out laughing.

"Someone thinks you're a sketchy fuck?" Aiden asks. "Do I want to know why?"

"It may have something to do with my methods of trying to track down Alex earlier today?" I mumble a little. "I'm not sure I can go back to that side of town anytime soon."

Now it's everyone else's turn to laugh. Fuckers. They were in on it when we planned to look around the neighbourhood. Shit, it was pretty much Travis' idea. They were with me the first night when we drove around looking for her place, hoping we'd get lucky and see her somewhere. If one of us is a sketchy fuck, then we all are. At least that's what I'm going to keep telling myself.

"It turns out that I wouldn't have even had to go to all that trouble, anyway. You know that gym that I go to? Mike, the old guy I've been training with for the last eighteen years, is Alex's grandfather. And he's hinted at setting me up with her in the past." I'm attempting to distract them from the stalking and get their attention back to the amazing coincidences involved in bringing Alex back into my life. "So I could have had you with me for the last eighteen years, babe." I move closer to Alex and pull her into a hug. I know I probably shouldn't be so touchy with her yet, but I can't stay away. I love how her body feels against mine.

"Yeah." Alex pulls away from the hug. She seems a little uncomfortable, so I let her go without making it a thing. "Let's get started on this dinner. If you're in my kitchen, you help. Anyone who's not good with that can fuck off right now. I will call you when it's ready if you're going to do something else."

"I'm going to do some work in the studio." Even though I'd be more than happy to help, I don't want to crowd her. It's been a day full of surprises for both of us. "I've been working on a song for a bit and I think I finally have a handle on some lyrics. You guys coming?"

The other guys all get up at once, except for Ryder and Devon.

"Not that I'm afraid of helping you, Alex," Travis lies. He hates cooking. And he's terrible at it. "But I really need to keep an eye on Connor in the studio. I have a feeling he's bursting with the desire to write love songs tonight, for some strange reason." He laughs and takes off, running down the hall toward the studio.

"I'm sure something's going to be bursting with desire later tonight." Johnny wiggles his eyebrows and throws Alex an exaggerated wink before turning to follow Travis.

"Do you see what I have to put up with around here?" Aiden sighs heavily. "It looks like you and I are going to be the only adults around here, Alex. Welcome to the crew." He grabs a beer before going after the others.

Ryder comes over to me and pushes me out of the kitchen. "We'll take care of her, bro." He says, before giving me a little shove and whispering, "You're crowding her. Give her some time."

I take one more look at her before going to the studio, too. I know it's best to give her some time, but my body wants to be right beside her.

35

I'd Like to Call a Friend

Alex

"ARE YOU DOING ALRIGHT?" Devon looks at me with concern in his eyes. "It feels like a lot has happened in this one day. Did you get the chance to talk to Becca yet?"

"Not yet." I'm concentrating on the sheets of pasta rolling through my pasta machine. "I didn't think I was supposed to mention anything to her until she's been cleared?"

"I think you'll be okay to talk with your best friend," Ryder says to me while he stirs our sauce. He's actually a decent helper in the kitchen. From his playboy rock star look, I expected him to be a lot less domestic. "I doubt she'll be running to the tabloids to sell us out."

"You should call her," Devon tells me as he combines the ricotta cheese with eggs for the middle layer. I like to keep lasagna pretty simple, especially when I'm feeding a bunch of guys. Ryder has the meat sauce and will grate the cheese, Devon has the ricotta layer, and I'm making the noodles. "You look like you need a little girl time, no offense."

"None taken. It has been a very surprising day. I need to talk to someone who's on my side. No matter how nice you guys are being to me, I know you're Connor's friends first."

"Hey now, you offered to be an ear for me, so that makes me your friend, too. Truthfully, those guys are always telling me to fuck off, so maybe I'm deciding to be *your* friend first." Ryder bumps my shoulder with his. He's smiling at me, so I can't really tell if he's serious or not. I mean, I have heard them tell him to fuck off a lot, but...

"Thanks, Ryder. I'll keep that in mind for next time. I think in this situation, though, I need some girl talk. With a girl." I grab the lasagna pans from the cupboard and gesture for Ryder to bring me the sauce and cheese. Devon sees what we're doing and brings me the ricotta layer as well.

The guys help me layer the lasagnas and we get them into the oven.

"You guys go ahead and do whatever you need to do now. The lasagnas need to cook for about an hour, so you've got some time."

"That's okay, Alex. We can stay and hang out." Ryder says as he grabs a beer from the fridge. "I don't want to leave you all by yourself."

"Don't worry about that." I hold my phone up. "I'm going to do what you guys said and call Becca for some girl talk."

"You sure?" Devon asks. "We don't mind staying. And that's only partly because it smells so much better in here than in the studio."

"Positive. I'll let you know when dinner is ready."

"Okay, see you in a bit, then." Ryder tips his beer towards me in a wave as he turns to leave. "Come on, Devon. Let's give Alex some privacy. I'm sure she doesn't want us eavesdropping on her gossip session with Becca."

Devon waves as he turns to follow Ryder. As soon as they're out of earshot, I pull my phone out and call Becca.

36

Take Your Time

Connor

"I won't take the chance of losing her again, guys." I'm pacing in the studio while the guys try to convince me I'm moving too fast. I sort of see their point, but I don't know how else to go about this. "She's been in my head for twenty years. And now she's here. I need her to stay."

"That is not something you need to worry about yet." Aiden stretches out on the floor, throwing one of his drumsticks in the air repeatedly and then catching it. "She's signed a six-month contract, so she'll be around for a little while. Get to know her again. It's been twenty years, man. You could both be completely different people now. You might not even want her to stay when you know her better."

"Shut up." I say, while flipping him off. There's no way I could ever see myself not wanting her to stay.

"Yeah, you don't want to overwhelm her. She recently got out of a relationship with some dude who she caught cheating. And from what Becca said that night, it sounds like it's happened more than that one time." Johnny is working something out on his guitar while talking to us.

"Do you think that would really matter?" She has to know that I would never do something like that to her, right? "If it's happened lots, and she keeps trying, then it can't bother her that much, can it?" I already know the answer to this. Of course it bothers her. I watched her run out of the bar at the mere mention of it, and I'm sure it's not because she just met most of the people there.

"Oh gee, I don't know, dude. If you'd been cheated on a bunch of times, would you be interested in starting up a relationship with someone? Let alone someone you could google to see evidence of the countless other people they've been with?" He's throwing my past in my face. It was a long time ago, but things on the internet never go away. I rarely regret the decisions I made in the past, but this is one time I wish I'd kept it in my pants a little more back then.

I sigh. "Yeah, that's a good point, Johnny. It will take some work to gain her trust. I can't seem to control myself very well when she's around. It's like my lips are drawn to her and I have to kiss her all the time. I've kept it innocent so far, but I can feel my willpower fading every time I see her."

"It's been less than a day!" Aiden says from his spot on the floor.

"I know! That's part of the problem," I agree. "I've been on edge since I saw her after the show and didn't get her number. I was so worried she would disappear again that as soon as I saw her today, my brain has been trying to come up with a way to make her stay. And my body is trying to get closer to her any way it can. I feel so out of control."

"You do seem to be a little out of it, man. Chill out. You may not have had a real breakup with her back then, but that doesn't mean that you can pick up right where you left off." Aiden gets up off the floor and comes to sit beside me. "You've both been with other people in the years since you were together. And in her case, some of those people betrayed her, and that has probably left a mark."

A stabbing pain hits me in the gut when he mentions the other people Alex has been with. If I'd been smarter when I was a kid, she'd never have been hurt all those times. Because she'd still be with me.

"And if you look at the stereotype of guys in our industry, it doesn't exactly scream 'will be faithful in a relationship', so you're going to have your work cut out for you if this is what you really want." Travis is joining in now, to really drive the point home.

The guys are right, though. I can't jump right back in. In the last twenty years, so many things have happened and yeah, for the first little while, I was out of control. Too many parties, too many women, and way too many photos as evidence of both. It will be hard for her to trust anyone, let alone someone in my position. Even now everyone expects I will sleep with any woman who looks my way. Hell, half of Devon's job is getting rid of groupies like the one who showed up in the bathroom after the show last week. So how am I going to prove myself to Alex?

I look up to see Devon and Ryder coming in. They're speaking too quietly for me to hear, but I see them both look at me, so I know what they're talking about. I'm hoping that Alex hasn't said anything bad. I'd hate to be starting at even more of a disadvantage than I already am.

"Hey guys, is dinner done already?" I call out to get their attention. "That seems pretty fast."

"Nah," Ryder answers. "The lasagnas just went into the oven. She fucking made her own noodles, man. I don't think I've ever had lasagna made with fresh noodles. You better not fuck this up."

I'm already worried about fucking it up, so I don't even respond.

Devon adds, "I'm going to need to start coming to the gym with you, Connor. If she feeds us like this for six months, I'm going to get too fat to move. Some security I'll be for you then."

He laughs a little. The guy works out more than I do, and he's the farthest thing from fat. He is just naturally bigger than the rest of us. I'd run if I saw him coming at me in a dark alley, that's for sure.

"So before Connor asks, did Alex say anything about him?" Johnny jumps right into it before I have time to. He's right though, that's exactly what I was going to ask next.

"Not much, man," Ryder says. "She's going to call Becca to talk, because Devon and I are your friends first. I let her know that I've dumped you, though. I'm officially team Alex from now on. She's way better looking than you are, and she cooks. It's a no-brainer, really." He comes over and flops down beside me. "I think I'm going to have t-shirts made. I'll wear them at our shows." His grin tells me he's not exactly kidding.

"She seems kind of confused." Devon adds, glaring at Ryder. "This has likely been too much for her to take in all at once. Not only does she know where you are now, she knows you've been trying to track her down. And she's now working for you. Being your employee might change things for her. All I know is that I like her. She seems super nice, and she's definitely way too good for you. I didn't come right out and tell her like Ryder did, but I'm probably going to need a team Alex shirt as well. You better not fuck this up."

"Well, you've been told." Aiden laughs. "But I happen to agree with him. She seems like a nice girl. If you're not serious, then back off. She doesn't need any more shit in her life."

"I am serious." I jump up and fist my hands into my hair. "I'm so serious that I would go ring shopping right now if I thought there was even the slightest chance she'd say yes." I sit down again and wipe my hands over my face. "And yes, I am aware of how crazy that makes me sound. But I can't help it. I'm fucking in love with her, guys. Tell me what to do."

"In love? You just met her." Somehow, Johnny doesn't look as incredulous as he sounds. "I'm not sure that's even possible?"

"I didn't just meet her. I've been in love with her all these years. I never thought I'd get another chance. I thought I'd ever see her again."

I lean back in my chair with my hands over my face. I have a pit in my stomach that I don't know how to ease. I'm scared Alex is going to disappear again, and I want to make sure that doesn't happen. Not sure how I can do that, though.

37

First Family Dinner and Then...

Alex

"You're working for Connor?" I think I've shocked Becca with the news. *"The Connor that you've been in love with since you were a teenager? The same one that you thought you lost again? We moved you into that Connor's pool house?"*

"That's what I'm trying to tell you. That's not even the craziest part. Apparently, he's been working out with Pops for like eighteen years." I'm assuming the studio is soundproofed, so I have Becca on speaker while I get some salad and bread ready to go with the dinner. I may be in crisis mode, but I still know how to feed people. And the routine of making a meal helped to calm my nerves some. "We've somehow never crossed paths in all this time. And how many times have I lived with you in that apartment in the last eighteen years? Probably has to be twelve times, at least."

"This is amazing. What are you going to do?"

"I don't even know. Did I tell you how he and Devon caught me taking pictures in the kitchen? I was getting a list ready to go to the store, and that's when they came in. I'm lucky he didn't call the cops on me, thinking I was a stalker. He joked about it, though, since I made such a huge deal out of it after the show last week."

"No way! How surprised were you? That must've been insane. I have to be honest with you. I'm having a hard time wrapping my

head around this. You guys have been circling around each other for years, then. Didn't you say a former client recommended you for this job, too? So that's another connection between the two of you."

She's making me more nervous about this than I already am. There's about half an hour left before we eat, and I'm still no closer to figuring this out. On a whim, I ask Becca to come to dinner.

"It's lasagna," I plead. "You love my lasagna, remember?"

"You want me to come eat with you and Connor? No thanks, I don't feel like being a third wheel."

"You won't be a third wheel. The whole band is here, plus Devon. Please?"

"Okay, I'll be there in about twenty minutes. I have to get ready." She seems pretty eager for dinner now. I wonder what's up with that? *"See you soon,"* she says before hanging up on me. That bitch didn't even say bye.

I busy myself in the kitchen for a bit before realizing I should tell someone that I invited Becca. It is Connor's house, so even though my first instinct is to text Ryder (he is the one who said it would be okay to talk to her after all) I text him instead.

Alex- I invited Becca to join us all for dinner. I hope that's okay?

Connor- Of course. She's always welcome to visit.

That's a relief. If he says it's okay, then we won't need to worry about the background check. A few minutes later, the guys start coming back into the kitchen.

"Anything we can do to help?" Connor asks. "We're not afraid to work for our dinner, you know."

If they're all going to stand there and insist on helping, then I will put them to work.

"Alright." I point to the salad that I've already made. "Bring that to the table, please. Someone else can set it. We'll need the cheese out with the small grater. There's a cheese board over there." I point to the back counter.

The guys get right to it, not hesitating at all. If I ever find myself in charge of a kitchen again, I might have to hire them on as my staff. If their whole famous rock band thing doesn't work out, that is.

"Lasagna will be ready to eat in about twenty minutes now. Do we have enough chairs for everyone?" I eye the kitchen table, noticing there are only four spots.

"I've set us up in the dining room." Devon points back towards the front of the house. "I sent Denise a message to tell her to join us, too."

Right then the doorbell rings, and Johnny jumps up to answer it.

"That must be Becca," Connor says. "Denise has a key."

While I wait for her to come back to the kitchen with Johnny, I take the lasagnas out of the oven and place them on the counter to rest. Throwing the bread into the oven to heat, I finish washing up the dishes I used when preparing dinner. I hate waiting until after to do all the cleaning. Though tonight I might get all these guys to help. They said they'd work for their supper after all, and I'm technically not working yet.

About ten minutes pass before Becca and Johnny come back with Denise in tow. Becca looks a little flushed, probably nervous to be hanging out with these guys again after my week long search for Connor.

"Hi, Denise." I greet the woman who hired me while getting the bread out. "It's nice to see you again. Did you get that issue all sorted out this morning?"

I notice her glance quickly at Ryder before she tells me she got it fixed right up. That's strange. Although with Ryder as a client, I'm sure most of the issues she has to deal with stem from him. He seems to be a bit of a troublemaker.

"Okay, well, now that we're all here, let's go ahead into the dining room. Everyone grab something and bring it with you, and then we can all eat." I direct everyone to take the things we need and soon we're all sitting around the table.

"No need to be shy. Everyone dig in." I serve myself the first piece. "I'm the chef. Serving the food isn't in my job description."

We make quick work of dinner, listening to the guys talk about last week's show and how the writing for the new album is going so far. Before long, Ryder is excusing himself, saying he has a date. Denise and Devon leave shortly after, followed not long after by Aiden and Travis.

Becca pulls me aside. "I have an early shoot tomorrow. Are you going to be alright tonight if I go? I really need to get some sleep."

"Yeah, that's no problem. The night's almost over, I'm sure I can manage. Call me after the shoot tomorrow and we can talk."

She says goodbye to Connor and thanks him for having her over, says bye to Johnny, and I walk her to the door. After giving me a hug, she leaves.

Johnny sticks around for a bit, helping me and Connor bring all the dishes back to the kitchen. He even loads up the dishwasher before needing to leave, too. Apparently, he also has a date tonight.

That leaves me here, alone, with Connor. I glance over as he comes back into the kitchen after seeing Johnny out.

"No sense in having a security system if we don't lock the doors and set the alarm, right?" he jokes. I watch as he runs his hands through his dark hair. How does messing it up more make it look even better? He comes over to the sink where I've already got the pans in soapy water, ready to wash.

"I'll wash and you dry?" He takes off the multitude of silver rings he's wearing and sets them on the bar above the sink. He also takes off a leather cuff that he wears on his left wrist. I can see something tattooed across his fingers, but I can't make out what it is from this angle. I pull a dish towel out from the drawer beside the sink and get ready for him to pass me the pan he's currently washing.

"Is it only these pans that we need to wash?" He asks after passing me the first one and starting on the second.

I grab the pan that he passes me, but I don't really hear the question because I'm too busy staring at his arms. The muscles flex underneath the full sleeve tattoos he has, and I can't look away. How did I now notice that his arms are covered in flowers, and many of those flowers are peonies? It's almost like we have matching tattoos.

"I'm sorry, what?" I sputter when he nudges me with his elbow.

"I said, are you going to dry that or keep staring at my arms?" My face heat as he looks at me.

"Oh, sorry." I look down and hurriedly wipe the pan I have in my hand. "I was noticing that we both have peony tattoos."

He finishes washing the other pan and gives it to me once I've put the other one back in the cupboard. After draining and rinsing the sink, he turns to look at me. I quickly turn and put the last pan away before turning back to look at him.

"They were always your favourite," he whispers, running his fingers down my arm where my tattoo is. "So I knew I wanted peonies on me permanently. That way, you'd always be close."

I feel the same tingles that I did that first night after the show. I release a long, slow breath.

"You got peonies tattooed on you because of me?" I've lost the dish towel somewhere and now I have my first two fingers on each hand tucked into his front pockets, ever so slightly. "I would have never thought that."

"I got them done after our first tour. The album was successful, and we all had a reasonable payday. By the time that happened, it had already been eight years since I'd seen you. I knew there was no way I was getting you out of my head, so I decided to go ahead and put you on my skin, too."

He looks down at my lips and then back up into my eyes. Oh god, he's going to kiss me. His hands come up to push into my hair while he cups my face and slowly tilts his head down, lowering his lips to my face. Warm breath caresses my mouth, and then his lips are on mine, kissing softly. He tilts my head with his hands, deepening the kiss, his tongue slowly massaging mine. Shit, he's good at this. My hands move of their own volition, exploring the hard planes of abs that I hadn't noticed in my prior appraisal of his body. Oh, those are nice. I'm going to need to explore those with my tongue later. My hands roam over his skin, moving from his abs to his chest, pushing his shirt as I go. Connor stops kissing me long enough to reach back over his head with one hand and pull his shirt off, giving me a view of what I've been admiring with my hands.

Tattoos may completely cover his arms, but he has few on his chest. He's smooth with a little chest hair, and a small trail leading down into the front of low-slung jeans. Holy shit, he has an adonis belt! I've always been a sucker for that muscly V shape that points directly to a man's package, but I've never been fortunate enough to see one in person. I am staring at it in wonder, lightly running my fingers along both sides, when Connor chuckles a little.

"See something you like, babe?" he leans down and whispers before slowly sliding his tongue down the outer shell of my ear, making me gasp when a bolt of desire shoots straight to my clit. I don't know that I've ever been this turned on before.

"I'd like to see a lot more," I breathe, my voice a little shaky. "But I also want you to keep doing that." He's started kissing and licking my neck now, with little nibbles here and there. He has one hand back in my hair, holding my head tilted so he has better access to my neck. With his other hand, he draws lazy circles on my thigh where my shorts meet skin.

"Is that so?" He kisses a line back up to my mouth, where he gently licks and sucks on my lower lip before stroking my tongue with his own. "I'd like to see a lot more, too." He slides his hands to my waist and catches the hem of my tank, easing it up and over my head, careful not to snag my hair. The shirt drops from his hand and he reaches around to unhook my bra, then stops.

When the bra doesn't easily slide off with a little tug, he pulls back and looks at me with his eyebrows drawn.

Fucking yoga bra.

"It has to go up and over," I mumble. What a way to kill the mood. I pull it over my head myself while he chuckles. "I, uh, wasn't really expecting anyone else to be undressing me today," I offer.

"Might I suggest you expect it from now on?" Connor reaches for me again, thumbs skimming my already pebbled nipples. The electricity I feel from his touch jolts through me once more. "Because I plan on undressing you as often as possible from this day on." His mouth is on my neck again. He begins slowly kissing down my chest, stopping to suck a nipple into his mouth, grazing it with his teeth and flicking it with his tongue, the contrast between hard and soft sending my arousal through the roof. He moves to my other breast, showering the nipple with the same affection he showed the first. One hand moves down to the button on my shorts while his lips make their way back to mine. He flicks it open and slowly slides the zipper down.

"I have wanted to taste you since I saw you at the show last week," he says against my mouth. I let out a small groan. "I haven't been able to get you out of my head. I've been stroking myself to thoughts of you every day while I shower. I've never come as hard in my life as I have from thinking of you." He punctuates every sentence with ever deepening kisses, our tongues sliding together more frantically each time.

Suddenly, my shorts and panties are on the floor and Connor's hands are under my ass, lifting me off my feet.

"Wrap your legs around me," he says. My hands are in his hair now, as we frantically kiss, and I can feel the hard ridge of his cock through his jeans. I rub myself against him as best as I can while he carries me to the kitchen table. When he sets me down on the edge, he whispers, "Lay back, baby. I haven't had my dessert yet."

Oh fuck, yes, please! He kisses me as he lays me back gently on the table and proceeds to kiss and lick a path down my body. He passes my breast and sucks a nipple into his mouth briefly, but doesn't stop there. He continues down, down, while I whimper softly, urging him to move to where I want him, where I need him. I hear a chair being moved when he lets me go for a moment.

"Legs on my shoulders, love." He sits down, positioning me closer to the edge of the table. And then his mouth is on me. He licks me from my entrance to my already sensitive clit, sending a jolt of pleasure through my entire body. The moan that comes out of my mouth sounds completely foreign. I know I've never made that sound before. "You taste as sweet as I thought you would," he says. "I am going to savour this." He reaches a hand up to my hip, holding me down, as he licks me entrance to clit again, before sucking that magical little nub into his mouth, his little licks and flicks driving me higher, the pressure building as I feel the orgasm just out of my reach. My hands reach down to his head, grabbing fistfuls of his soft hair and holding him right where I need him.

"Greedy girl," he says against me with a small chuckle. I can feel a slight rumble as he groans while sliding first one finger, and then two, inside me. "God, Alex, you are so wet for me." He hooks his fingers a little, slowly stroking inside me, until he finds that little spot that nearly makes me explode all over his hand. His mouth locks on to my clit again as he sucks it between his lips, his tongue flicking faster in time with the movement of my hips as I ride his face.

"Oh fuck, Connor, yes. Don't stop. Like that, don't stop, don't—" a strangled scream escapes my throat as he strokes, and sucks, and licks me through my orgasm. Explosions dance behind my eyelids as my core pulses with my release, squeezing his fingers as he continues to stroke his fingers inside me. He licks me once more, his tongue flat and wide, taking in all of me, before I feel him stand up. He slowly slides his fingers out of me, and I watch as he sucks them into his mouth, licking them clean. A ripple of my orgasm flashes through me at the sight.

"You taste fucking amazing, babe. I would do that all day, but I'm about to make a fool of myself. If I don't stop right now, I'm going to come in my pants or climb up and fuck you right on this table." His eyes are black with lust and his breathing is quick, and I can see the truth of his words. I sit up and reach for him.

Grabbing his waistband, I slide my hands to his belt buckle, undoing it. I look into his eyes as I flick open the button on his jeans and slide the zipper down, reaching in to palm his hard cock. Oh fuck, he's naked under his jeans. A groan escapes my lips.

"You *better* get up here and fuck me, Connor," I say, pushing down his jeans and sliding back a little on the table. "Right fucking now."

38

Twenty Years in the Making

Connor

ALEX PUSHES DOWN MY jeans and slides back onto the table. I'm not even sure that I heard what she said, but the intent is clear. She wants me inside her now. And I won't keep her waiting any longer. I push down my jeans, grabbing a condom from my pocket before stepping out of them. Moving closer to Alex, I tear open the condom and she takes it from. She strokes my cock with one hand before rolling the condom on and leaning back on the table. I climb up after her, kissing my way up her body, finally settling myself between her legs. Teenage me is losing his fucking mind right now. Alex has always been my ultimate fantasy, and having her like this after all these years is everything.

Her eyes look up at me, and she pulls me down into a kiss, her tongue thrusting into my mouth eagerly. I line the head of my cock up with her entrance, pushing in slightly. Her hips lift off the table, drawing me in a little more. A small moan escapes her lips. Sparks cloud my vision and I'm on the verge of coming without making it all the way inside of Alex. Her eager hands scrabble at my back as she tries to pull me in farther, but I need a minute.

"Feeling impatient?" my hand moves between us and I use my thumb to make circles on her already sensitive clit. She bucks off the table beneath me, and it's my turn to groan as I slip a little farther in. "I've been waiting a long time for this, babe. I don't think I'm going to last long."

Her breath quickens, her hands tightening in my hair as she moans into my mouth. "Please Connor, please," she whispers between moans.

"Please what, love?" I press a little harder with my thumb, making the circles a little faster. "What do you want, Alex? I want to hear you say it."

"Please, fuck me." I can feel her muscles tightening, her orgasm so close already. I slide my cock in slowly until I'm fully seated, then I pull almost all the way out and slam back in, making her arch her back and moan louder. Fuck, she feels good.

"Is this what you want?" I pull out and slide in more slowly this time, getting into a rhythm, continuing to work her clit. She's climbing, her orgasm closing in, as she nods excitedly. I take her lips in mine, kissing her again and again, feeling her panting against my mouth. I could listen to her make these noises all night. But I feel the pressure building in me as well, and I know I'm almost as close as she is. She needs to give up another orgasm for me before I will let myself go, though. It felt amazing on my fingers, but now I need to feel her come all over my cock.

"I'm going to need you to come for me again, baby. I can't hold out. God, you feel so fucking good." I thrust steadily, using my body to push my thumb against her clit more, until I feel her orgasm begin to surge through her. I move to grab both of her hips, pumping toward my own release, feeling her come beneath me as her orgasm pulses around my dick, pulling my orgasm from me. It's endless. Pulse after pulse, my orgasm continues, while Alex moans beneath me. My forehead drops to hers, and I kiss her deeply as our bodies both experience the aftershocks, as the last brief surges of the most intense orgasm of my life rush through me.

"That was…" she starts.

"Amazing? Brilliant? The best sex you've ever had? I know babe, me too." I smile as I climb off the table and go dispose of the condom in the trash. The giddiness of finally getting to be with her has brought out my goofy side. I walk back to the table to help her down and turn to pick up her clothes for her. "Here you go, love."

"Thanks," she says, pulling on her panties. "Ummm, I wasn't planning on that happening so soon. I don't normally move this fast."

"Alex, this thing between us is twenty years in the making. I don't think twenty years is fast at all." I pull my jeans back on but don't bother doing them up before wrapping my arms around her, bringing her in close enough to rest my chin on her head. "And it was better than I ever could have imagined." I step back so she can finish getting dressed.

When she's dressed, I lace our fingers together. "Let's go sit outside on the deck and talk for a bit before we turn in. I'm not ready to let you go yet."

I probably should have asked her about it before I climbed inside of her, but I'm hoping she'll open up to me about the cheating exes now. Because if anything gets in the way of us, it will be that.

39

Eight is Too Many

Alex

"I DON'T REALLY FEEL like getting into it." Connor is asking about the story Becca told that caused me to leave the bar in such a hurry last week. "It's depressing, not to mention completely embarrassing."

"Being cheated on is nothing to be embarrassed about," he tells me with concern in his eyes. "It means something was wrong with the other person, not with you."

"I could see that being the case if it were only a couple of guys, Connor, but numbers don't lie. I am the common factor in all these relationships. Something must be wrong with me." I don't think he's going to let this go. It doesn't feel like he's going to laugh at me, but I'm still a little hesitant to tell him the extent of it. I mean, I want him to know, but it's hard to admit out loud that eight out of the eight men that I've been with have cheated on me. And what if he thinks I'm damaged goods after he finds out? What if he thinks maybe those eight guys were on to something and I'm not worth the trouble of finding out for himself? I don't think I'm okay with letting him go after tonight. Being with Connor feels like home.

I shiver a little in the cool night air. Now that the sun is down, my shorts and tank aren't really warm enough. We're sitting on the deck off the kitchen, cuddled up on a large sectional. I see an outdoor kitchen off to our right that I'd love to make use of one of these days. There's also an enormous fireplace on the opposite side of the deck that I didn't see the other day. Connor gets up to light it and then motions that he'll be right back. He goes back into the house, coming out a few minutes later with an armload of blankets and pillows. Laying them out in front of the fireplace, he calls me over.

We snuggle down into the nest of blankets he's made, and between that and the fireplace, the chill of the evening doesn't feel so bad. I lay my head on Connor's shoulder, feeling his arm come around me to pull me in tighter. We lay quietly, listening to the crackle of the fireplace for a long time. I can't remember the last time I felt so comfortable.

Finally, Connor speaks again. "I won't judge you for what happened, Alex. I want to know so I can understand where you're coming from and how I can help you. You were laughing at the Derek story last week, but I could still sense that you were hurting. Betrayal is always hurtful. When someone you love and trust turns out to be an asshole, it can make you second guess your own judgement. But know that people like that are very good at making others see them how they want to be seen. There is nothing wrong with you for believing someone who is obviously very good at lying."

I take a few minutes to think about what he's said. I wish I could believe him, but eight guys are a lot different from one or two.

"Connor," I sigh. "You say that now, but when I tell you, you might feel differently."

"I couldn't feel differently about you, Alex."

I take a deep breath and sit up. I need to face him and see his reaction in his eyes if I'm going to believe what he says about it after. I'm not totally convinced I can trust my judgement about any guy, but I feel like I know Connor. Or at least I did. I don't think I've changed too much, so hopefully he hasn't either. The way he makes me feel hasn't changed, that's for sure.

I fill my lungs and blow out a hard breath, attempting to calm myself. "It was eight men," I finally admit. "I've had eight boyfriends, and all eight of them cheated on me. Some were public, some were private, some relationships were more serious than others. But the result was always the same. They cheated, I found out, and I left." I can't even tell what he's thinking. Looking at him during my confession didn't help at all.

He sits up now too, and I can see he is thinking. He pulls me close and wraps his arms around me. When he finally opens his mouth to talk, what comes out is nothing like what I expect.

"So, you must go through a lot of umbrellas then, hey?" I can feel his smile pressed against my forehead. I'm stunned for a moment. And then I laugh.

"You'd think so, wouldn't you?" I shake my head. "Unfortunately, it was only Derek who ever got that reaction. I think after all the other times, and finally trusting him enough to move in with him, I snapped when he turned out to be a cheater, too. It doesn't bode well for whoever is next, that's for sure. I might move on to actual baseball bats. Becca had one for me last time, but Derek ran too fast."

Connor lays back down and tugs my hand a little, so I join him again. He pulls the blankets up around us, and I settle my head onto his chest. My body is fighting fatigue after such a long day and the heaviness in my limbs is dragging me down. I struggle to keep my eyes open even as my breathing steadies. Fingers trace circles on my back, and Connor his other hand with mine.

"I know you have no reason to trust me, and I know we haven't even talked about what this is." I hear him through a fog as I sink into the beginnings of sleep. "But you never have to worry about me hurting you like that. You're the only woman

I've ever truly wanted. And now that you're here, I'll never let you go again."

40

Mine Now and Time to Clean Up

Connor

I'M NOT SURE IF Alex heard what I said as she fell asleep, but I'm not about to wake her up to tell her. We can talk when she wakes up. The crackling of the fireplace soothes me as my thoughts drift to what Alex confessed.

How could anyone, let alone eight different guys, ever turn their back on this woman in my arms? When she left, it broke me. It would have never occurred to me to be the one to do the leaving. I could never have cheated, because other girls didn't even exist to me. And for a horny teenager, that's saying a lot.

Even apart, she's been the driving force in my life. Almost every song I ever wrote was about her. She's been my muse since the first time we met, whether or not we were together. She's the reason Sleeping Dogs has seen any success at all.

But even the success we had seemed hollow. I'd always thought making it would feel better than it did, but it wasn't the accomplishment I'd hoped it would be. I didn't know Alex was what was missing. I tried to fill that hole with the drugs and women my success afforded me, but they didn't fulfil me. Apparently, all I needed was for Alex to come back into my life. It makes sense now that I think about it.

But now, with Alex in my arms, things are finally falling into place. Her warm body pressed against mine has my eyes growing heavier. It really has been a long day. I started out searching for

Alex and I'm ending it with her in my arms. I slip right into sleep with thoughts of how everything is finally falling into place.

"WELL, ISN'T THIS SWEET?" Devon is at the house bright and early, and I hear him through the mist of my dreams. He kicks my feet and wakes me from where I've fallen asleep on the deck with Alex. "You'll need to install a high fence around the property if you two are going to be falling asleep outside like this." He's joking but he has a point. Staying out here all night wasn't exactly my smartest move. I'll need to get Denise to find a contractor to get the fence started. Now that Alex is living here, I won't take any risks with security.

Alex is still asleep on my chest. I brush the hair off her face and lean my head down to kiss her. "Wake up, babe. Devon's here and there's some stuff I need to go over with him." She wakes up slowly. Hopefully, she slept as well as I did. For sleeping on a hard surface, I feel surprisingly well rested. Must've been the company. I catch myself smiling as Alex sits up and stretches.

"What time is it?" she asks. "Do you guys want breakfast?"

I can tell Devon wants to say yes, but I cut him off before he gets the chance. "No, baby. If you need more sleep, you should go back to bed. It's only eight o'clock. We're not usually up this early around here." I stand up and grab her hand, pulling her up with me. "Do you want me to walk you to the pool house? Or do you want to go inside and sleep in my bed?"

Her cheeks visibly redden as her eyes cut to Devon at the mention of her sleeping in my bed. She's so adorable I have to kiss her again, a little more seriously this time. Even with her slight embarrassment in front of Devon, she lets me kiss her deeply, her tongue sliding easily with mine while her hands reach up to the back of my neck. Before I can stop myself, I've got one hand fisted in her hair and the other on her lower back, pulling her against me. She lets out a little moan as I grind my erection into her stomach, letting her feel what she does to me.

"Okay, so..." Devon says quietly. "I'll let myself in and go make some coffee. Talk to you guys soon." The next thing I hear is the door opening and closing behind me.

"Let's go grab a shower at your place." I grab her hand and start dragging her across the grass to the pool house, frantic with the need to be inside her again.

"What about Devon?" she blurts while jogging along beside me. I slow down a little, letting her catch up. I might be a little too eager. "Won't he be mad at having to wait for you?"

"Nah." I grab her keys and unlock the door. "He gets paid well enough to wait. I'm sure the other guys will be here soon enough to keep him occupied. Plus, I'd be taking a shower either way. This way, I also get to see you naked again and give you a proper good morning."

I disarm the alarm and pull her inside, kicking the door shut once she's clear. As soon as she's inside, I turn around and get my lips on hers again. Leaning in, I push her up against the wall, both of her hands in one of mine over her head, my thigh between her legs, lips on hers in a deep kiss. My other hand reaches around her back, grabbing her hair and tugging down gently, giving me easier access to move my lips down to her neck. I'm driven by a need to consume her, make her mine, mark her so everyone knows she belongs to me. I'm pretty sure the last time I ever left a love bite it was on her and I'm doing it again right now. She's moaning while grinding against my thigh, her heat and heart beating on my leg.

"Fuck, Alex. I need to get inside you again. Now."

I let her arms go, reach under her ass, and pick her up. She gasps, then chuckles as I spin her in a circle.

"Arms around me, baby. We either go to the shower right now or I fuck you against this wall. It's your choice." I'm sure she realizes that I'm fucking her either way, but she can decide where it happens. This time. I'm reserving the right to fuck her in the shower and against the wall at a later date, possibly even later today.

"Shower," she whispers against my ear. "We can get dirty, then clean." She tries to get her legs out of my grip, but I won't let her.

"Hold on tight baby, I'm not putting you down yet." And I kiss her deeply again as I walk. It's a good thing I'm familiar with the layout in here or else I'd bump into a lot more than I do. Alex, of course, laughs against my mouth every time I have to correct our course after running us into an obstacle.

"Maybe you should put me down for the stairs? So we don't break any bones or, you know, die?"

"Fuck no," I growl. "Lock your legs around me. I'm carrying your fine ass up the stairs, too." That's easier said than done, though, since I try to continue kissing her while climbing the stairs. We almost fall twice, and I have to use one hand on the railing in order to keep balance. Alex laughs at me the entire time, and it's the most beautiful sound. Finally, we make it to the master bathroom, and I put Alex down on the counter.

I lean into the shower and turn the water on to warm up. Turning around, I reach and grab the back of my shirt, pulling it over my head in one smooth motion. I walk to where Alex sits on the counter and gently pull her shirt over her head as well. I unfasten her bra and earn myself a grin when I remember it needs to be pulled over her head. Seeing her perfect little dark pink nipples, I can't stop myself from leaning down and pulling one and then the other into my mouth. Letting her go with a slight graze of my teeth, I bring my lips to hers again and push my pants to the floor. Breaking the kiss, I lift her off the counter, undo her shorts, and push them off and kick them over with my own. Her legs are smooth, as I trace up them with my fingers before settling my hands on her waist. She grabs the back of my head and pulls me down into another kiss while I maneuver us into the shower.

The water rains down on us from the double sized rain shower head, warming our bodies. I push Alex to the back of the shower where the bench is. "Turn around and put your hands on the bench, baby." I tell her. "And wait there for me." I leave the shower to grab a condom from my pants and quickly roll it on. "I promise I will take my time with you later, but right now I need to get inside you."

I approach her from behind, sliding my fingers around her hip and down past her clit, feeling the wetness pooling between her folds. A groan escapes my throat. "You are so wet for me, so ready." Lining my cock up with her entrance, I slowly rock my hips and ease my way in, inch by inch. Once I'm fully seated, I roll my hips, slightly pushing against her ass while I hold her to pull her onto me a little more, grinding in as deep as I can go. A small whimper comes from Alex and she pushes back into me a little harder.

"Connor..." she whispers, "please."

"Please what, love? Tell me what you want. I want to hear you say it." I can feel what she needs, but I want her words. I want her to tell me how she wants me to fuck her.

"Harder, Connor," she pleads with a moan. "Please fuck me harder. I want to feel you slamming into me."

I spread her legs a little, tilting her ass up more, before pulling out nearly all the way and thrusting in forcefully. She groans my name and I nearly lose control. "Is that how you want it, baby?" I ask as I pull out and slam back in. "Is this okay?" I ask as I reach forward and gently squeeze her throat, pulling her back up and toward me a little more. She nods, but I need more than that. "I need you to say it out loud, Alex. Is it okay if I hold your throat like this?"

"Yes," she pants as I drive my cock in again. "Yes, Connor, do that. Fuck me like that."

"Fuck. babe. You're so tight, so wet. I can't fucking get enough of you."

I can feel her orgasm building, her pussy contracting tightly, and she pushes back against me, urging me on. Pressure is building in my back, my balls are tightening, and I need to focus to hold my orgasm back. I think of anything I can to stop myself from coming: inappropriate old ladies, vegetables on pizza, the many, many times I've seen Ryder's dick against my will. None of it helps. I thrust in deeply again, squeezing her hip tightly with one hand, grasping her throat with the other, when I feel her orgasm rip through her. [Thank god.] She throbs around my dick, coaxing me over the edge, and I come with her. A guttural yell comes from my throat as Alex squeezes me tightly, a yell escaping from her as well. I rock my hips, pumping us through our orgasms before I still completely, letting the aftershocks of her orgasm squeeze my dick, sending waves of pleasure through me as well.

Pushing kisses up her spine, I pull out and remove the condom, tying it off and putting it on the shower ledge to dispose of after. Right now, I need to hold this beautiful woman. I turn Alex around and pull her into my kiss, wrapping my arms around her as I slowly stroke her tongue with mine. She kisses me back, her arms going up and around my neck.

"You are amazing," I tell her. "How are you so perfect?" I pull back and look into her eyes. She tries to protest, but I stop her, holding her chin so she doesn't look away. "Everything about you is perfect. I will spend every day for the rest of my life doing everything I can to make sure you believe that." And I kiss her deeply, feeling her slick body sliding against mine.

Stepping aside, I grab her shampoo and pour some into my hand. "But now that we've gotten dirty, I think it's time I get you clean. Turn around." She turns her back to me, and I work the shampoo through her hair, massaging her scalp.

"That feels incredible." She tilts her head back, letting me massage her scalp. "You're hired."

I laugh. "I would be happy to be your shampoo boy, love. The only accepted form of payment is sexual favors, though." I move her under the water and start rinsing. "Now let me finish this or I'll require payment immediately."

She laughs. "Just Put it on my tab. I promise I'm good for it."

I can't help but laugh, too. "Still such a smartass. God, I've missed you."

41

Unlikely Allies

Alex

Alex- Breakfast is ready. Tell the guys.

Connor- Be right there

It's only Sunday and I'm not technically working yet, so I load up my plate and sit at the kitchen table to eat while I wait for the guys to come out of the studio.

My body heats as my brain strays to thoughts of Connor and me in the shower this morning, both the activities before and after we started getting clean. I'm so distracted by thoughts of how he felt inside me, and of the three more orgasms I had, that I don't even notice when the guys come into the kitchen. I realize they're here when Connor tips my head back to kiss me.

Probably would've been a pleasant kiss too if I hadn't nearly pissed myself in surprise when he did it. And if I hadn't immediately started choking on the food in my mouth.

"Oh shit, you okay?" Connor rubs my back a little while I nod and continue to cough.

The rest of the guys laugh while I cough my food up into my napkin. Assholes. "A little warning would be nice next time. You know, so I don't choke to death." I give everyone a death glare, and all I get in return is more laughter.

"I take it back," I tell them. "No breakfast for you pricks."

The guys are already filling up their own plates, so they clearly can tell I'm not serious. I look around at everyone and notice that Ryder is missing today.

"Where's Ryder?"

"No idea," Johnny answers. "He's probably still passed out somewhere. He's been doing a lot more drinking than usual lately."

"Poor Denise. She finally gets a boyfriend who is okay with her job schedule, and we're home so she can see him, and she's constantly having to leave to get Ryder out of trouble."

The guys talk a little more about Ryder and his drinking issues. When I'm done with my breakfast, I take out my phone and text him.

> **Alex-** I made breakfast at Connor's place. You should come have some. The rest of the guys are almost done, but I'll be in the kitchen.

I'm surprised that he responds right away. I guess he's not passed out somewhere after all.

> **Ryder-** I'll grab a shower and be there in a bit.

I don't know what's going on with him, but I think he might need that ear that I offered him. Everyone needs a friend and I know for a fact I am a great one.

BY THE TIME RYDER arrives, the other guys have all finished their breakfasts and are already back in the studio. Connor left me with a deep kiss that is still lingering on my lips nearly half an hour later. And he made sure I didn't have a mouthful this time, which made it even better.

"Hey Alex," Ryder greets me on his way to grab a plate. "What's this I hear about breakfast?"

"Right on the counter. Load up a plate and come sit at the table. Want a coffee?" I offer to get him one since I'm refilling my own.

"Sure, that would be great. Cream and sugar, please."

He gets himself a plate of everything I've made, piling it up as high as he can without it falling over.

"Hungry guy."

"Yeah, I may have had a lot too much to drink last night. I need to refuel."

"Makes sense." Now's as good a time as any to offer that friendship again. I take a deep breath and jump in. "Hey, is everything okay? What I said the other day still stands. I am a great friend, and a fantastic listener."

"Ahhh. I see what this is about now." He leans back in the chair and wipes his mouth with a napkin. "You had ulterior motives for the breakfast invite." He smiles at me, so I take that as a sign that he isn't mad.

"Yes, and no." I take a sip of my coffee. "I wanted to know why you weren't here when the other guys were and they mentioned something about you drinking more lately."

Now he looks a little irritated. Not mad yet though, so that's good.

"But they also mentioned something about Denise not being able to spend time with her boyfriend because she's so busy getting you out of trouble. Despite what the other guys might think, I'm pretty sure you're a considerate guy. I don't think you'd be causing her this kind of trouble unless you had a reason. And I have a feeling your drinking isn't actually out of control. So... do you want to talk about the other thing?"

His mouth drops open in surprise, and then he laughs.

"You've been around for two days and you've figured this out already? And these other assholes still have no idea, and they've been around me for years."

"Sometimes it takes a woman to see something like this. Love is a funny thing, and a lot of dudes have blinders on when it comes to seeing it in other people. I may be shit at my own relationships, but I have pretty good intuition about everyone else's love lives."

He nods and drinks some of his coffee. "I appreciate the offer." He pauses a moment before continuing, "but I'm not ready to talk about it yet. I didn't realize I was causing Denise *this* much trouble, though. I'll try to keep myself in line, or at least keep my antics out of the papers."

"I'm sure she'd appreciate that."

Ryder and I talk some more while he finishes his plate and gets himself another helping of breakfast. He tells me about when he joined the band, being raised by a single dad, and about what got him started in music. I tell him about my parents' deaths and about moving to the city to live with my Pops. By the end of our conversation, we know a lot more about each other.

I'm glad I extended that offer of friendship. He's a pretty cool guy, and I'm happy to have someone else to talk to about my Connor troubles. Not now, though. I'll save that for another day.

42

Burgers and Guys

Connor

"So? You gonna tell us what that kiss was about, man? Looked pretty intense." Johnny waited about three seconds after we got back into the studio before letting his curiosity get the better of him. "You guys a thing now?"

"I wasn't going to say anything, but when I got here this morning, they were sleeping all snuggled up together in a pile of blankets out on the deck."

"Fuck Devon, really?" I throw him a dirty look before turning back to Johnny. "We haven't really talked about it yet. I'm hoping to spend some time with her after you all fuck off today."

The door swings open and Ryder walks in.

"I really like her," he says. "She's legit a nice person. You did good choosing her, Connor."

"Uh, thanks, man." I look around at the other guys, the confusion on my face mirrored on theirs. "When did you get here? No one could get a hold of you this morning."

"Oh yeah, I was ignoring you. I was way too hungover to deal with you assholes today." He tries to make it sound like he's joking, but there's at least some truth behind what he's saying. "But then Alex sent me a text telling me to come for breakfast and now here I am. She's easy to talk to. I've claimed her as my friend." He looks me dead in the eye as he says this last part, and

I can tell that he's serious. "If you fuck this up, I'm going to take her side. Just so you know."

"That's great, Ryder. I'm happy she could get you to join us. And that you guys have found a friend in each other." I give him a warning look. "But if you try to take it further than friends, there will be trouble. I've been obsessed with her since I was a kid and I'm not losing her again."

He actually laughs at me. "You don't have to worry about that, man. I have my own love life to worry about." He looks around at the rest of the guys, a little more seriously. His shoulders sag. "And I know I've been a huge asshole lately. I'll get it under control."

He stuns us with that, and we're all silent for a beat. That's as close to an apology as we're likely to get. When we gather our wits, everyone gives him a nod or a word of approval. We've been talking about it a little and he has been out of control. But if he says he's got it, then we trust him.

"Are you all ready to get started? I've been doing a little writing, and I have some stuff to share with you." I pull out my notebooks, changing the subject, and forcing us to focus on work.

We spend most of the day locked away in the studio, piecing together some new material. It feels like something big is happening here.. The guys have some great ideas and we get three new songs nearly complete. We have some things to work through regarding composition, but lyrically, and mostly musically, we are confident that they are some of our best songs to date. The new album is going to blow all of our others out of the water.

Sometime around mid-afternoon, we break for lunch. Alex is out somewhere and not answering her texts, so the guys and I go out to eat at a local diner known for the best burgers in town. I don my customary disguise of a long-sleeved shirt and baseball cap, and the other guys put on similar stuff. We don't get recognized all the time, but it's happening often enough now that we all have to disguise ourselves a bit when we don't want to be disturbed. Sometimes it's nice to eat our food without constant requests for autographs and selfies. I plan to enjoy relative anonymity for as long as I can.

Devon drives us all to the restaurant in the Escalade, and we take up a couple of tables in the back of the place. There's no sense in calling more attention to ourselves than necessary, and the back tables are perfect for that purpose. The hostess gets our drinks and sends our server over. After she takes our orders, we sit around and talk for a bit.

"Does that server keep looking over here?" Johnny asks while darting his eyes over in her direction. "I think she recognizes us."

"It's been happening a lot more. We've done way more press recently, so it makes sense that people will know who we are."

I look over to see if I can get a look. She's looking right at me when I look up, and she flashes a big, somewhat sheepish looking, smile before looking away. She looks familiar, but I'm not positive I know her. I smile back politely anyway.

"Hey Devon, does our server look familiar to you?"

Devon barely glances over. "You don't remember? She's that groupie that was in the bathroom after the last show."

Shit. This could get awkward. I hope she doesn't do anything weird while we're here trying to eat. Maybe we should request a different server?

Before anything can happen, she comes over to the table and explains that she is going off shift and someone else will take care of us. She tells us all to enjoy our lunch and to have a great day, and then she's gone. She doesn't even let on that she knows who we are, though I'm sure she does. I thought that was going to be way messier than it was. Maybe she's embarrassed about how she acted that night? I know I would be if the situation were reversed.

After our new server brings our food, the conversation turns to me and Alex.

"So what are you going to do?" asks Devon. He seems to have a soft spot for her, like Ryder does. I love the fact that she gets along with my friends. These guys practically live with me, so it's important to me they can be friendly with her.

"I'm not sure." I think about while I eat some of my burger. "She told me a little about her past relationships and they were all pretty bad."

"What does that mean, exactly? She wasn't hurt or anything?" Aiden's concern shines from his face. He has experience with domestic violence and it is a cause that is dear to his heart. He even volunteers with a shelter in town and does a lot of fundraising for them.

"No, nothing like that," I clarify. "All the boyfriends she has had have cheated on her."

"You cheated on her?" Ryder nearly jumps out of his chair. "Why would she want anything to do with you now?"

"No, no. Not me. We didn't sleep together. Hell, we didn't really even break up. We were trying the long distance thing, but my stupid mother changed our phone number. I thought she'd decided not to call, and she thought I didn't want to deal with her grief. It was a big clusterfuck." That reminds me, I still need to confront dear old mom about that. I'm not sure I'm ready for that now, though. I'm still too mad to think about it clearly. Besides, she might be using again, so it's not like I would get a straight answer out of her, anyway.

I really need to check on the girls again and see if they can give me an idea where Mom's head is at.

"Okay, good." Ryder is visibly relieved. I should probably be concerned that he's so invested, but I actually like that he is already so protective of Alex. "She's way too nice for anyone to do that to her. And she's pretty hot, too. Why would anyone want to step out on that?"

"You're asking the wrong guy, man. She's not really even mine yet and I already can't see me wanting anyone else, ever." I'm not even a little surprised at the truth in my words. Why would I deny I feel serious about her? Might as well embrace it.

"Maybe she's a terrible lay?" Johnny adds in what I'm sure he thinks is a helpful way.

"No, that's definitely not it." All their eyes swing over to me. "Not that I'm giving any details."

"I knew it! You guys were way too cozy this morning to not have fucked already." Devon grins. "Plus, you took way too long to come into the house after I left you on the deck."

"Yeah, that's not up for discussion anymore." It's best to warn them all now. What I do in bed with Alex is none of their business. I will not talk about it. "Let's just say that the assholes didn't cheat because she's a terrible lay and leave it at that."

"Well shit then, it's a mystery. But you've got your work cut out for you. It's hard to come back from being cheated on once. If it happened to me more than once, I'm not sure I'd ever trust anyone else again. Not for more than a night, anyway." I can agree with Travis on this point. Alex must be amazingly strong to have tried again this many times and kept going back. I plan to make sure she never has to do it again, though.

"Okay, that's enough of this talk. I want to finish up and get back into the studio for a bit. I'm taking the evening to be with Alex, though. You guys can stay in the studio or go somewhere else, as long as you don't bother us."

The guys all promise to give me time with Alex, and then we go back to our food. After finishing quickly, we pay and go on our way. We drive straight back to the house and go into the studio, where the guys and I get to work.

43

Good Advice

Alex

Connor- I'd like to take you out to dinner tonight if you're interested? The guys and I will be done in the studio by 7 and then we can go if that works for you.

Alex- That sounds good. I'll see you then.

I'M ACTUALLY SURPRISED THAT Connor wants to take me out. I was a little worried that he would be done with me completely after the amazing sex we had. Looks like my swearing off of men hasn't lasted very long. I do sort of wish we'd talked a little before we jumped into bed—or onto the table, as it were—but it felt so right being with him that my brain wasn't working all that well. Then once he started kissing me, my brain took a complete vacation.

I've got a few hours before I need to think about getting ready, so I call Becca to kill some time. She answers after a couple of rings.

"Hey, girl. What's up? How was it after we all left last night?"

"It was... interesting." I say, drawing out the last word.

"Oh, how interesting are we talking here? Kissing on the couch interesting? Or having your world rocked by the sexy rockstar interesting?"

Leave it to Becca to get right to the nitty gritty.

"Um, more of the second one." I can feel my face turning red as I say it.

"You little slut! Good for you!" Becca is so loud that I have to pull the phone away from my ear. *"So... what are you doing talking to me? You should be banging that dude all over his huge house right now."*

I can't help but laugh at her. Becca is very sex positive, so I know when she calls me a slut she doesn't mean it in a bad way, but it always takes me by surprise when she says it.

"The guys are all down in the studio right now, but he is taking me out tonight when they're done working."

"Oooh, a proper date."

"I don't know about that. Maybe?" I say. "Do guys like him even date?"

"Well, he asked you out on a date, so I'm going to have to say yes. They date."

"Going on dates is different from dating, Becca. Of course he goes on dates. I mean, is a guy like him capable of being in a relationship. I'm not interested in being cheated on. Again."

She thinks for a few minutes, and the silence is more than I can bear. "C'mon Becca, you're killing me here."

"Sorry, sorry. I think what you're asking is if someone in his position, a musician in a successful band, can be faithful to one person? And I think that, yes, it is possible. But I don't know

Connor well enough to say that he, specifically, is capable of that. That is something you will need to judge for yourself as you get to know him better. I hear that's what going on dates is for." She chuckles. For as sex positive as she is, she doesn't go on a lot of dates. She sees guys one time, and for one thing only.

I heave a sigh. I know she's right. But I'm so tired of getting to know guys and then trusting them, only to have them betray me, anyway. And it's more complicated with Connor, because I work for him and live on his property. I've only been here for a couple of days. I don't want to leave already.

"I know that. It somehow seems a little different in this case. Connor and I have a history. You remember when I first moved here? How wrecked I was about not being able to contact him? Even while grieving my parents' death, I was still heartbroken about Connor. Not to mention the fact that I'll be living here for the next six months. I'm not sure if this is complicating things unnecessarily."

"Let's think of it this way. How would you feel if you didn't at least try? Especially now that you know he didn't actually change his number to avoid contact with you. You have a chance that most people don't get. I think you should take it and see where it goes."

I think about that for a second. Could I turn away from this without giving it a chance? We've slept together already. What more could it hurt if we get to know each other again? He seemed sincere when we were talking last night. Becca's probably right. I need to see where this leads.

Well, shit. Guess I'm dating a rockstar now.

"Yeah, you're right. I'll text you soon to let you know how the date goes."

"Yeah, sure, girl. I fully expect not to hear from you until tomorrow. But then I want all the details. And by details I mean we'll talk about all the amazing sex you're having with the sexy

rockstar." She's still laughing as she hangs up without even saying goodbye. That bitch.

Becca is right. Going on some dates and getting to know Connor again is the best way to go about this. I can't let myself be blinded by the feelings I used to have for him, though. His life has changed drastically since then, and he might be a completely different person.

It's that thought terrifies me.

This comes so soon after Derek's betrayal that I probably shouldn't even be considering it, but the chance to get to know Connor again is too tempting. And after all the coincidences that have been circling around us all these years, I have to admit my curiosity is piqued. I can't handle not knowing what this could be.

I only hope I can handle whatever happens if it all falls apart.

44

Jealousy and Friendship

Connor

I'm knocking on the pool house door before seven o'clock. From somewhere in the house, I hear Alex yell for me to come in.

"Are you almost ready?" I yell up the stairs. "I made a dinner reservation for eight o'clock."

"Yep, five more minutes."

I busy myself by having a look around at what she's done with the place. I was too distracted by her ass in my hands this morning when I was carrying her up to the shower. In a couple of days, she's made it feel like her home. Too bad I'm planning to get her to live in the main house with me as soon as possible. But I have to admit she's made this place her own. I see pictures of her and Mike, who I still can't believe is her Pops, and some of her and Becca. She has a few vintage kitchen tools displayed as well. She's added some interesting themed cushions to the couch. I can't say I've ever seen any that say 'fuck this shit' or 'more coffee, less talky' before. I like how she doesn't seem to take things too seriously.

"Oh, you like those?" Alex catches me chuckling at her decor choice.

"Yeah, they're kind of fun…" I turn around and my words fail me. Alex looks amazing. Her long, dark blonde hair is down and wavy. She's wearing tight jeans, another of those off the shoulder shirts that show off her tattoo, this one is a Rammstein shirt, and studded short stiletto boots. "Holy shit."

"Is this okay?" She seems a little unsure of herself. "I didn't know what you had planned, but I wasn't expecting anything too fancy. I can run up and change if I need to." She jerks a thumb behind her toward the stairs, showing her readiness to put on something else.

"NO!" I startle her with my loud answer. "You look so fucking hot. Perfect." I lean in and kiss her. "I think maybe I need to go change so I can look like I belong with you." I'm dressed casually tonight. Jeans, black tee, black combat boots, and my usual rings and bracelets. I'm way outclassed.

"Haha, very funny," she says, looking at me with heat in her eyes. "You look sexy, as you're well aware."

I smile at her admission. "I look not bad. You look like we should skip dinner and stay in. I'm sure Denise doesn't want to deal with the aftermath of me getting into fights trying to stop guys from asking you out right in front of me." I step into her, shove my hand into her hair, and lean in for a kiss. She turns her head to give me access, allowing me to slowly explore her mouth with my tongue. Once she's panting and grabbing my shirt to pull me closer, I let go of her hair and end the kiss. "But I said I was taking you out, and that's what I intend to do. Let's get going, so we're not late for our reservation."

Her hair is messed up and her lips are swollen with my kisses, but her smirk promises all sorts of great fun to be had when we're back later tonight. "Oh, that was mean," she giggles at me. "I'm going to have to do something about that later." She looks me up and down again and pulls her lip into her mouth. She reaches up and strokes my face as she leans into me to whisper in my ear. "You'll see," she says, before grazing my earlobe with her teeth. She brushes the front of my jeans with her hand as she turns and walks to the door. "Come on, Connor. We don't want to be late," she calls out as she steps outside.

Fuck, I think I love this girl. I rearrange my now erect cock in my pants and follow behind her. I'm going to be hard all night if we keep this up. And part of me really hopes that we do. Alex is going to destroy me in all the best ways, and I can't wait.

WHEN WE GET TO the restaurant, the hostess seats us immediately. I'm not disguised tonight, but I requested a table with a little of privacy to hopefully prevent too many interruptions.

"Excuse me?" Alex is getting the attention of the hostess before she goes back to seat more guests. "What is your executive chef's name?"

"It's Marcus Anderson, ma'am. He is very accomplished. He actually did his culinary training right here in town." The hostess seems used to answering this question. I know why Alex would be curious, but I can't understand why someone who isn't in the industry would care.

"I thought so," Alex smiles. "Can you ask him to come to our table when he has a moment? Tell him Alex Wilson is here."

"I surely will, ma'am. I will tell him right away." The hostess turns and makes her way to the kitchen.

"I take it you know the chef?"

"Yeah, we actually went through culinary school together. He's a talented chef. And a really fun guy." Alex is looking over the menu while she tells me about her history with Marcus. She seems to have spent a lot of time with him over the years, and I'm a little jealous.

"Sounds like he's a good friend." Jealousy drips from my words. Fuck.

"Yes." she eyes me as she takes a sip of water. "I'm friends with his husband as well."

I wish I could say that I wasn't relieved at that statement, but I'd be lying if I did. And she can see it too. She actually laughs at me.

"Jealous of my friends?"

"I am a little, actually. They've been able to spend time with you over all these years when I've been so close, but we somehow never crossed paths."

"Oh." she breathes.

"Alex, girl! You're finally coming to check out my restaurant!" This must be Marcus now. He's huge, burly, bearded, and friendly. He immediately sweeps Alex up into a bear hug, lifting her right out of her seat and off the ground. He looks over at me and says, "This isn't Derek." Great, already that asshole is being brought into this date night.

"No, Marcus, this is Connor, he's my—"

"Boyfriend," I interrupt. "I'm her boyfriend, Connor Ashley. It's great to meet such a good friend of Alex." I reach my hand out to shake his, but he pushes it aside and pulls me into a big hug too. Alex mouths 'boyfriend?' at me while Marcus is hugging me. He doesn't quite get me off the ground, but he still makes me feel like a small dude. Not an easy feat, considering I'm six feet tall, but he's got at least five inches on me. Like I said, he's a big guy. He and Devon could almost be twins.

"A new boyfriend?" He sounds more excited than surprised. "That's fabulous news. I never liked that Derek. Something always bothered me about him. I'm so glad you finally got rid of him, Alex."

"Yeah, he was a scumbag, after all, Marcus. You and Domenic were right."

"Domenic and I have an excellent track record with sniffing out scumbags." He looks me over while he says this, probably trying to detect any scumbag tendencies. "We should have the two of you over for dinner sometime soon."

"I promise I'm not a scumbag, just a musician. Although, some might say that's close enough," I say, throwing my hands up in surrender. "But I would love to join you for dinner sometime."

Alex laughs at her friend's attempts to vet me. I understand it though. If he knows her history, then he probably feels protective of her. I know I would if we were just friends.

"Wait, a damn minute! Did you say you're a musician? I thought you looked familiar. You're *that* Connor Ashley? From Sleeping Dogs? My husband loves your music."

"Okay, that's probably enough, Marcus. I'm sure you need to get back to the kitchen before your staff burns it down." Alex is so sweet. She's trying to protect me because she knows I hate being recognized in public. But Marcus is her friend and because of that, I'm confident he can act appropriately.

"Oh, girl. My staff is so well trained I can leave them for another ten minutes at least." He laughs. "But tell you what. How about I go back and I'll make you and your man here something extra special for dinner? I've been working on some new things for the menu and I'd love your input? Connor, it was great to meet you, man. And I'm sure I don't need to tell you to look after my girl here or you *will* be sorry. Domenic was special forces and knows how to hurt a man in many indescribably painful, yet completely undetectable, ways. I'll have to tell him the glorious news about Derek, too." He smiles while he threatens me, so I'm not sure if he's serious or not. Luckily, I have no intention of hurting Alex, ever, so I'll never have to find out for sure.

"Noted. I will treat her like the angel she is," I say, but he's already almost all the way back to the kitchen. I look over at Alex. "He seems nice."

She chuckles. "He really is. He's just protective. He sort of thinks of me as a little sister and hates that I've had such shit luck with boyfriends."

"Well, that unlucky streak is over, babe. I'm not doing anything to fuck this up. You're it for me."

45

Panic and Run

Alex

"WELL, THAT UNLUCKY STREAK is over, babe. I'm not doing anything to fuck this up. You're it for me."

I let the silence take over for what felt like five whole minutes before I excused myself to go to the washroom. Actually, I think what I really said was, 'I need to piss. Now.' And then I ran. But I'm sure he didn't notice how awkward I was, right? It plays worse in my head than it really was, I'm sure.

I sit in the bathroom stall thinking over what he said. I wish I'd brought my phone with me in here so I could text Becca. What does he mean that I'm it for him? That sounds serious. Serious is scary. Serious is where guys cheat on me and I get hurt. We are supposed to be going on dates and getting to know each other.

There's a knock on the main door, and then it opens. "Hello? Alex?" It's Connor. Shit, how long have I been in here? "Are you okay, babe?"

"I'm here, I'm fine." I stand up and open the stall door, plastering a smile on my face. "Just, uh, needed a minute." I walk to the sink and wash my hands. I may not have actually used the toilet, but I'm not going back without washing up first.

He chuckles at me a little. "I gathered with how quickly you jumped up and ran away." He grabs my hand and we walk out into the hallway together. "I didn't mean to freak you out by saying that you're it for me. I wanted you to know that I'm serious about not hurting you, and about us. I'm not proposing or anything. Not yet, anyway."

I take a deep breath. "I know that. It still seems fast. We hardly even know each other."

He pulls me into his arms and looks deep into my eyes. "We know each other, Alex. You're a part of me, like I'm a part of you. I may not know every little thing you've done for the last twenty years, but I know your heart. And you know mine." The kiss he gives me, barely tickling my lips with his, makes my body relax and I melt against him.

"Now, let's go back and see what Marcus has cooked up for us. I've heard great things about the food here and now that we're getting special treatment, I really can't wait to try it."

We make our way back to our table, with Connor holding my hand the entire way.

"Marcus is incredibly talented. I'm so glad this is where you made a reservation. It's been so long since I've seen him, and even longer since he's cooked for me. I think you're really going to enjoy this meal."

"I enjoy anything that I do as long as I'm doing it with you, Alex. But I am happy that coming here means I got to meet another one of your friends tonight." He knows what to say, this guy. I am in so much trouble.

As much as I'd like to say that the meal was the best part of the evening, I spend the night more interested in everything Connor has to say than what is on our plates. I'll have to come back so I can give Marcus' cooking the attention it deserves.

"Wait, so you pay for all of your sisters' school stuff? Like, everything? What does your mom do for a living?" I can't understand why Connor would have to provide everything. I could see helping out, but...

"It's not that I mind paying for the girls, really," Connor says, "but my mom expects me to take care of everything. She stopped working a while ago and now only calls me when she wants money. The other day, she was asking for money for Sadie's tuition and books. The thing is, though, I had already paid the school directly for those things. She was asking for money that Sadie didn't need."

"That seems a little weird." I don't know why, but I'm surprised to hear his mom did that. "What do you think she wants the money for, then?"

"I don't know," he sighs. "But I suspect that she's using again. It's been years, but I don't really know what else to think. I've asked the girls, but they haven't said much. I don't know if it's because there isn't much to say, or if it's because they're trying to protect mom. I've hinted at it to her, too, in a text, but she hasn't responded to me since then. I'm probably going to go over sometime soon to check on her."

This conversation has taken a depressing turn, and even though I have no issues with being a sounding board for Connor, I kind of get the feeling that he'd rather not talk about this. I don't blame him. It sounds like he's been looking after his mom and sisters for quite a while, being the parent the girls needed.

"Okay," I say cheerfully, completely changing the subject. "Let's get out of here. What are we doing next on our big date?"

Connor's eyes brighten a little. "Yes, let's go. We can do whatever you like. We can go home and go for a swim? Go grab a coffee? We can go have a drink with the guys and Denise?"

"Oh? Denise is out tonight? I actually wouldn't mind going for a drink then if that's okay? I'd like to get to know her a little better." My mind goes back to the conversation I had with Ryder the other day. I want to see how he acts when she's around. "Is her boyfriend coming?"

"Ummm." Connor looks at his phone. "I'm not sure. The text that Devon sent doesn't mention him, though."

"Well, let's go and have one drink, and then we'll leave. I don't want to spend the rest of our date with everyone else, but I wouldn't mind hanging out for a little while." I actually haven't said all the things I've wanted to say yet. I still want to talk about what Connor meant by saying that I am it for him. That sounds pretty serious, and I can't decide if I'm more scared or excited by it.

46

A Strong Drink

Connor

WE GET INSIDE THE bar and see the guys sitting in our usual booth in the back. Bill usually keeps it reserved for us when he knows we're in town because we often come by to do surprise sets. The fans love it, and Bill loves the money it brings in.

"I'm going to run to the ladies' room." Alex leans in and kisses me. "I'll meet you at the booth. Grab me a beer, please. Whatever's on tap. I think I need a break from whiskey." And then she's gone, around the other side of the bar and down the hall where the bathrooms are. As I watch her ass sway in those tight jeans, I'm tempted to follow her into the bathroom and get her out of them. Too bad I know that fucking her in a bathroom stall is not the way to convince her I'm serious. Once she trusts me, though, I'm fucking her everywhere we go.

I don't know how I've kept my hands off of her so far tonight. We better stick to one drink and then go, because I'm not sure I'll be able to control myself much longer.

"Hi Connor," an unfamiliar voice says from beside me as I wave at Bill at the other end of the bar. "I knew you'd be back here, eventually."

It's that groupie from the bathroom, the one who was our server at the diner. "You came here after the show, so I figured you guys came here often."

"Oh, yeah, hi... um..." I don't remember her name. Or if she even told it to me, for that matter. Once I saw Alex that night, everything else faded away.

"Sasha," she fills in for me, an exaggerated pout on her face.

"What do you need, Connor?" Bill comes over and asks.

"Hey Bill, nice to see you. I'll have my usual, and I also need a beer for my girlfriend, please."

He cocks an eyebrow. "Girlfriend, hey? Coming right up." He pours my whiskey and puts it in front of me before turning to pour Alex's beer. I grab a fifty dollar bill from my pocket and throw it on the counter. That Sasha girl leans in close when I do.

"That's generous of you," she says. "I'm sure your drinks don't cost that much."

"Yeah, well, Bill is a friend. He tries to give me drinks on the house but now that the band is successful I always refuse. I like to be sure my friends are taken care of." This chick is awfully close to me, so I grab my drink and take a step back. Throwing back the whiskey, I call out to Bill that I need another one. He's very busy tonight and I don't mind waiting for a bit. I'm willing to bet there's a line at the bathroom, and I'll be waiting on Alex, anyway.

"That's really nice of you. You're such a good person. And you're so hot too." She steps closer to me again, and I take one more step back. "I've loved your music for so long. I always imagined that you were singing about me."

"That's great, uh, thanks..." I'm really feeling that drink now. I must've had more wine at dinner than I thought, if this whiskey is hitting me this hard already. Alex and I had a bottle of red wine with dinner, but I don't think we even finished it. "It's fucking hot in here tonight."

"Oh, yeah?" the girl in front of me says. What the fuck is her name again? Where's Alex? "Do you need to go outside for some air?"

"Air?"

"Yeah, you said you're too hot. Do you want to go outside and cool off for a minute?"

"Shit, yeah. That's a great idea." I grab the front of my shirt and pull it away from my chest, allowing the cooler air to float across my sweaty skin. Oh shit, I think I'm going to puke. I turn around and walk towards the door, bumping into a few people on my way. "Oh, sorry dude," I say to each of them. Actually, one of them might be a chair.

I step outside and immediately feel cooler. The girl walks me over the wall so I can lean against it, and the brick feels amazing against my back. [Who is this chick again? Why isn't Alex here?]

47

Should Have Seen That Coming

Alex

"Hey guys," I greet everyone as I slide into the end of the booth. "Hi Denise, it's nice to see you again. I feel like we haven't had much of a chance to talk."

"Hi Alex, so you're settling in alright?" She gives me a little wink. Damn, all these guys have big mouths.

"Yeah, I guess you could say that." I laugh. "It's a pretty cosmic coincidence, hey?"

"You can say that again. I never would believe it if it weren't happening right in front of me," Devon adds from the other side of the booth.

"What coincidence? What's happening?" A boring looking guy sitting beside Denise asks. He looks completely out of place here. Dress pants, polo shirt, preppy hairstyle. He looks like a lost kindergartner wearing his new big boy clothes.

"Alex, this is my boyfriend, Andrew." Denise makes the introduction. I hear a snort from Ryder. Interesting. I would never have pictured Denise with a guy like this.

"Alex and Connor were childhood sweethearts, and now Alex is working as Connor's chef. Connor is madly in love with her still, but no one knows exactly how Alex is feeling. Isn't that right, babe?" Ryder directs this last question at me, but he stares at Denise throughout his brief speech.

The way he slurs his words makes me think he's had a lot to drink. Never mind the extensive collection of empty drink and shot glasses sitting in front of him that pretty much confirms it.

"Let's dance, Alex," he says before climbing up over the table and coming down beside me and dragging me to the dance floor.

"You okay?" I ask him when we're out of earshot of the rest of them. "You're pretty trashed."

"Andrew is a dickhead," he says with a shrug, like that explains his drunkenness. Although, maybe it does. "Did you see his stupid hair? And that shirt? He's the complete opposite of Denise. She's so hot, and edgy, and cool. He looks like a math teacher. A boring one." He snorts at this last part, like it's a tremendous insult. "I'm surprised he even spoke out loud. Usually, he looks around uncomfortably and whispers in Denise's ear instead of talking to the rest of us."

"Ah, I thought that maybe that was it. You can admit that you have a thing for Denise, you know?"

"What?" he laughs, like it's the most ridiculous thing anyone has ever said to him. "Why would you say that? I just think that guy is a loser, and she's way too good for him is all."

"Yeah, okay." I look up at him as he runs a hand through his hair. "She looks happy enough to me, though."

He lets out a huge breath. "Yeah, she does."

"But..." I prod.

"But I'm not. Not if she's with him." I stare into his eyes, urging him on. "If she's with him and not with me." Finally, he admits it.

"There you go," I say. "Was that so bad? I'm your friend, remember? You can talk to me about stuff. Especially girl problems. I myself am a girl problem, so I know all about that shit."

He can't help but laugh at me calling myself a girl problem. "Not tonight, though," he says. "Connor was really looking forward to your date tonight. Where is he, anyway?"

I look around, not seeing Connor anywhere. "He was grabbing drinks and was going to meet me at the table. I don't see him now, though." That's weird. Even with how busy it was at the bar, he should have made it to the table by now.

"Meh," Ryder says, pulling me into him to dance. "He probably had to piss. He'll turn up."

We end up dancing to another song before going back to the booth, where there is still no sign of Connor.

"Did Connor make it over here yet?" I ask everyone.

They shake their heads or say no. Devon offers to come with me to the bar to see if Bill knows where Connor is.

"Hey Bill," Devon yells so Bill can hear him over the crowd. "Have you seen Connor? He was supposed to grab drinks, then come sit with us."

Bill walks to our end of the bar. "He went outside about ten minutes ago, looking a little out of it. Some little chick was walking with him. He said he was grabbing a beer for his girlfriend. I assumed that was her."

My stomach drops and a pit forms in the hole it leaves behind. He left in the middle of a date? When he'd just finished telling me he wouldn't hurt me? What the fuck?

"That fucking asshole! 'You're it for me,' my ass. FUCK!" I yell. "I can't fucking believe him!"

I knew this would happen again. *I knew it.*

I run outside, with Devon following close behind. I scan up and down the block that Rough Mix is on, but I don't see Connor anywhere. His car is still parked right out front, though.

"Devon, can you drive me back to the house?"

"Sure thing, darlin'." Devon can see the gears turning in my head. "Listen, I don't know what's going on here, but Connor is crazy about you. I don't think this is what you think it is."

"Save it, Devon. I've seen this before. Many times. I should have known better. He said the right things, but he's just another asshole."

I pull out my phone and text Becca.

Alex- meet me at my place. Bring boxes.

Becca- WHAT!? That fucking asshole. On my way.

Becca- And I'm bringing the bat.

"Let's go, Devon. I'm done." I stomp my way to the parking lot. I don't t know where he's parked, but he catches up and turns me in the right direction.

"You need to believe me, Alex. I don't know what this is, but Connor is deadly serious about you. He mentioned not being able to lose you again."

"He should've thought of that when he was going off with some random to get his dick wet then, I guess, huh?"

I hear Ryder calling out for us. "Alex, Devon. Where are you going?"

"Back to the house," I yell back. "You're welcome to come with and help me pack."

"Pack?" He pants as he catches up to us at the truck. "Why are you packing? Moving into the big house right away? Not even going to wait for the ring, hey? I like it. Living in sin is the way to go."

"No, Ryder. I'm going back to Becca's. I can't accept the chef's position anymore. It's too complicated with the whole Connor thing. I can't spend six months being miserable and watch-"

"I keep telling you, Alex," Devon interrupts. "I really don't think he's off fucking that girl. There has to be something else going on."

"Oh shit! He left with some chick?" Ryder sounds more surprised than Devon. "I can't even remember the last time he took someone home. It doesn't make sense that he would do it now. He's pretty hung up on you, Alex."

"Okay, cool. Thanks for the input. Now whoever is coming better get in the truck. We need to go. Now. Becca is already on her way to the house to meet me."

We all get in the truck and Devon reluctantly drives us back to the house. Ryder sits in the back the whole time, trying to puzzle out what the hell Connor was thinking. I wish I understood it too. He promised me, mere hours ago, that he wouldn't hurt me. Didn't take long for him to break that promise, did it?

Despite traffic being light, takes way too fucking long to get to the house. It always seemed like it was right in the city when I was admiring nature in the backyard, but this drive makes it seem like we're going to another planet. Ryder talks the whole way, mostly to himself. I wonder if he'll still be my friend when I move out? Or if Devon will? I've only known these two for a few days, but I'm pretty fond of them already.

I occupy myself with these thoughts until we're pulling into the property. Right there, pulled up right by the front door, is an unfamiliar car.

"What the fuck? He came here?" Devon looks confused as he hops out of the truck.

Becca pulls in right behind us and jumps out of her car. "He's here?" She stops and reaches into her back seat, pulling out the baseball bat she brought. An evil grin lights her face. "Good. Time to play ball, girl," she says while tossing it over to me.

"Fuck it," I mumble, gripping the bat tightly. "Let's do this." And then I storm into the house.

My ragtag group of friends follows along behind me while I call out threats to Connor. I'm pretty sure I look like some less mentally stable Harley Quinn wannabe with the way I'm dragging my bat across the walls and doorways. I realize during the search that I actually haven't been in Connor's room, so I don't even know where it is.

"Bedroom?" I snap at Devon, pointing my bat at him.

"It's the one at the end of the hallway," he says. "But please don't kill anyone with that bat."

"No one is going to die," I promise. "At least not at the scene. I'm not responsible for anyone who dies later at the hospital, like a little bitch. CONNOR, WHERE THE FUCK ARE YOU?"

Ryder runs ahead of me and opens the door that Devon said was Connor's. I hear a woman's voice, but I can't really make out what she's saying. Sounds like she's having trouble with a condom. Good. I hope she's riddled with STDs and he catches them all. Ha! Like STD Pokemon.

"Oh, babe." Ryder turns around and blocks the door. "You don't want to go in here. Let's go get some boxes and I'll help you pack up your stuff."

"Move, Ryder. Now." I'm not interested in his bullshit. I'm sure he's trying to protect me, or Connor maybe, considering I'm the one with a baseball bat, but I need to see this so I can get closure. It's amazing how much easier it is to make a clean break when you see your boyfriend balls deep in some other woman.

It's like metaphorical relationship scissors to sever all ties. Snip, snip, motherfucker.

I think I need a drink.

He reluctantly moves out of the way, and I walk up to the door. Looking in, I see a beautiful room with a wall of windows overlooking the backyard, including the pool and the pool house. Really, there's a beautiful view through that window. The part of that view that isn't beautiful is some chick obviously trying to ride Connor. He's not even attempting to get up and tell me bullshit lies about the situation, either. He's lying there, letting her do whatever she wants.

I lose my shit right there, a white hot rage running through my veins. For the first time ever, I go for the chick instead of the guy doing the cheating.

"GET THE FUCK OFF HIM!" I scream at her before I drop my bat, grab her by the hair, and pull her right off the bed. Throwing her down on the floor, I jump on top of her and unleash my fury. I punch her in the face over and over again, not even noticing if she tries to defend herself. I don't stop hitting her until Ryder drags me off and pulls me out of the room.

"Let's go, girl." Becca says. "I'll drive around and bring the boxes. You and Ryder go out and start gathering up your stuff."

I'm silent now, and a little stunned. Ryder takes over, directing me through the house to the side door that will lead us out to the pool house.

"I'm so sorry, Alex," he says to me. "I know it's difficult to see the person you love with someone else, no matter how many times it's happened before. You deserve better than that."

I nod my head and keep walking. I've heard that countless times, but there's one minor problem; I *deserve* better, but I never *get* better. This is what I get for letting myself have hope. Especially with a rockstar. Even though it was Connor, he's clearly not the same guy I knew when I fell in love with him the first time. I wish he'd given me some sign that he'd changed so completely. This wouldn't be such a surprise, then.

Ryder takes my keys and lets us into the pool house. After I go in and disarm the alarm, I head upstairs to start. He comes with me and we make quick work of the contents of my bedroom and the master bath. All soft items are thrown down the stairs, and the few things that I can't throw get stacked in the hallway. Moving downstairs again, we climb over the pile of clothes and get to work taking down all the personal pictures and decorative items. Ryder has been in the pool house before, so he knows what goes and what stays.

It's sad that I've had so much practice at moving out that we're nearly done already. Maybe I can start a moving company so I don't have to go back to restaurant work? It seems like a waste to not use these skills ever again, now that I'm really swearing off men forever.

"Boxes are here." Becca brings in her stack of well-used boxes and some packing tape. "I'll get the kitchen stuff sorted."

"Cool, thanks. Oh, shit. Actually, everything stays in the kitchen. My knife roll is the only thing that's mine from in there."

"Nice. That makes it easier. I'll get started on that pile at the bottom of the stairs then."

I get a box ready for Ryder and he packs up the pictures and things that we've taken down. Becca packs up all my clothes and bedding while I run up and get the stuff I left in the hallway. We take the boxes out and put them into my car, with extras going into Becca's. I go back into the pool house to do a quick walkthrough to make sure we didn't miss anything.

Connor being an asshole aside, I'm sad to be leaving this little house. I may have only been here for a couple of days, but this place felt like home. I'm really going to miss the back deck and how peaceful it is out there.

Becca and Ryder are waiting for me in the living room when I get back from checking the upstairs areas.

"Devon sent a text. He wants us to go back to the main house before you leave. Says there is something you need to see. That it isn't what it looked liked. Are you up for it?" Ryder looks up from his phone. "I told him I'd ask you, but that I wouldn't make you go."

"I don't think I can. They always say it's not what it looks like. And it's always exactly what it looks like. I'm not up for dealing with that again. I'm really broken this time, guys." Tears well up in my eyes and I try to blink them away before they fall. "I don't want him to see that he hurt me so badly. I need to get out of here before I fall apart."

Becca and Ryder both wrap their arms around me. At least I'm pretty sure now that Ryder will still be my friend after all this. I may have gotten my heart broken, but I can always use another friend.

I walk to the door and leave the pool house for the last time. After letting Becca and Ryder come out, I set the alarm and lock the door.

"Thanks for all the help, guys. Becca? See you at home?"

"Yeah, girl. See you there." Becca gives me another little squeeze and then she's getting into her car. She gives us a wave as she drives away.

"Can I get you to give these back to Denise?" I pass the keys and the company credit card from my wallet to him. "I'll call her and explain everything soon, but can you also let her know she'll need to hire someone else right away?"

"Sure, babe. If you're sure this is what you want? You could still work here, you know. You shouldn't be out of a job because Connor's a prick." He looks hopeful when he tells me this. I think maybe he's liked having a friend around too. I shake my head no. There's no way I could stick around here after what Connor's done to me.

"I'll call you soon, too." I give him another hug. "You've been a good friend."

I take another look at the main house and then one more at the pool house. With a deep breath to calm myself, I get into my car. Starting the car, I turn on my angry music playlist and pull out of my parking spot. Ryder waves as he walks back to the main house.

As I pass the car that must belong to the chick Connor brought home, I notice again how closely it's parked to the front entrance. She nearly drove it right through the front door. I guess she couldn't wait to fuck the famous rockstar, Connor Ashley. *The famous fucking asshole is more like it.*

As I'm driving away from the property, I allow a few tears to fall. Screaming along with angry music helps, so I crank up my stereo and start yelling. The road is busier now, but everyone is heading in the opposite direction from me. There must be an accident somewhere too, because I pass by a couple of cop cars and an ambulance going that way.

It doesn't take long to get to Becca's place, and soon I'm pulling up to park in front of the building. Becca is walking up to the door when I get out of the car. I watch her bend over and pick up a rock from the doorway, which she then throws it down the street. That's strange. She's swearing to herself when I get out of the car and walk over with a box.

"I'll help you bring your stuff up," she says. "I've already brought up the boxes from my car." She comes over and gives me another huge hug. "And I have lots and lots of liquor in the apartment. We're getting absolutely drunk off our asses after, no exceptions."

I laugh at her through my remaining tears. "I could use a few drinks. Or maybe a dozen."

"Done! Now let's get this shit inside and start drinking. I have already warned the neighbours that it's going to get loud, so I'll even let you pick the music. We can scream along all night if we want."

She's lying, of course. One great thing about these apartments is despite their rundown appearance, they're well made and have excellent sound proofing. She wouldn't have needed to warn the neighbours because they won't be able to hear us, anyway. It's still a nice of her. As is her allowing me to move back in. Again.

While we bring my stuff, I think about Connor. I need to get drunk immediately. It won't make me forget, but drowning my sorrows seems like the best thing to do right now. I can't believe I let myself fall for him again. I knew better than to trust him.

Fucking men. They're all the same.

48

Such a Fuck Up

Connor

"Dude, wake up. Connor. CONNOR." Someone is yelling at me, and I can hear crying in the background. And sirens. What the fuck? Where am I?

"CONNOR!" A different person is yelling at me now. "What the fuck were you thinking? Alex left. She packed up all her shit and moved back in with Becca. How could you do this to her?"

WHAT? Alex left? Why? What the hell is going on? I'm trying to open my eyes, but they don't really want to cooperate. I'm so fucking tired. I'm trying to sit up, but my arms don't want to do what I'm telling them to. And why am I laying down, anyway? And who the fuck is that crying?

"Shut up, Ryder." I recognize Devon's voice now, so it was Ryder who was yelling about Alex. "Go to the front door and wait for the cops and paramedics."

It's then that I feel the all too familiar roiling in my stomach, that sloshy feeling, and then the saliva is pooling in the back of my mouth, warning me of the puke that is already on its way up.

"Fffrowww ummmm," I mumble, unintelligibly, but it's already too late. I'm throwing up while laying down. Hot liquid is running down my face, into the folds of my neck and into my ears.

"Oh shit. You're okay, Connor. You're going to be fine." I hear Devon whispering to me as he turns me on my side. "What the fuck did you take?" He's not really asking me this question, he's merely speaking out loud to keep us both calm. *Good thing, too. Because I'm about to lose it.*

"You need to let me go." A female voice, from the side of the room somewhere. "You can't keep me here like this. We're in love. That's not a crime."

Devon is moving something around on this side of the bed, which I'm thinking must be my bed, if Devon and Ryder are both here. I crack my eyes a little and see that he has a bucket beside me on the floor, lined up where my face hangs over the side of the bed.

"You shut up," Devon tells the woman. "He's not in love with you. He doesn't even know who the fuck you are. You may have wanted to sleep with him, but it was plainly obvious that he didn't want to sleep with you. Never mind that he is completely out of it and in no position to consent to having sex, anyway. He can't even talk, for fuck's sake."

"You still can't tie me up like this. That's against the law." Huh? Devon has a woman tied up in my room. What the hell is going on? I was on a date with Alex. What was it that Ryder was saying about Alex? She moved out? That makes no sense.

"I'm Mr. Ashley's personal security," Devon explains. "I am detaining you until the police arrive, and that's it. They will handle everything from there. So sit still, and they'll be here any minute. They'll get your face looked after, too. You're going to need some stitches, at the very least."

It's then that I hear Ryder coming back into the room with the sound of footsteps following him. Devon explains to someone who the girl is, and I hear other voices coming over to talk to me.

"Hi Connor, I'm Patrick. I'm going to help you, okay?" Must be a paramedic. I'm in terrible shape if Devon called emergency services. "Can you tell me what you took tonight?"

"Uffinnn, dooot nuffi." Shit, that sounds nothing like what I'm trying to say. "Nnnnnooooo duuugggss." The words seem to slide out of my mouth on top of each other, but it's better, I think. No drugs.

"You're saying you took nothing? No Drugs?"

"He was on a date at a restaurant, and then they came to meet us at Rough Mix. His date said he was ordering a drink and joining us at the table, but he didn't show up. He's never really been one for drugs, and I don't think he'd start right now." Ryder is trying to help explain to the paramedic.

"Hey officer," Patrick calls out. "Can you ask his date what he took? Or how much he had to drink?"

"Oh no, that's not his date." Devon speaks up now. "But I have seen her around a few times. She showed up half naked, hiding in a bathroom after the show last week, and then we saw her at the diner yesterday, too. Remember Ryder?"

"Shit, yeah, now I do." He sounds excited about something. "Actually, I think I saw her at Rough Mix a few times this week, too. She could have been there tonight, even, but I'm not sure about that. You'd have to ask Bill if she's the girl he saw talking to Connor at the bar."

My stomach gets sloshy again, and before I can say anything, I'm puking over the side of the bed. My eyelids are so heavy that I stop fighting to open them and I leave them closed. Around me I can hear too many voices, and no one is saying anything that makes sense. The only thing I can think about is Alex, and why she's not here.

AFTER WHAT FEELS LIKE five minutes, but must be more, I open my eyes. All I see is white. And curtains. I try to move my hands, but I feel a tug. I look down and see that I have an I.V. line, and from the looks of it, it's saline. What the fuck happened last night?

"Hey man." Ryder is sitting on the chair beside my bed. "How're you feeling?"

"Like I drank the entire bar last night." I run my hands through my hair. "Why am I in the hospital? What happened?"

Ryder's eyebrows are low over his eyes, and his mouth tenses a little before he speaks. "You don't remember anything from yesterday?" he finally asks.

I think back over the day. "I remember Devon waking me and Alex up after we'd fallen asleep on the deck. Then we went to the pool house and showered together," which was so hot I'm getting hard now thinking about it. "Alex made breakfast for everyone. Then we worked in the studio. Lunch at the diner. Shit!"

"We ate at the diner and the server was looking at us funny. I have an image of her talking to me outside of Rough Mix. Did I go to the bar last night?" I'm mumbling to myself more than I am talking to Ryder. Sifting through my muddy thoughts while he listens.

I go back to the part about lunch at the diner. "The server left, and we had a different server after that. The rest of the afternoon we spent in the studio. I went and got ready for my date with Alex, then walked to the pool house to pick her up. We went for dinner and it turned out her friend was the chef, so he prepared something special for us. We split a bottle of red wine that we didn't finish. And then… then we… It's kind of mixed up after that."

"I see us parking in front of the bar. She went to the bathroom, and I was going to get drinks. But it was so hot in there I was burning up, so I go outside. Then… I'm in a car? Then I'm at home, trying to get to my bed so I can lie down, but I'm stumbling so much that someone has to steady me. And that's it. That's all I've got."

Ryder swipes his hand down his face. "Fuck dude."

"Where's Alex?" I ask with a sinking feeling. Something has to be wrong if she's not here.

"Ah fuck." Ryder leans forward in his chair. "I was pretty drunk last night, and I wasn't exactly beside you for all of it. But I'm going to fill you in on the parts I know. Don't get pissed at me, though. We were all acting on the information we had."

"What the fuck happened, Ryder? Where is Alex?"

"So," he starts. "You and Alex went out, and you came to the bar to meet the rest of us. You stopped to get drinks, and she went to the bathroom. You were supposed to meet her at our table, but you didn't show up. Devon talked to Bill, and he said you went outside with some chick."

"What the fuck?" I left with someone? Alex must be so mad. What the hell was I doing last night?

"We couldn't find you, and Alex flipped out. Given how her relationships in the past have gone, I couldn't blame her. So we went back to the house. Devon and I went with her, and Becca was going to meet us there."

"When we pulled up, there was some car pretty much parked right in the door. Becca came in behind us and gave Alex a baseball bat. That was pretty hot, actually. She was fucking pissed and looking to do some damage." Ryder chuckles a little at the memory. I'm sure Alex did look hot, but that's not what I'm concerned about right now.

"Hurry up, man. What happened next?"

"Right, so we hear noises from your room, and I run ahead and open the door." He lets out a huge breath before continuing. "You were flat on your back with some chick straddling you, man. I tried to keep Alex out, but she had a bat. She saw you with that chick on you and went nuts."

"Oh, shit." I check out my arms and legs. I don't feel any bruises and nothing seems broken. She didn't hit me? "Did she kill that chick?"

"Nah," he laughs. "Alex dropped her bat and snatched her right off of you, though. Threw her on the floor and started beating the shit out of her. It was impressive. I thought you said she wasn't much of a fighter, but man..."

I bet it *was* impressive. If I weren't the cause of it, I would have loved to have seen it. I lean my head back on my pillow and shut my eyes tightly.

"I can't believe I fucked around on her. Why would I do something like that? I love her, man."

"I know you do, Connor." Ryder smiles at me. "But the good news is, we don't think you actually slept with that chick. Based on how everything went down, the cops actually think that the chick may have drugged you. The doctors are doing some tests, and Devon is getting the security footage from Bill."

"That's... fucking nuts. She roofied me? So... she raped me?" Holy shit, this is not something I ever thought I'd have to think about. I'm a guy. I didn't think guys could get raped. At least not by a woman.

"Well, it's not for sure, but I overheard the chick telling the cops that she didn't sleep with you. And Devon saw no evidence to the contrary, if you get my meaning. No used to condoms, no wet spots, and the chick seemed to be having issues when we walked in. You even had all your clothes on, for fuck's sake.

Devon said you were pretty much passed out and didn't appear to be at all… uh, interested."

"Yeah, but that doesn't mean much. Maybe she flushed a condom before you guys got there?" I don't know why I'm trying to convince him I could have slept with this chick. I really don't want that to be the truth. I need to talk to Alex. She must be going crazy thinking I cheated on her. She really has had the worst luck with relationships. I don't imagine she had a difficult time believing that I took that woman home, based on all her experiences with men who said they cared for her. No matter what I said, I haven't earned that level of trust from her yet.

"It's possible, I guess," he says. "But when we talked to Bill, he said you'd left about ten minutes before us. For this chick to get you into, and out of, a car, into the house, and then into your bedroom, in the state you were in?" He shrugs, like he's not sure about it.

"There wasn't enough time for anything to have happened? Oh, thank god." A feeling of relief washes over me. I didn't cheat on Alex. I didn't really believe that I would have, but I remember so little from last night. "I need my phone. I need to call Alex."

"Yeah, about that. I've tried that. Her phone's off. I've sent a million texts and left several messages, so hopefully she calls me when she gets them."

"Why the fuck would she call you?" Is Ryder trying to move in on Alex already? I'm going to kill him. "Stay away from her. She's not some slut for you to stick your dick in."

"Fuck you," Ryder spits at me. "She and I are friends. You already know that. She told me to call her, and we'd hang out. She's been a better friend to me in the last few days than you fucks have been in years." He takes a breath and lowers his voice. "I called her for you when I figured out how unlikely it was that you fucked that chick."

Ryder is really friends with Alex? I thought he meant they were casual friends, not good friends, like they appear to be. And she's a better friend to him than the rest of us? I guess I can see that. She's such a great person, and we've all been pricks to Ryder this last little while. He's clearly got something going on and all we could do was bitch about his acting out.

"You're right, man. I'm all messed up right now. I'm mad and I shouldn't be lashing out at you." Now I feel like a dick for being a shitty friend. Today is not my day to feel good about myself, it looks like. "I haven't been good to you at all, and here you are trying to help me out of this shit now. Thank you."

"Yeah, you're an asshole sometimes. But you're forgiven. I won't even make you beg for it." He laughs. "And since I am such good friends with Alex, and you, I am going to help you fix this. Because that girl loves you, too. And she deserves to be happy."

He gets up and throws a bag at me before going to the door. "I brought you some clothes. Have a shower. You puked all over yourself last night. I'll let you know when I find Alex."

And then he leaves me to wallow.

Fuck! How will I ever be able to fix this with Alex? Even if she learns the truth of what happened last night, will she be willing to risk something like this happening again? Being famous isn't all it's cracked up to be. And I would walk away from it all in a heartbeat, if it meant I could have Alex with me.

49

I Feel No Pain, Until I Do

Alex

BANG BANG BANG! BANG bang bang! Bang bang bang!
 What?! What the hell is that?
 Bang bang bang! "Alex, open up. It's Ryder."
 Ugh, what is he doing here at this ungodly hour? It's only…
What? It's already two in the afternoon? I've got some fuzzy
memories of drinking way too much after Becca and I got back
here last night. I feel kind of okay, though. Maybe I'm getting
so good at drinking that I don't get hangovers anymore? That's
a cool side effect of being heartbroken.

I sit up in bed. "Coming," I yell out so Ryder stops banging
on the door. I sway on my feet a little when I stand up. No wonder I feel fine. I'm still drunk. I pick up the whiskey bottle that I
left on my dresser when I finally went to bed early this morning.
Might as well stay drunk for the rest of the day and put off my
hangover until tomorrow. That seems like the responsible thing
to do.

I walk over and throw open the door while taking a big drink
of my whiskey. "What?" I spit at Ryder not all that nicely. I turn
around and leave the door open for him to follow me in. "How
did you know where I live?"

I flop down on the couch and grab a cigarette from the pack
that I bought last night. I dig around in the couch to find a
lighter, but Ryder helps me out first. I tilt my head to accept

the light that he offers and take a long drag. I give him a nod of thanks and then point to the couch for him to sit.

"That looks like the breakfast of champions there, girl." He chuckles at me. "And you're not exactly dressed for company."

"I wasn't expecting any company." I grumble. I have to look down at myself to remember what I've got on. Oh, I guess he has a point. I don't normally open the door wearing my underwear and an old sweatshirt. "Hold on."

I go back to my room and grab some old grey joggers that are so big I have to pull the drawstring tight. That's the best he's going to get. It's not like I invited him here, after all.

"So, what are you doing here, Ryder? Come to get drunk with me? I have a pretty decent head start, so you've got some catching up to do, if that's the case." I look down at my nearly empty whiskey bottle. "And I'm not sharing, either."

"That's okay, doll. I'm actually not here to drink. I came to talk to you about Connor."

"Hard pass," I say, while dropping my cigarette into an empty glass on the coffee table. "I'm still drinking away my sorrows; I'm not really interested in talking about assholes right now."

I get up off the couch and walk into the kitchen. Oh look, Becca left me a fresh bottle of whiskey. I spin the cap off and take a nice, big drink. Mmmm, refreshing. The burn of the alcohol almost drowns out the burning feeling of rage in my stomach.

"You want coffee or something?" I'm still an excellent hostess when I'm angrily drinking. I am a chef, after all, hospitality is my job.

"Nah, I'm good. Thanks."

I throw myself back down onto the couch and grab another cigarette. Nothing like furiously chain smoking when you're mad, am I right? My lungs and throat are going to feel this tomorrow, but for now, I gesture to Ryder for his lighter. He tosses it to me this time, and I light my own cigarette.

"So as I was saying," Ryder begins. "There was more to what happened last night than we saw back at the house."

"I don't want to fucking hear it. I don't." My love life has been a never-ending series of disappointments. It seems fitting that it started with Connor and is now ending with Connor. "I've had more than my share of the same bullshit over the last twenty years, and I'm finally fucking done." I hold my bottle up in a toast and take another huge swallow.

Ryder slides closer to me on the couch, takes the bottle from my hands, and places it on the coffee table. He grabs a cigarette from his own pack and lights it before leaning back beside me. Both of our heads are resting against the back of the couch, our eyes pointed toward the ceiling.

"I understand where you're coming from, babe. I really do. But what you're feeling right now is based on what you *think* happened last night. But it didn't happen the way you're thinking. Connor didn't leave with that girl."

I sit up and look at him. "What do you mean? Of course he did. We both saw him under her, in his bed. I wasn't drunk at that point. I remember it clearly. It's burned in my brain." I hold my fists out to him, knuckles up. "And my knuckles tell the story of what I did to her face."

Ryder grabs my hands and inspects them closely. They're swollen and bloody still. He's looking at a deep gash on my right hand that's still leaking a small amount of blood when he says, "Holy shit, Alex. This looks bad. Did you have this cleaned up yet?"

"Uh, no. We came here and started drinking immediately. First aid wasn't exactly high on my list of priorities, given my mental state."

"I think I should take you to the clinic to get it looked at. It looks like you cut yourself on her teeth and it could get infected if you don't get it cleaned out properly. You probably even need a couple of stitches." He looks me in the eye. "Why didn't you say something last night before you left Connor's?"

"Oh, you know," I attempt to gesture nonchalantly with my injured hand, but I'm stopped short by the pain. Shit, it must be bad if I can feel it now, even though I'm still a little drunk. Funny how I didn't notice the pain before. "I had other things on my mind. I didn't even realize my hands were this bad until you looked at them, actually. Must've been the adrenaline."

"Well, get your shit. I'm taking you to get looked at right now."

I try to protest, but Ryder isn't listening to it at all. He looks around the apartment and finds my wallet and phone. My keys are harder to track down, but he finally finds them in the freezer. Huh, must've put them in there when I was getting ice last night. He even helps me get my shoes on since, now that I've felt how much my hand hurts, I can't seem to not feel it.

We get out to the car, and he even has to do up my seatbelt for me. Fuck, I really hope I did some damage to that chick's face for all the trouble it's causing me now. I'm betting I broke my hand. I've seen enough boxers' fractures in my life because of Pops' gym that I think I'm qualified to make that assessment. I distract myself on the way to the clinic by talking to Ryder some more. But not about Connor.

"So how did you know where I live, anyway?"

"I got Johnny to ask Becca." He looks over at me, as if to gauge my response.

"What? Johnny?" Johnny and Becca are talking? That is new information. She didn't tell me that. We are so having words when she gets home from work.

"Yeah, I had him text her for me. You weren't answering calls or texts from anyone, and I needed to get in touch with you." He points to my hands. "And it looks like it's a good thing we found you before that cut gets any worse."

"Yeah, you're probably right about that. Hey," I say, brightening up, "Maybe they can help me fend off the hangover that's bound to hit me soon. I've seen people on TV use IV saline or something like that. My plan was to stay drunk for the rest of the day, but going to the clinic right now has put a wrench in that. I'm sure they'd frown upon me drinking during an examination."

"Here." He passes me a bottle of water that he pulled out from behind my seat. "Drink this. It will help. I have painkillers in my pocket too, if the doctor doesn't prescribe something for you."

"Thanks, Ryder."

He really has proven himself to be a good friend. In fact, he's an even better friend than I thought. After pulling up at the clinic, he brings me right in and helps me fill out the paperwork. As I suspected, the doctor sends me for an x-ray and while waiting for the results, a nurse cleans out the wounds and puts some butterfly bandages on. She thinks I will need stitches but wants to wait until we know if I need a cast for a break.

We don't have to wait long before we find that I have, in fact, broken a bone in my hand. The doctor wants to put a cast on it, so we stick with the butterfly bandages, since I won't risk opening the wound by moving my hand.

"Well, this sucks," I say, as we're on our way out. I hold up my sparkly black cast. "This makes it a lot harder to find a new job. Guess I'm taking a six-week vacation. Good thing Becca doesn't expect much rent from me."

I glimpse my reflection in a window as we walk outside. "Shit, you let me leave the house looking like this?" I point at the bun resting loosely on the side of my head, amidst a nest of loose and tangled strands, and then at the mascara that has very obviously been cried off my eyelashes and onto my cheeks. "You're lucky they didn't call the cops on you. It looks like we got into a fight."

He laughs at me. "I honestly didn't think of that once I saw your hands. I just wanted to get you here to get it looked at." He bends down into a professional-looking fight stance and pretends to throw a couple of punches at me. Huh. I wonder if Ryder does any training at Pops' gym? "Plus, you did get into a fight. It just wasn't with me."

I think about that for a second as we get back into the car and Ryder buckles me up again. If I hurt myself this badly, that girl must have at least some bruising. I could be in big shit for what I did last night, regardless of the circumstances.

"Do you think that chick is going to press charges?" I ask Ryder, seriously. "I assaulted her, and I imagine she's hurt pretty badly." I'm kind of worried now. Last night I was so mad that I didn't even think about what could happen. What even possessed me to attack the girl and not Connor? When I caught Derek, I went right after him. I never blame the girl, because it's the guy who I expect faithfulness from. The girl usually doesn't even know there is a girlfriend in the picture.

"About that." he looks over at me. I guess we're talking about Connor after all. Shit. "Connor has Denise and the lawyers working on it. They're pretty certain that you're fine, since you were protecting Connor from a crime."

I nod. "That's right. I was—wait, what?"

50

Just Desserts

Connor

Saying I was surprised to wake up in the hospital after what should have been my date night with Alex would be the understatement of the year. Finding out that the groupie from the bathroom at the concert had roofied me and dragged me home in order to rape me has me seriously fucked up. I would have never believed that someone would have the ability to do such a thing to a guy, let alone actually attempt to do it to *me*. She had to move fast once the drug started to take effect, otherwise she'd never have been able to get me out of her car. I could already barely walk when I got there, if I can trust my memory at all. Imagine what another five minutes would have done.

Of course, if I'd been stuck in her car at the house, then Alex would have seen the state I was in and I wouldn't be in this mess with her.

The police questioned the girl, and she confessed to drugging my drink at Rough Mix and then getting me outside and driving me home. Apparently, she followed us back to my place that day that we saw her at the diner. She faked sick to go home and then waited for us to leave so she could follow us. Bill told us she'd been at the bar every night for the last week. I guess she was waiting for her chance to put something in my drink. The surveillance footage shows her leaning over me when I'm looking towards the bathrooms, so the police assume that is when she did it.

"Hey asshole," Devon's here at the hospital to pick me up now that they've discharged me. "All set?"

"Yeah, let's go." I still feel nauseated, but it's nothing I haven't experienced before. It feels like a bitch of a hangover. At least I was able to shower and change into the clothes that Ryder brought for me earlier. Nothing smells worse than day old vomit.

"Ryder went to find Alex, so you don't need to worry that she's got her phone turned off."

"What the fuck? How does he know where she lives?" I didn't think they were that good of friends yet.

"Johnny got the address from Becca, apparently."

"I *knew* that fucker was interested in Becca." Johnny has been hinting about wanting to see Becca again. I wonder when he pulled it off. "He better not do anything to hurt Becca and wreck my chances with Alex. I mean, any more than I've wrecked them already."

"Ryder will talk to her." Devon seems pretty confident in Ryder's abilities to convince Alex. Then again, he's also made fast friends with her, so he probably knows what he's talking about. "Plus, you didn't do anything. The woman who drugged you is responsible for this."

"I still can't believe that Alex beat the shit out of that chick. Guess Pops taught her a thing or two, after all." I'm not looking forward to talking to him about this mess, that's for sure. He might not look so kindly upon how I've hurt Alex, even though it's a misunderstanding. "Did Denise take care of that? Alex isn't going to get in shit for it, is she?"

"Nah, she's good." Devon says as he unlocks the doors to the truck. "She was protecting you from a crime, so she won't be charged. I called a cop buddy of mine, too, and he said they're not interested in pursuing charges against her."

As we're getting into the truck, we both receive a notification ding from our phones. It's Ryder.

Ryder- I'm with Alex now. She's drunk. Has been since last night, looks like.

Ryder- She answered the door wearing her underwear and drinking straight from a bottle of whiskey. Alex is so pissed off at you, Connor.

Connor-Tell her to turn her phone on so I can call her.

Ryder- She won't even talk about you dude, there's no way she's going to talk to you right now.

Fuck. How am I ever going to apologize if she won't even talk to me?

Me- Fine. Let me know when I can come by.

Ryder doesn't answer right away. If I don't hear from him in the next couple of hours, I'm going to go over there. If I can get Johnny to give me the address, that is. Becca probably made him promise not to give it to me.

I get Alex wants some time, after what she thinks happened last night, but I can't stand the thought that I might lose her because of a misunderstanding. I'm burning with the need to explain. When I said I would never hurt her, I meant it. Too bad there was no way to predict some chick would force me into a situation like this. I wonder what Alex will think when she finds out she protected me from a rapist?

"Did you want to stop anywhere on the way home?" Devon asks before he turns out of the hospital parking lot.

Should I go see Mike right away? I should try to own up to what happened instead of letting Alex tell him. Even if she learns the truth before she talks to him, he seems like the kind of guy who would appreciate it if I come and tell him about it myself.

"Yeah." I look over at Devon. "Take me to the gym. I need to talk to Mike. When he hits me, you can drag me back to the truck." I attempt to laugh at my little joke, but the truth is, I know even at seventy-five-years-old Mike can still do a little damage. Especially since I won't defend myself if he punches me in the face. Hell, I'd even let him get one of the trainers to do it for him if it makes him feel better. I feel like shit about how I made Alex feel, even though I was merely a bystander. I didn't want her hurt, whatever the reason. But I *did* hurt her, and I'm ready to let Mike deliver whatever punishment he sees fit.

"You sure about that? That old guy is pretty tough, and I'm sure he has a soft spot for Alex the size of a football field. He's going to be pissed at you, even though you didn't really do anything."

"I know that, but I think this will sound better coming directly from me. He told me what would happen if I hurt her. I canonly hope he believes what I have to say about the situation. He's pretty old school. The idea that a woman would attempt to rape a man might be hard for him to wrap his mind around."

"Either way, it's your funeral, man," he says, already driving in that direction. "I'm going to put 'here lies a dumbass' on your tombstone, FYI."

I chuckle at that. "Yeah, sounds about right."

The hospital is near the gym, so it doesn't take too long to get there. Devon parks right in front, which is great since I'm still a little out of it. I'm not interested in walking a long way to get my ass kicked. Devon opens the door and lets me go in first.

"Mike, you here?" I yell out as soon as we walk in. "I need to talk to you for a minute. Where are you?"

"Up here, kid," he yells out from his office. "Come on up."

"Wish me luck." I turn to Devon. "I'll either walk down in a bit or he'll throw me down those stairs in a couple of minutes."

Devon gives me a nod and goes to the desk to talk to the trainer that's working. He'll keep himself occupied for as long as he needs to. I don't think this will be a quick conversation. I take a deep breath and walk up the stairs to the office.

"Hey Mike," I greet him as I walk in. "Mind if I sit?"

"You bet, kid." He gestures to a chair. "What's going on? You asking for Alex's hand already?" He laughs like it's the most hilarious joke. It's not funny to me though. If I can get Alex to trust me after this, I will be getting a ring on her finger as soon as possible. "Wait. Why do you look like shit? More than you usually do, I mean."

"Not yet, Mike." I run my hand down my face. "Something happened last night that I need to talk to you about. I hurt Alex unintentionally, and I wanted you to hear it from me first."

"What do you mean, you hurt her? You didn't hit her, did you?" He's already standing up, getting ready to teach me a lesson.

"No, no," I say. "Nothing like that."

I take a few minutes and explain the whole situation to the best of my ability. I still don't remember all the details clearly. I can see how women wouldn't want to come forward after being raped. It's hard enough for a person when people don't believe you, even when you can remember all the details. Having a spotty memory seems like it would make it that much harder to convince people of what happened. Victim blaming is such utter bullshit. I don't even know how I would feel about it if my friends hadn't been there to stop her last night.

"Okay, so what I'm hearing is, you went out with Alex, some girl drugged you, and then Alex followed y'all home and beat the crap out of her?" It's kind of freaking me out how little he seems to care about this. I was expecting a swift punch to the face, not whatever this is.

"Yes, sir. Alex thought I was cheating on her with the crazy chick and she pulled her off of me and basically beat her senseless. I didn't see her after the fact, but apparently the chick looked like something out of a horror movie once they pulled Alex off of her. And then Alex packed up and moved out of the pool house before the cops even showed up."

"That's my girl," he laughs. "Where is she now?"

"I'm not sure. She has her phone turned off right now. But our friend, Ryder, is with her. He says she's been drinking since last night. She was already drunk, or still drunk, when he got there this morning."

"Whiskey, straight from the bottle?" he asks.

"Apparently."

"Yeah." He barks out a laugh. "She's real pissed off, kid. Best to let her calm down a bit before you try to talk too much."

"Ryder says she won't even talk *about* me yet. He's not pushing her, just letting her vent, I guess."

"Hey guys," Devon yells out from downstairs. "Ryder says we need to get to Alex's place now. He's bringing her back from the doctor's office. She broke her hand or something."

Mike looks over at me. "You weren't kidding about her doing a number on that other girl. Let's get over there and see how she's feeling. She might look a little more kindly on you if I come along, too."

We both get up and walk downstairs to where Devon is waiting for us.

"I'm assuming you know where she is?" I ask Mike. "Want to ride with us?"

"Good one, kid. I didn't know you were in such awful shape that you couldn't walk next door."

My jaw drops to the floor.

She's been living right next door, off and on, for the entire time I've been coming here?

Fuck my life.

51

It's a Trap

Alex

"I ALREADY TOLD YOU, Ryder. I'm fine." He's insisting on coming up to the apartment with me instead of dropping me off when he drives me home from the Doctor's office. "I can handle having a cast on my hand. It's not like I won't be able to do anything at all."

"I understand that, babe," he says, walking with me to the door of the building. "But you're still drunk and I'd rather not have you hurting yourself more because you can't fully feel the pain that you're in yet."

"Gah, fine. Come on up." After he told me about how I stopped an attempted rape last night, I wanted some time to myself to figure this out. I guess it's good they're not charging me with assault. But I really thought Connor had cheated. That's a rollercoaster of emotion that I can't erase.

"I knew you'd see it my way." He gives me a little side hug. "You're going to love having me as your friend and nurse today. I'll even wipe your ass if you need it." He winks at me.

"Ew, gross." I laugh. "I think I can manage that with my left hand, thanks."

"Well, the offer stands. Let me know what you need from me."

I give him my keys. "I think unlocking the door will be enough for now."

"You got it, babe." He lets us into the apartment and the stench of stale whiskey and cigarette smoke is heavy in the air.

"Wow, I really did my best to turn this place into a bar last night, didn't I? Do me a favor and open the windows?" I walk over and grab the cigarettes from the coffee table, pulling one out of the pack and placing it in my mouth. I grab the lighter and try to light it left-handed, but I'm not that coordinated, apparently. Ryder laughs and comes over to light it for me.

"You'll be rethinking that ass-wiping offer soon, I think."

"No way you're getting near her ass, dude."

I snap my head over to the door where Pops, Devon, and Connor are standing, and sway on my feet a little.

"Whoopsie. Guess I forgot to lock that when we came in." Ryder doesn't look guilty at all. I'm pretty sure he didn't lock it on purpose.

"Let me see your hand, Lexi Girl." Pops says, walking over to me. "And put that cigarette out. It stinks in here." I pass my smoke to Ryder to deal with and give Pops a big hug.

"What are you doing here, Pops?"

"Well, that sketchy fuck over there"—he grins and jerks a thumb over to where Connor is standing—"came to me and told me you rescued him from an attack last night. He was concerned that he'd hurt you and came to collect the beating that I promised him if he ever did that."

"Even you're calling me a sketchy fuck now? I *really* need to go talk to Tino."

"I'm fine, Pops. Ryder took me to see the doctor. I had x-rays. Typical boxer's fracture plus a cut that they could have stitched but didn't. It's in a cast for probably six weeks. The doctor said I didn't feel it last night because I was drunk before the adrenaline wore off." I show him my sparkly black cast. "Check out this sweet cast, though. I'm all fancy now."

"That's good, girlie. I'm glad to hear you're okay. Knew you would be." He pulls me in for another hug. "I really wanted to come over with Connor to ask you to give him a chance to explain what happened. It seems to me like that boy has some powerful feelings for you and I would consider it a favor to me if you would hear him out?"

"I don't know, Pops. Even if it wasn't his fault, it still hurt me." I know he's itching to get back to the gym now that he knows for sure I'm okay. Physically, anyway. I'm not so sure how my heart is faring yet. But if Pops thinks I should listen to Connor, I suppose I could at least try. Maybe. "I'll stop by and see you soon."

"I'll be expecting you. Love you, Lexi Girl. "

"Love you, Pops."

Pops pats Connor on the shoulder on his way by.

"Well, I think my work here is done, too." Ryder claps his hands together and then mimes dusting them off. "Devon. You need a ride, man?"

"Sure, that would be great." He tosses Connor his keys. "You can drive the truck home."

Ryder walks to me and hugs me. "You okay to talk to him now?" he whispers. I shrug then nod in response.

Devon comes over and hugs me, too. "Thanks for taking care of our man last night. I'll tell you anything Connor can't remember next time we talk. Call me when you're ready."

Devon and Ryder leave the apartment together, and then I'm alone with Connor. Whether I'm ready for it or not.

"Hey, babe," he says, hands in his pockets. "Can we sit?"

I turn and sit on the couch, leaving room for him to sit beside me.

"Thanks." He chuckles a little. "Actually, wait a second. Before we start, do you really need help with the bathroom? I can do that for you, you know."

I shake my head and laugh. "I'm fine right now, thanks."

52

There's Still Hope

Connor

TURNS OUT ALEX ALREADY knows most of what I tell her. Ryder already explained how the girl drugged me, trying to get me to sleep with her. Actually, let's call it what it is; She was attempting to rape me. I was too out of it to consent, even if I had wanted to sleep with her. Which I absolutely did not.

"I know it's going to be hard for you to trust anyone," I say. "But I promise I will never hurt you like that. I'm so sorry that it looked like I did. I can't even imagine how you felt, thinking I had left with someone else. And with what Devon said about how you found me, with her on top of me like that? I just... I can't say enough how sorry I am."

"I understand it wasn't your fault, Connor, but it hurt. It hurt so much. We've only been back in touch for a few days and it felt like you had deserted me all over again." The tears are trailing down her cheeks and I have to stop myself from reaching up and wiping them away. She's not ready for that yet, and I won't push her. "And I was so fucking angry. I don't think I knew I could get that mad. I felt out of control."

"Never, Alex." I promise. "I will never desert you. And I'm sorry I gave you reason to feel so angry." I lean forward, resting my elbows on my knees. "I haven't felt complete since I lost you when we were kids. But I didn't know it until you showed up in my life again. When I touched you after the concert, I felt like I was slamming back home into my body. Like I'd been floating outside myself and you finally came and anchored me to my life again."

Alex looks up at me, tears still on her face. "That's how I felt. I didn't know any of my pieces were missing until you were there, putting me back together."

I slide over to sit next to her and wrap my arms around her. Fuck not being ready yet. I can't let her cry and not hold her. She rests her head on my shoulder and puts her hand on my chest. I finally release the breath it feels I've been holding since I woke up in the hospital and heard what happened last night.

"I'm sorry that I automatically assumed you would be cheating. It's not even like we said we were together." She inhales a big, shuddering breath before continuing. "I don't know if even know how to trust after all the shit that has happened to me."

"You have nothing to be sorry for, Alex. Not a thing. None of this is your fault. I know you've had some shitty relationships. I know they will probably color anything that you and I have together, at least for a while." I turn her face toward mine, needing her to really hear me. "But I felt like you were mine as soon as I saw you after the show last week. And if you will try this with me now, I promise I will spend every moment of every day doing everything in my power to prove that I'm worthy of your trust."

"It's been a crazy few days, hasn't it?" She says with a yawn. "It feels like it's been so much longer. I'm exhausted, honestly. I don't think I'm in any frame of mind to decide something that big right now. Can I sleep on it?"

"You can take as long as you need, love. I will be trying to prove myself to you, regardless. I know you feel something for me too, so I can wait for as long as it takes."

"Sure." She yawns again, then she completely changes the subject. "Can you get me some water and painkillers?"

"Of course," I laugh while getting up. She must really be exhausted. And I'm sure her hand hurts like a bitch. "Point me in the right direction and I will get anything you need."

She points to the bottle of painkillers on the counter and to the fridge. "Over there."

I bring it all back to her and sit back down, hope blooming in my chest as I work up the courage to ask her for something I have no right asking for. "I have a request. Don't be afraid to say no."

"Okay," she says slowly, looking confused. "Shoot."

"I sort of got sick all over my bed last night, apparently. Whatever that chick slipped into my drink made me so sick. I'm having a new bed delivered tomorrow. But I was hoping you might let me stay with you tonight?" Please say yes, please say yes. I don't know if I can be away from her tonight, not after all that's happened. I want to hold her, to convince myself that she's real.

"Oh, gross." She thinks for a couple of minutes. "Yeah, you can stay. But no funny business. Only sleeping." She waves the hand with a cast on it in the air. "I'm injured and need my rest."

"No funny business. Got it." I help ease her off the couch, avoiding her broken hand. "But wait. One question. Does this count as funny business?" I ask, sliding my hands up and pushing them into her hair, bringing my mouth to hers, kissing her. God, that feels so right. Until this moment, I wasn't sure I'd ever get to kiss her again. I place another soft kiss on her lips and pull back slightly, looking into her eyes. Her breath quickens slightly and her lips part, inviting my kiss again. I place my lips on hers, slipping my tongue into her mouth, devouring the soft moan that comes from her throat as I do so. Her hands slide up my chest, gripping my shirt and pulling me closer. I deepen our kiss, exploring her mouth with my tongue while she eagerly kisses me back. She tastes like whiskey and cigarettes, and I can't remember when a kiss has ever tasted better. My dick is trying to get in on the action, and she's pulled me so close that I know she feels it, too. But I gradually end the kiss, knowing it's not the right time to be doing more.

"As much as I want to be inside you right now, love, I think you're right about the no funny business. It's probably best for both of us if we rest tonight. You broke your hand protecting me, and I'm still feeling the aftereffects of whatever that bitch dosed me with." My voice is heavy with regret. I rest my forehead against hers, placing soft, chaste kisses on her lips while we both allow our breathing to return to normal. "Would you prefer I sleep on the couch tonight? If it makes you more comfortable, I will." It kills me to ask, but I'm not forcing my way into her bed, even if we won't be doing anything but sleeping.

"No." She wraps her arms around my waist and rests her head on my chest before releasing a shuddering breath. "I'd like you to sleep beside me, if that's okay? I think I will sleep better with you there."

"I was hoping you would want that. Lead the way, love. Take me to bed." I lace my fingers with hers and she turns to lead me to her bedroom. Moving boxes are stacked neatly along one wall and the bed is against the other. I can't believe things got so screwed up that she felt her only choice was to quit and move out. I'm kind of impressed at how quickly she managed to do it, though. It had to have been less than an hour between when she got back to the house and found me and when she was here and getting into the whiskey.

I can't shake the guilt for not seeing what was happening with that dumb bitch at the bar. She'd popped up enough times that I should have suspected something was going on. How did I allow myself to get drugged like that? I know it's not actually my fault, but that doesn't make me feel much better. It's all bullshit, but the worst part for me is how it made Alex feel. I need to figure out how to earn her trust again. That she's letting me sleep beside her tonight is a good sign. I hope, anyway.

Alex walks over to the far side of the bed and starts taking off her pants. I spin away because her gorgeous legs are too tempting. My poor dick can't take much more of this. How much harder can it possibly get? God, this woman is so bloody sexy. And it seems like she doesn't know that she is. She pulls off her sweatshirt, revealing a thin white tank underneath. I wonder if she knows I can see her hard little nipples right through it. This is going to be a long night for my dick, I think.

"Nice jammies," I joke, trying to lighten the mood a little, even though I'm inexplicably nervous. Good thing false bravado has always served me well. "I'm afraid mine won't be nearly as appropriate for our purposes this evening."

I reach back and pull my shirt over my head, exposing the chest and abs that I've worked so hard for at the gym. From the way Alex licked her lips, I think she still likes the view. My hands move down to my belt buckle and her eyes follow, widening ever so slightly. As I loosen my belt and undo the top button of my jeans, I can see her swallow as she remembers, and readies herself to see what I wear under my pants.

Nothing.

53

Why Her?

Alex

WHAT IN THE HELL was I thinking when I said no funny business? Did I forget what he looked like naked? How can I stick to that when this man is standing in front of me with eyes full of lust as he stares at me in the tank top and panties I had underneath my clothes? I think I can feel the heat coming off of him from here. I know for damn sure that my panties are flooded already, even though we've only kissed, and he's still dressed.

"Nice jammies," he says, looking me up and down, "I'm afraid mine won't be nearly as appropriate for our purposes this evening."

He pulls his shirt over his head, and I lick my lips at the view. That kiss-worthy V is on display above his low-slung jeans and his abs and chest look like Michaelangelo chiseled them from marble. That's one thing to be said about a fighter's body. They're often well muscled and lean enough to see it. And I can tell Connor has been doing a lot of fight training lately.

His hands move down to his belt and start working the buckle before moving on to the button of his jeans. He stops and looks at me. I can feel my eyes open wider in anticipation. I know what's under those jeans. And it's not boxers *or* briefs. Connor goes commando, and I'm about to see exactly what that V is pointing at.

Connor pulls the zipper apart and pushes his pants down to his feet. His cock is hard, long, and thick, and pointing at me like some sort of desire compass. Pre-come is glistening at the tip already, and it's taking everything I have in me to not walk over there and lick it off. Kicking his jeans the rest of the way off, he walks to the opposite side of the bed.

"Get in bed, baby. If you keep looking at my dick like that, I'm not sure I can be held responsible for what happens next." His voice is husky, deeper than normal, and how badly he wants me is evident in the growl that teases the edge of his words.

I go to the door and flip the light switch, but there's still more than enough light to see by. My curtains are open and the light from streetlights and signs in the neighbourhood is almost as bright as leaving the overhead light on would be. Connor is already laying in bed, the sheet he's covered himself with doing nothing to disguise his impressive erection. I make my way back to my side and crawl under the blankets, turning to face him.

He turns on his side to look at me and rests his hand on my waist. His other arm is under his head and I can feel him twirling my hair in his fingers. That's going to make it an even more tangled mess than it already is, but it feels so good I can't bring myself to care.

"Can I ask you something?" He's looking into my soul. Of course he can ask me something. At this point, he could ask me anything and I would answer.

"Why did you pull that girl off? Instead of going after me? I know with Derek the, uh, position? was different, but you still could have easily gotten to me instead of her."

"I'm not entirely sure," I admit after a moment. "I haven't blamed the woman in a situation like this before. My belief is that it's the person in the relationship who is doing something wrong. My partner is the one breaking my trust, not the other woman. But before I could even think, I had that girl by her hair and didn't stop hitting her until Ryder pulled me off and got me out of there. And from the broken hand I'm sporting, I can tell that I didn't hold back. I'm just glad I dropped the bat, or that bitch might be dead right now."

"Do you think somehow you knew something was wrong with the situation? Like somehow, deep down, you knew I wouldn't do that to you?" He whispers. I give it real consideration before I answer.

"It all happened so fast, but I recall a flash where I thought 'he's not even moving'. When you and I have been together, you were a very active participant. And last night you jus... weren't. I know now that it's because she'd drugged you and you were nearly unconscious."

He uses his grip on my waist to pull us closer together. "I think you knew." His whisper ghosts across my skin, sending a pleasant shiver up my spine. "I think you knew, and you were protecting me, even though your experiences were trying to convince you that something else was happening." He leans in and kisses my forehead. "Thank you, Alex. You're my hero." He says with a smile, but under the joking tone, I know he's serious. That shit last night scared him, and he is grateful that I was there for him.

I think he might be right; I think I knew.

I push him over onto his back and slide over to lay my head on his chest. His heart is beating a gentle rhythm and soon his breath steadies and slows. I match my breath to his, and before I know it, I'm asleep.

54

Derek the Dickhead

Connor

I DON'T REMEMBER FALLING asleep last night, but when I wake up, I'm wrapped around Alex. The sky is starting to lighten outside, so I know that it's early still. I slide my arm out from under Alex's head, careful not to wake her. Going out into the kitchen, I find her a bottle of water and painkillers and take them back to leave on her nightstand. After tracking down her keys so I can lock the door, I head out in search of breakfast.

The diner down the street is open, so I go in and order us two full breakfasts and coffees to go. Good thing these guys don't know about my day of stalking or they might have refused to serve me. I guess Tino isn't spreading the word as much as I thought. Breakfast is ready in about ten minutes and I turn around a go back to Alex's place.

When I get up to the apartment, there's some angry-looking guy banging on the door.

"Alex, let me in. I want to talk to you."

"Uh, hey pal, can I help you?" I ask him. My arms are loaded with stuff and he's kind of in my way.

"Get lost buddy, this doesn't concern you." the guy says to me. "I'm trying to get my girlfriend to open the door."

"Oh, you must be Derek." Now I understand. "I got bad news for you dude, she's not your girlfriend. I would have thought she made that pretty clear when she took an umbrella to your ass. Now, if you'll excuse me, I need to get in there. I brought my girlfriend breakfast."

I push my way around him and pull the keys out to unlock the door.

"You look familiar," Derek says to me. "Aren't you that guy from that band? Are you dating Becca or something?"

"Yes, I'm that guy." I open the door. "And no, I'm not dating Becca." Once inside, I kick the door closed behind me, right in his very surprised face.

Alex is sitting on the couch, looking nervous, but still gorgeous in her panties and the sweatshirt she had on yesterday.

"Hey, baby." I bend down and kiss the top of her head, and then put the bags on the coffee table. "I brought breakfast and coffee."

Her face lights up when I say coffee, but before she can answer, there's more pounding on the door. "Alex, answer this door. You're dating that guy? What about us? I said I was sorry. Give me another chance."

"What do you want to do, babe? Want to tell him to fuck off? Do you want me to call Devon to get rid of him?" I sit beside her and grab her hands. "Before you decide, you should know that I kind of gave him the impression that we're dating. I hope that's okay."

She takes a deep breath and runs her hand down her face. "Open the door. I don't know how I could have been any clearer than hitting him with an umbrella and moving out, but I guess he's a lot dumber than I thought."

I stand up with her, and together we go to the door. Before she opens it, I pull her into me and devour her mouth with a passionate kiss that leaves us both breathless. It's a little childish, but I need her to know she's mine before she sees this dickhead again. I know she'd never consider going back to him, but knowing she'll have my kiss fresh on her lips when she talks to him makes me happy. Not to mention that I want him to see the desire in her eyes and know that it's not for him. Okay, so it's more than a little childish. I'm okay with that.

I lean into her. "I want to fuck you so bad right now," I whisper before I lick up the side of her neck. "Maybe I should fuck you right here against this door? Hmmm. Should we do that before you get rid of him? Or after?" I push her up against the door and kiss her, pressing the hard ridge of my cock into her thigh. When she moans into my mouth and I know she's as turned on as I am, I pull her away from the door and open it, dropping our kiss as I do.

"What do you want, man? I'm trying to have some alone time with my girlfriend." I have my arm around Alex and she's leaning into me, breathing a little too heavy.

"Derek," she says, sounding exasperated. "Why are you here? I made it pretty clear that we're done."

"What the fuck, Alex. You're leaving me for this guy?" He looks between me and Alex, trying to make sense of what he's seeing. It's hard to misunderstand this situation, considering I have my arm around her and she's wearing underwear and a sweatshirt, but I think this guy might be delusional. Seems he didn't get the memo that she's been gone for more than a week already.

Alex shakes her head. "No, Derek. I dumped you [*last week*] because I came home to find you fucking some bitch in our bed."

"I said I was sorry." Poor Derek seems confused. It's almost like he really thought this would work. Even if I weren't here, I know Alex wouldn't fall for this guy's bullshit. "I miss you."

"Well, I don't miss you, Derek. You need to leave."

Derek stands there, looking like he's trying to think of the right thing to say so that Alex will forgive him.

"Alright, man. You've had your say. Alex has said she's done with you, so it's time for you to move along." I've almost got the door closed when Derek pushes it hard, and somehow he hits Alex in the face with it.

I spin and face her, grabbing her shoulders. "Are you okay, baby?"

She looks a little dazed, but she nods. "Yeah. I'll be fine."

"I didn't mean to-"

"Shut up." I bite out. "You're done here." I step out into the hallway and grab him by his shirt. "Let me show you out."

I drag Derek down to the main doors, where we run into Devon and Ryder.

"What do we have here?" Ryder asks with a chuckle. "Taking out the trash?"

"Hey guys, you're right on time. Let me introduce you to Derek. He thought he would come by today to see why Alex was leaving him for me, and to win her back." I throw Derek on the sidewalk in front of Devon. "And then he tried to push the door open as I was closing it, and it hit Alex in the face. We decided it would be best for everyone if he left."

"Looks like that plan worked out real well for him." Devon laughs. "Need some help?"

Derek cowers on the ground, looking up at the three of us as we have this conversation around him.

"Yeah, that would actually be great. I need to get back to Alex. I just brought her breakfast from the diner up the street when this asshole showed up."

"No problem Connor, we'll take care of this and then come back." Ryder gives Derek an evil look. "I love taking out this kind of trash."

I turn around before I head back into the building. "Oh, don't come back at least this afternoon. I'm planning to keep Alex occupied for a few hours after we've finished our breakfast and gotten our energy up." I give Derek a little wink. "You guys can come and help move all her stuff back to my place later."

I rush back to the apartment, walk straight over to where Alex is sitting and grab her face in my hands, checking to see if there's any damage from where the door hit her. Luckily for Derek, it didn't leave a mark.

"Is everything okay?" she asks, pointing her fork at the door. "Did he leave?" I notice she's already halfway through her breakfast and raise an eyebrow at her. "Sorry," she says with a fresh mouthful. "I was starving and couldn't wait."

I chuckle and sit down beside her, grabbing my breakfast from the bag. "That's fine, babe. That's why I went and got breakfast. I knew you'd be hungry after the last few days. A diet of straight whiskey isn't very nutritious."

She nods while stuffing a big bite of pancakes into her mouth. "You ain't kidding."

"I ran into Devon and Ryder outside. They are dealing with Derek. He won't bother you anymore." I look at her out of the corner of my eye to gauge her reaction.

"They wouldn't do anything that would get them in trouble, would they?" God, this woman is amazing. I love that her first thought is concern for Devon and Ryder.

"No, babe, nothing like that." I lean back. "They'll come back in a few hours to help move your stuff back to my place."

Her head jerks up in surprise. "Back to your place? I can't do any cooking for at least six weeks, Connor. I won't be much use. Plus, you'll need the pool house for whoever Denise hires." She waves her sparkly cast at me to remind me why she can't cook.

I take her fork and set it down. Cupping her cheek with one hand, I look deeply into her eyes. "I'm not asking you to come cook for me, Alex. I want you to move in with me. Live *with* me. As my girlfriend, not as an employee."

"I... wow... what?"

"We've wasted so many years already. I don't want to waste any more. I know it's fast, but I meant it when I said that you're it for me. I know that you're the only one I'll ever want." Shit, why did I ask this already? I should have waited. She's probably freaking out. We've been together for mere days and there's already been a crisis. Her hand is broken because of me. Why would I think this is the best time to ask her to move in?

"Yes." She looks up at me through her eyelashes. "I will move in with you."

55

Finally Mine

Connor

"Yes?" Did I hear that right? She's actually going to move in with me? After the shit show the other night, she's able to forgive me and move on. "You are the most amazing person I've ever met, Alex. I feel horrible over what happened last night. I didn't mean to blurt that out, but I'm so glad I did."

"You have no reason to feel bad, Connor." She leans closer and hugs me tightly. "I've had some time to think it over and I'm confident that you wouldn't have done anything with her. She drugged you. She's the one who did something wrong."

"What did I do to deserve you?"

"I don't know, but it must've been something good, because I'm awesome." She laughs, grabbing her fork again and shoving another bite of pancakes into her mouth. "Now, let me finish my breakfast before I starve to death."

Shaking my head at her, I grab my coffee from the table and take a drink. "I'm going to drink this coffee, and when I'm done, I'm taking you back to bed. You better finish your breakfast by then, because you're going to need the energy." I let my gaze travel down her entire body while my hand makes little circles on her thigh. I feel her shiver under my touch.

She swallows hard, dropping her fork and pushing her plate away at the same time. "I think I'm all done." She takes my coffee and puts it back on the table, then swings a leg over mine to straddle me there on the couch. "I found something I'd rather have now, anyway."

"Is that so?" I say, reaching to pull her to me for a kiss. "And what would that be?"

I hold her head in my hands, tilting her to deepen our kiss but it's not enough. Sliding one hand down her back, I grab her ass and pull her closer, grinding her onto my hard dick, showing her exactly what she does to me. She groans at the contact, rocking her hips and increasing that delicious friction. Her hands play with the hem of my shirt before she breaks our kiss and pulls it up over my head. She toys with my nipples, pinching them hard enough with her soft fingers that it's just this side of painful.

I lean forward to kiss her more, while my hands push her shirt up over her head. She has the same little tank underneath that she was wearing last night, barely keeping her breasts from my view. I pull the top down so it pushes her tits up, bending down to pull a nipple into my mouth.

"These tits, Alex. I can't get enough." I lick around her nipple, grazing it with my teeth while she continues to grind down onto me, making me harder than I thought possible. Alex moves her hands between us, undoing my pants and releasing my cock. She pulls my face up and brings my mouth to hers, kissing me wildly. Without breaking the kiss, she stands up and pushes her panties down her legs, kicking her way out of them before straddling me again.

"Condom?" she asks against my mouth, rubbing her slick heat over the length of my dick, pushing me to the brink.

"Front pocket," I mumble before grabbing her hair and plunging my tongue into her mouth again. I feel her reach into my pocket and pull out the condom I put there when I was praying she would forgive me, before I even hoped that she'd agree to move in with me.

She tears open the package without breaking our kiss and rolls the condom on me without even looking. Pushing up onto her knees, she lines my cock up with her entrance and impales herself on me in one swift movement.

"Oh, god Alex," I growl. "You feel so fucking good." I slide my hands down to her hips, thrusting up to meet her, and she grinds onto me. I angle my hips, making her clit rub against me fully, and her breath quickens as her pussy tightens. I can already feel the tension building at the head of my cock, my release threatening to come hard and fast.

"Yes, Connor, like that." She moans into the air, throwing her head back as she climbs closer to the edge of her orgasm. "Don't move, don't stop, just..."

Her entire body tenses, her pussy clamping down on my cock, threatening to take me over the edge with her. Through sheer force of will, I control myself and focus on helping her ride out her orgasm. When she leans forward against my chest and kisses me once more, I reach under her ass and lift her off the couch. I kick my pants off fully before carrying her back to her room and lowering her to the bed.

I follow her up onto the bed, settling myself between her thighs, and slowly slide my length into her fully.

"Connor," she whispers. "Kiss me."

I dip my head and taste her swollen lips, kissing her slowly, savouring her. Her kiss is unbelievably soft as she mirrors my desire. Supporting myself with one arm, I hold myself over her while reaching down and pulling her leg up. With her knee over my shoulder, I slowly rock into her, the new position allowing me to slide even deeper than before, enjoying the slick feeling of my flesh against hers.

As I push into her, all I can see is my future. Alex is the one I want by my side, forever.

"I meant what I said before," I whisper in between kisses. "You're it for me, Alex."

She pulls back and searches my eyes with her own. I slow my rhythm even more while she looks for the truth in my words. She must like what she sees.

"I love you, Connor," she whispers back. "I think I always have." And then her mouth is back on mine, our kisses growing deeper, our need for each other becoming stronger with each thrust of our tongues. I pick up my rhythm again, rocking into her a little more forcefully.

Her body chases her release as she meets my rocking motion with her own. She rubs against me, hands gripping my ass and pulling me into her, her orgasm insistent, until she's screaming her release beneath me.

As her pussy contracts around me, I pull up her other leg and place her knee up over my shoulder, lifting myself up on both my hands. I plunge my cock into her deeply, and she takes everything I have to give. The remaining pulses of her lingering orgasm throws me into my own. As I thrust, and finally still, deep within her, my balls tighten as I let go and she wrings every last drop of come from me. The orgasm seems endless, my arms and legs shaking from holding myself up as jet after jet of my release fills her.

My name is on her lips when I finally lower her legs and roll to the side, exhausted.

I remove the condom and tie it off, throwing it into the wastebasket beside her bed. Rolling toward her, I gather her in my arms, pulling her into my chest, and kiss her forehead.

"I love you, Alex," I whisper. "You are amazing."

"I love you too, Connor." She tilts her head up and kisses me softly. "Now sleep. We've got a big day ahead of us, moving me in and then getting on with our lives together. I don't know about you, but I need a nap before we deal with any of that."

I laugh, squeezing her closer to me while pulling the blankets up around us. "Yes, ma'am," I say. "I can't wait."

56

Second Chance

Alex

HE ASKED ME TO move in. And I said yes. We celebrated with amazing sex. And a nap. We were getting out of the shower when Devon and Ryder showed up to help move my stuff.

"Thanks guys," I say when they start grabbing boxes. "Sorry to make you do this again so soon."

"Aw, darlin'. If it means we get to keep you, we'll move your stuff over and over again." Devon drops his box on the table to come give me a hug. He whispers in my ear, "and if he ever hurts you, call me and I'll beat him senseless and move you anywhere you need to go. He might pay me but that doesn't mean I'll be on his side."

Connor laughs. "I heard that, dickhead. Let's see who gets a Christmas bonus this year."

"Ha! I didn't get one last year, fucker. You owe me two this time around."

"Nice try." Connor shakes his head. He looks over at me. "He's very well compensated. Still, I know he would be on your side should anything ever happen. The man has no sense of loyalty."

Devon shakes his head in his direction. "See?" he says to me. "I've got you, girl." He winks and grabs the box up again, taking it outside.

Ryder comes to me next. "Don't forget that I'm also on your side. Us bitches gotta stick together, okurrr," he says in his best drag queen voice, which is absolutely terrible. "We can go get mani/pedis and gossip."

"Sounds good to me." I give him a hug. "Thanks for being here for me."

"Anytime, babe. I'm firmly Team Alex in this situation."

"That's the last of the boxes, babe." Connor passes a box to Ryder. "We'll meet you guys back at the house. Put those in my room."

"You got it, boss." Ryder's voice is dripping with sarcasm. He winks at me before taking the box out the door.

"Are you ready for this, really?" Connor looks at me with concern in his eyes. "I don't want to rush you. I have a few spare rooms that you can move into, if you prefer."

I laugh. "Well, it is kind of fast, but I don't want to be away from you anymore. It's strange, but it feels like all of my past failed relationships were merely filler while I was waiting for you to come back to me. I can't imagine not having you in my life."

"I'm so glad to hear you say that, baby. I plan on never letting you out of my sight again. You're stuck with me now, Alex. There is nothing I wouldn't do to keep you." Connor pulls me into his arms, and his mouth finds mine in a sweet kiss. It's full of apologies for the past and promises for the future. It's the beginning of our second chance.

57

Settling Into a New Life

Alex

AFTER EVERYTHING I'VE BEEN through in my life, I feel like I'm finally on the right track. I have the love of my life beside me, good friends, and a plan for the next year. I'll be travelling with Connor on tour and eating all the best food in the places we visit. When we get back from that, I'll decide what to do next.

Connor's finished up in the studio for the day, and I'm already in our bedroom. The bed Connor bought after the attack is amazing, and it's the best place to relax and read a book when I need a little time to myself. Since I've moved in, Connor has encouraged me to make his house my own and I've added all sorts of art and decor. The other guys seem to find my expletive adorned throw pillows as amusing as Connor did when he saw them the first time.

I even convinced him to make our own art for the bedroom by covering our naked bodies in paint and having sex on an enormous canvas. Admittedly, it took very little convincing, and now it hangs on the wall over the head of our bed. My face never fails to heat up thinking about that day.

Even better than making the canvas was getting cleaned up in the shower afterward.

"What's on your mind, baby?" Connor asks, eyeing me from where he leans against the doorway.

"That I'm a lucky girl to have such an amazing boyfriend."

"Oh?" He says, walking toward me while pulling his shirt over his head. Fuck, he looks so good when he does that. "How amazing?"

I crawl down to meet him at the end of the bed. Reaching my hands up to his hair, I pull him down and brush my lips gently against his. Trailing kisses along his jawline and down his neck, I use my hands to explore his chest. Kissing Connor is one of my favorite pastimes. Laying more kisses down his chest, I pull a tiny nipple into my mouth, flicking it with my tongue, then biting down softly. Connor's sharp intake of breath, followed by a low groan, sends a flood to my panties, getting me ready for him. But that's not what I'm interested in right now.

I reach for his belt, undoing the buckle before opening the button on his jeans and sliding them down to the floor as I sit on the edge of the bed. I kiss down his abs, along both lines of that sexy V, before licking my way to its end.

"Fuck," Connor moans his approval, "You're killing me, baby."

I taste the bead of salty pre-come that glistens at the end of his penis, and he groans again. I roll my tongue around the head of his cock before taking it into my mouth, licking and swirling around it fully, the taste making my mouth water. Reaching out for Connor's hands, I place them on my head, encouraging him to grab on. He fists my hair; the sting sending a thrill through me as I reach around to grab the backs of his thighs and pull him toward me, shoving his cock right to the back of my throat and making me gag a little.

"Fuck, Alex, that feels so fucking good." Connor pumps into my mouth hesitantly. "Is this okay, baby?"

I let his dick go with a pop and look up at him. "I want you to fuck my mouth, Connor," I say, sucking his cock back into my mouth, right to the back of my throat. I have to remember to breathe on the out stroke so I don't suffocate, but I love it so much that I moan low in my throat, the sound reverberating through Connor's cock.

"How the fuck did I get so lucky?" I hear Connor ask as he pumps into my mouth a little more forcefully. "Every time I think you are as perfect as a person can get, you surprise me with something else."

I look up at him as I move my hands up to squeeze his ass, feeling the muscles flex as he rams his dick into the back of my throat. Even through the tears running down my face, I can see that he's looking at me with nothing but love. Every groan I make is met with a deeper one from him.

He starts to pull back. "Alex, I can't hold back anymore," he says, to warn me he's about to come, but I pull him deeper into my mouth. His release explodes into my throat, forcing me to swallow each spurt as it comes. Swallow after swallow, I take him in, until he's completely spent. I release his dick with a pop, then look up at him and grin while wiping my mouth with the back of my hand.

He drops to his knees and pulls me into his arms. Using his thumbs, he wipes the tears away from my face and kisses me deeply, tasting himself on my tongue.

"I am definitely the one with an amazing girlfriend," he says, a look of awe on his face. "I can't even believe you're real sometimes, Alex."

Meant To Be

Alex

Three Months Later

Becca, Ryder, and I have spent a wonderfully relaxing afternoon at the spa. We booked massages, waxing, and mani/pedis. Imagine my surprise when Ryder took part in everything.

"I can't believe you actually got waxed, Ryder," Becca laughs. We're sitting on the patio of a pub down the street from the spa, enjoying some appetizers and a couple of drinks before we all head our separate ways. "You should have seen that poor girl's face when she realized Ryder Sullivan, world famous lead guitarist for Sleeping Dogs, was up on her table with his ass in the air, waiting for her to wax his butthole." Tears run down her face as she pictures it again.

"Why did we think it was a good idea to have a group appointment? I think I need to have my eyeballs bleached after that." I laugh too.

"Forget your eyeballs. I had her bleach my asshole. But it's all good, because I asked her out after."

I spit out my drink. "You did not! You asked her out? What did she say?"

"I'm picking her up at seven tonight." He smirks. "So I'd better get home if I want to have time to get ready."

"What do you even need to get ready?" Becca asks. "You've waxed your junk and bleached your asshole. You should be good to go."

Ryder is like the rest of the guys in the band. They aren't much for dressing up. I think black shirts make up most of all of their wardrobes, fancy or otherwise.

"I'll have you know that I like to look good for my dates. Plus, I need to shower and make sure all traces of wax and bleach are gone. I don't want her to encounter any of that when she's not at her day job." He wiggles his eyebrows suggestively.

"Such a gentleman." I joke.

"I always take care of my lady friends," he says with a bow. "And with that, I will leave. See you guys another day. Thanks for inviting me to join you today. I love a good girls' day." He gives Becca and me both hugs and the next we see him, he's driving by the pub and giving us a wave while he drives away.

Once he's gone, Becca and I get up and leave the pub as well.

"So what are you up to tonight?" Becca asks. "Big plans with Connor?"

"Nah, we're staying in tonight. The guys have been so busy in the studio that we haven't had a lot of time for ourselves." I'm actually surprised that Ryder joined us today. The other guys must've been giving him too much shit again, and he needed to get away for a bit. They're a little too hard on him, from what I can tell. "What about you?"

"Oh, I have a photo shoot tonight. Some band is doing a small show. I was going to see if you wanted to come, but you've already got plans."

"Maybe next time."

"I'll hold you to that." Becca flags down her own cab. "Let me know when you're free this week and we can hang out." She gives me a hug before getting into the cab.

I wave at her and flag down another cab to take me home.

I unlock the door and disarm the alarm, calling out for Connor as I walk through to the kitchen. I don't get an answer, but on the countertop in the kitchen, I find a note.

HEY BABE,

BILL ASKED IF ME AND THE GUYS COULD PLAY AT ROUGH MIX FOR A BIT TONIGHT. MEET ME THERE AT TEN.

LOVE YOU, CONNOR.

I'm a little disappointed that we won't get to hang out, just the two of us, but I'd love to see them play. I go upstairs and grab a quick shower (thanks to Ryder for the reminder to get off any stray wax) and dry my hair a little. I've got some time to kill before I need to get dressed, so I pull out a book and settle into the bed to read for a while.

By the time I need to get ready, I've finished my book and had a quick nap. Good thing I set the alarm on my phone or I would have slept all night. Lately, it seems as though I could sleep all night and half the day too. I hope I'm not getting sick.

Hopping out of bed, I change into my favourite ripped skinny jeans, a Sleeping Dogs tee I stole from Connor and turned into a cropped shirt, and some black Chuck Taylors. I put on my standard mascara and lip gloss, grab my phone and wallet, and then I'm out the door.

I drive my car there because I don't feel like taking a cab again right now. If I need to leave my car there overnight, so be it. A new playlist of music that Connor made for me makes the drive better. I get to listen to some of the music that he's enjoyed over the last twenty years we've been apart and it makes me feel so close to him. It's like an old school mix tape without all the hassle of actually doing any recording.

When I get to Rough Mix, I park in the side lot and walk around to the front. There's a bouncer at the door tonight, which I find a little strange. I don't remember that from the last time we were here. Maybe the incident when Connor was drugged has caused Bill to increase security?

"Good evening, Miss Wilson," the bouncer says as he opens the door for me. "Have a great night."

Now that's weird. Connor and I have been careful to keep me out of the public eye, so nobody knows who I am yet. We fully expect our privacy to be violated once the next tour starts since I am going on the road with the band, but so far we have kept our relationship quiet. This bouncer shouldn't know who I am.

Walking in the bar I'm met with... silence? And candles? What in the hell is going on?

Suddenly, a trail of candles lights up, leading from me to the stage at the far end of the room. I'm clearly meant to follow, so I start walking. Shortly I'm met with a set of stairs leading me onto the stage and to a stool. Before I can look around, more candles light up the stage and I see Connor sitting on a stool close to me, and the rest of the guys are a little further back, set up with their instruments.

"Hi, baby," Connor says, his eyes never straying from mine. "I sort of lied to get you here. The guys and I aren't really playing a show tonight. We have one song to play and it's a new one. It's called *Meant to Be.* I hope you like it."

The rest of the guys start playing while Connor grabs his mic and comes closer to me. He takes my hand and starts the song, looking into my eyes while he sings.

Circling around you
Not knowing what was missing
I wasn't whole
Until you starting kissing me
Circling around you
So close but not enough
Emptiness inside me
Waiting for your love
You make me whole
You fill me up
I'll keep you with me
Because we're meant to be
Lives Intertwined
Spinning around you
I'll keep you with me
Because we're meant to be
Circling around you
Because to me you are the sun
Circling around you
Because for me you are the one
You make me whole
You fill me up
Please stay with me
Because we're meant to be

He leans over and presses a kiss to my lips before handing the mic off to one of the guys. My heart is racing after the sweet serenade, and I'm not sure what happens next. The rest of the band leaves the stage, leaving me alone with Connor. He's holding both of my hands now, and kisses me again before he begins.

"Alex, we've been circling around each other since we were kids, and even when we were apart, there were parts of our lives that remained intertwined. We've nearly reconnected so many times over the years, but the fates must have decided that the timing wasn't right yet. Then the most amazing thing happened; I saw you in the dressing room backstage after a show."

"When you passed me that whiskey bottle and our hands touched, I knew instantly that this was something special. It was like a bolt of lightning coursing through my body, telling me I was finally home. Because you are my home, Alex. I've been lost for so long, but then you walked back into my life and I knew where I belonged. With you. Forever."

Connor pulls a small box out of his pocket and kneels down on the stage in front of me.

"Alex, I love you. I've never stopped. All these years I've been missing you and I didn't realize it. But I know it now, and I never want to miss you again. I want you to be my home, my wife, and my life forever. Alex, will you stay with me? Will you marry me?"

He opens the ring box to reveal a stunning black diamond ring in a simple rose gold setting but I can barely see it through the happy tears that are now pouring down my face. I stand up, put my hands on either side of Connor's face, and pull him in to kiss me. I hold his face to mine and kiss him deeply, then I pull away slightly, looking into his eyes.

"Yes," I whisper against his mouth, the grin creeping up to take control of my cheeks. "Yes, I will marry you. I love you Connor, you're my home as well." Then I pull him in to kiss me again.

He wraps his arms around me and lifts me off the floor, deepening the kiss. I pull my legs up to wrap around him, wanting to get closer, to get him inside of me, and then I hear it. Rustling and movement at the sides of the stage.

"Ahem, ahem." Pops clears his throat. "As horrifying as it would be to stand here and watch y'all get down to business, I believe I need to congratulate my granddaughter now."

I quickly lower my legs and end my kiss with Connor. As I'm looking around for Pops, some of the bar lights come on and I can finally see something other than Connor and candles. Everyone is here: all the guys in the band, Becca, Pops, Marcus and Domenic, Denise and her boyfriend Andrew (even though I thought they broke up?), and Devon.

All the people I care about are gathered here. It makes me wonder where Connor's family is. Not for long though, because soon I am getting hugged and kissed and loved on by all these people, as they congratulate us on our engagement.

Pops comes over and gives me a huge squeeze and a kiss, then he shakes Connor's hand.

"This ups the stakes, kid," he tells Connor. "If you hurt her now, you won't get off with a beating. Don't think I don't know how to make a man disappear, for good. You've been warned."

"POPS," I gasp. "Don't threaten to kill him. We've been engaged for a few minutes." I smile over at Connor. "At least wait until tomorrow." I'm sure Pops isn't serious. At least, I think he isn't.

Pops wanders over to the bar and everyone takes their turn to come and congratulate us. Becca and Ryder confess they were in charge of distracting me today.

Ryder apparently didn't actually ask the waxing technician out. I'm glad about that since he's finally come to terms with his feelings for Denise.

Becca didn't lie about having something to shoot, though. She's been taking photos of the proposal this entire time. We make a plan to schedule some engagement photos and then she goes off to mingle with the rest of the band. Johnny moves over to let her sit and passes her a drink before they all start laughing and joking again. It's so nice that all of our friends get along as well as they do. Even Marcus and Domenic are here. After grilling Connor over dinner one night, they determined that he is, in fact, not a scumbag.

Connor has been standing with me throughout all the congratulations, and now that we're finally alone, he leans over and whispers in my ear.

"You look so beautiful." He breathes against my neck. "I need to get you home and taste you, and I don't know how long I can wait." His fingers stroke my back above my belt line and he peppers kisses down my neck to my shoulder. I tilt my head to the side to give him better access.

"Well, what are we waiting for?" I whisper back. "Time for my fiance to take me home and fuck me."

He grabs my hand and begins pulling me to the door while I laugh at his eagerness.

"Not even going to say bye before you sneak off?" Devon yells out from the other side of the room. "Fine, have fun then."

"Love you guys, bye." I flip him off as Connor continues leading us to the door.

CONNOR DRIVES US HOME in my car and before long, we are naked in our bed.

"God, I love you," he murmurs while he kisses a line up my body. He wasn't lying when he said he couldn't wait to taste me. As soon as we walked into our room, he stripped me out of my clothes and threw me on the bed, kneeling in front of me for the second time tonight. Instead of proposing, though, this time he's eating me like it's his job, and giving me three mind-blowing orgasms before crawling back up my body.

"I'm going to spend my life loving you and worshipping your body as often as I can."

His fingers tangle in my hair and he places his forehead against mine, looking deep into my eyes. I reach down and line up his cock with my entrance and then grab his ass and pull him into me, a soft moan escaping my lips.

"I love you, Connor." I whisper against his lips while he rocks himself slowly into me, again and again. "Fuck, that feels so good."

Connor leans back and looks down at our bodies, watching himself slide in and out of me.

"Look at us, babe," he tells me. "See where we're connected, where we're joined."

I look down and watch his cock slide into me slowly before he pulls back, only to do it all again. I can feel myself responding to the sensuality of it, pumping out more wetness, rolling my hips to meet his, as my orgasm builds again.

"I've always felt something was missing, and when you came back, I realized it was you. You make me whole, Alex. I'm not me without you."

His words are making me too emotional. I can't speak, so I lift my head and meet his lips with mine, pulling him into a kiss. We match the languid rhythm of our kiss to the unhurried pace of our love-making until we are both climbing toward our release. My climax builds and builds as we continue to rock our bodies against each other until finally it explodes from me with incredible force. Stronger than anything I've felt before, it truly feels like we are becoming one being in this moment. Stars explode behind my eyes as I contract around Connor, pulling him over the edge with me. He groans my name as he comes, filling me, his cock pulsing over and over again. When we both finally still, he rolls to the side and pulls me to him.

I relax into his embrace, loving the feel of his skin against mine. I can't believe we're going to get married. All these years after Connor first became a part of my life, now he's going to be part of it forever.

"Shit!" He leans up over me. "We forgot a condom."

"Oh." I say quietly, surprised.

"I'm so sorry, baby, I've never done that before. I was so caught up with how wonderful everything felt, and with you agreeing to marry me." He bends and kisses my forehead. "Are you okay?"

I chuckle a little. It's not funny, but it's also not the end of the world. "I'm fine, Connor. I'm sure everything will be fine."

He visibly relaxes. "I love you, Alex," he says as he takes my mouth again.

"I love you, Connor," I say with my lips pressed against his. "Now shut up and kiss me like you're making me your Mrs."

He barks out a laugh. "You got it, wife. Come here." He kisses me with everything he has while rolling onto his back and pulling me with him.

I know that this time, there is nothing that can happen that will keep us apart. Now or ever.

Epilogue

Connor

"Babe, can you get the door? I need to get Allie and Mollie into the bath right now if we're going to make it to Travis and Finn's wedding on time."

Alex's voice drifts down the hallway, rousing me from my song-writing stupor. Okay, I may have been drifting off a little, but last night was my night up with the twins and they're currently going through a sleep regression. Can you blame me for closing my eyes for a few minutes after getting approximately sixteen minutes of sleep? Yeah, I didn't think so.

I shake myself the rest of the way awake and make my way to the door, unsure who would be showing up at my house right now, considering everyone we know should be getting ready for Travis and Finn's wedding too. When I throw the door open, I'm shocked by who I see standing there.

"Sadie? Amanda?" My eyes scan past my younger sisters to take in the pile of boxes sitting on my front steps. "What...what are you doing here?"

Amanda looks down at her feet and shrugs.

"It's a funny story," Sadie says, pushing past me into the house. "Mom called me at university and told me she was leaving town with Ted. Can you believe that? Apparently, they're moving to Vegas to help Ted's makeup business break into the drag queen market. As if those queens don't already know not to use the pyramid scheme makeup he's hawking."

I guess that is kind of funny, considering I thought she was on drugs when she first started talking about Ted last year. I was so relieved when I found out he was selling makeup instead of dragging my mom back into the drug addiction she worked so hard to overcome that I even invested in his business. Well, I gave him a onetime loan to buy product, fully expecting to be hit up for money again and again, despite his promise to pay me back with interest. I haven't heard a word from Ted since, not even to ask for more money. He has a surprising amount of integrity for a guy I once thought was a deadbeat. He's even got my mom working on something other than getting money out of me. Like abandoning my little sisters, apparently.

"So, can we crash here until we figure something else out?" Amanda asks from the same spot on the porch. "I have a job interview with a toy factory this week. I should have some money saved up to move out in a couple of months."

I snort a laugh and step out beside her, wrapping an arm around her shoulders. "You're welcome here as long as you want. I'm not forcing you to move out. As if I would make you move into a crappy apartment when I still have the guys bedrooms set up in the basement. They never stay over anymore, not now that they all have families to go home to, so the rooms are just sitting there. We can redecorate however you want."

Sadie laughs. "Told you he'd say that," she says to Amanda. "We didn't even need to offer our babysitting services."

"Did I hear someone say something about babysitting services?" Alex, her arms full of wiggly babies wearing hooded towels, joins us in the hallway, passing Mollie to me. "I'll never say no to Auntie Sadie and Auntie Amanda's babysitting."

Allie wriggles in Alex's arms, reaching for Amanda, who grabs her up and squeezes her in a hug.

"Of course I'll babysit these little cuties," Amanda says. "It's the least I can do for you letting us stay here."

Alex's eyes cut to me and she tips her head in a slight nod as if to say, "You didn't ask me, but yes, it's okay that your sisters move in".

"Perfect. Can you feed them while I get myself into the shower? If I don't get a move on, I'll be going to the wedding in my sweatpants." Alex gestures to her baggy jogging pants. "I'll wear them just about anywhere, but I draw the line at wearing them to a wedding. That's going too far."

I pass Mollie into Sadie's waiting arms. "I need to get ready, too," I say, trying unsuccessfully to hide my excitement at being able to get Alex alone. With twin six-month-old babies in the house, we don't get to spend much time together. "We won't be long."

Ignoring my sisters' matching eye rolls, I follow Alex through the house and to our master bedroom.

"Finally alone," I say, spinning her to face me. I lower my lips to hers and kiss her deeply, just as in love with her today as I was the day we met all those years ago. My forehead drops to rest against hers. "So, are you sure it's okay if my sisters move in? I could get them their own place instead, if you would prefer."

Alex chuckles and wraps her arms around my waist. "We're not sending them away," she says, her face buried in my chest. "They're still so young. Besides, we have the space. Now we just have a bigger family to fill it."

I nod, enjoying the feel of having her wrapped around me like this. It's been so long since we've been able to just enjoy being with each other. "Thank you."

"Now," Alex says, pulling away. "Last one in the shower is on dirty diaper duty for a week." She rips her shirt off, shoves her pants down, and strikes a pose in all her naked glory, sending all the blood in my body straight to my dick. "Catch me if you can." She takes off to the bathroom, leaving me to catch up.

Joke's on her, though. I don't care if I'm on diaper duty for the next year. Showering with my wife, knowing our twins won't be interrupting us, is worth it. And now that my sisters are going to be living with us, we might get to do this more than once every six months.

I guess my mom has finally come through for me, after all. Too bad she let my sisters down in order to do so, but I plan to make up for it. Just as soon as I've spent some quality alone time with my wife.

The End

Keep Reading for a Sneak Peek of Face the Music (Sleeping Dogs Book 2)

Chapter One – Creepy Andrew and a Pity Party

Ryder

"Can I just tell you again how happy I am you two worked out your differences," I say around a mouthful of prime rib. "Your weekly dinners are the only time I eat well all week."

Ever since Alex and Connor reconnected, and then made it through the bullshit that was that groupie drugging and trying to rape Connor a couple of months ago, Alex has been hosting weekly family dinners at their house. She's a professional chef and loves cooking. And I am a semi-professional eater who is more than willing to eat any of the delicious things she makes.

My dad wasn't much of a cook while I was growing up. His specialties were mac and cheese and takeout. I never went hungry, but the food probably could have been healthier. It's not his fault, though. Being stuck raising two young boys all alone because their mom wants nothing to do with them is tough. He did the best he could with us. It's just really hard to compete with an actual chef.

"I'm happy that you all come every week and give me a chance to feed you. It's been tough since I haven't been working. Who knew that taking ten weeks off would have such an impact on my employability?" Alex is serving up extra Yorkshire puddings that she's pulled from the oven. I immediately put my plate up to grab a couple of those crispy little golden puffs of goodness. Maybe it's a good thing that Dad couldn't cook like this. I'd never have been able to maintain my girlish figure.

"How is your hand feeling now that you've had your cast removed?" Denise asks. She's sitting opposite me, next to her clean-cut looking doofus of a boyfriend. Dude hardly ever talks, unless he whispers something into Denise's ear. She never looks pleased with what he's said when he does that, either. The guy gives me a weird feeling, but I can't put my finger on why. Mostly, he gives me the creeps.

"So much better. I can shower without help now, which is nice. I can't believe they made me keep it on for nine weeks."

Connor comes up behind Alex and runs his hands around her waist as he pulls her toward him. "Oh babe, you know I'm still going to help you in the shower."

"Get off me, perv." Alex laughs while pushing Connor away.

They've come a long way in the ten weeks since Alex broke her hand defending Connor from that groupie. It was subconscious since she didn't know that Connor had been drugged, but she beat the chick so hard she fractured her hand and saved Connor from sex that he didn't want. They're so happy together it's gross, but in a good way.

I hope one day that I can find love like they have, but since I'm only interested in one person and she is dating a stupid asshole named Andrew, I don't think that's likely to happen. You could say my crush on Denise is the reason I have a problem with Andrew, but it's not. Well, it's not the only reason, anyway. He's not quite right.

I look across the table at Denise. She's got her long black hair tied up in a red bandana with only her long bangs hanging down over her forehead. It goes great with the tight jeans and flannel shirt she's wearing tonight. She looks like a pin-up queen out for a casual stroll. That idiot Andrew leans over and whispers in her ear while I'm looking. Denise looks at him and shakes her head a little before he whispers to her again. She looks away from him and rolls her eyes while letting out an enormous sigh.

"Well, I hate to say it. We're going to have to get going now. I've got early meetings tomorrow, and there are some things that I need to get sorted tonight in preparation." Denise stands and places her napkin beside her still full plate. She spent more time wiping her fork with her napkin than she did eating. Every time she took a bite, she'd make a face and then wipe her fork again. It was weird, yet oddly adorable. "Thank you so much for dinner, Alex. It was delicious, as always."

"You're leaving already?" I stand when Denise does, a remnant from when I was a kid and my brother, Hunter, and I would spend half of every summer vacation with my grandmother. She drilled into me the importance of being a gentleman. I may be an asshole, and I may drink too much, but I still use my manners, especially with women like Denise. Standing when she does is the least I can do.

"Yes, Ryder," she says, a look of irritation on her face. "Can you please try to behave tonight? I don't have time to bail you out of jail again."

That only happened once. However, she has had to rescue me from other towns, public parks, private homes, and the occasional possibly haunted hotel. Like I said, I drink a lot more than I probably should.

"I will be on my best behaviour tonight, love. Just for you." I wink and give her a little bow. That's probably too over the top, but it gets a laugh from her, so it's worth it.

"Good." Andrew sneers in my direction. "I plan to keep her very occupied tonight."

Ugh, that guy is such a creep.

"Yeah, we'll see," is all Denise says. She looks a little uncomfortable. "See you all later."

Denise and Andrew leave, and the rest of us stay to enjoy our dinner.

Alex looks over at me, checking if I'm okay. She knows I have a thing for Denise, and she knows that I'm doing my best to stay out of her business with Andrew. What she doesn't know is how hard it is for me to see them together every week at family dinner. The way he acts makes me want to punch him in his stupid math teacher-looking face.

"That was a weird." Aiden is sitting to my right. He's noticed my crush too, but he hasn't come right out and said anything. "I'm not sure I really like Andrew."

"Me neither," Alex says, still looking at me. "Why is he always whispering in her ear? She always looks uncomfortable when he does it. There's something weird about him."

"Agreed." I put my napkin on my plate. I've had three helpings already. There's no way I could fit anything else in my stomach.

"I have crème brûlée for dessert," Alex offers. "I'm so excited to try my new torch."

"Leave it to my girl to want to play with fire for the sake of dessert." Connor's pulled Alex down to sit on his lap, and he's kissing along her jaw while she tries to stand.

"I'm going to have to pass, Alex. I couldn't eat another bite if I tried." I'm already going to need to open the top button on my jeans the second I leave. I'm overly full, but it was totally worth it.

"Well, I'm going to get a few ready, anyway. Connor, can you help me?" Alex gets out of Connor's grip and she walks out of the dining room.

"You guys can see yourselves out." Connor jumps out of his chair and runs after Alex, stopping only to throw her over his shoulder. "Leave the mess," he calls out over his shoulder while running out with Alex giggling the whole way.

"Yeah, so... I don't think dessert is on the menu anymore, guys." Aiden laughs.

Travis is already on his way out, leaving only me and Aiden at the table. Alex's friend Becca had to work tonight, shooting someone's Sunday wedding, and Johnny and Devon weren't able to make it, either.

"See you, Trav."

"Bye guys," he says without turning around.

Aiden waves at Travis before turning to me. "Sit for a minute."

"Um, okay?" I say, taking my chair again. "What's up, man? Everything alright?" Aiden is the oldest member of our band, and he's also the quietest. He doesn't normally talk unless he really has something important to say.

"I know how you feel about Denise," he says to me. "And I also know how we all feel about Andrew. There's something wrong with that guy."

"Right? But what can we do about it? Denise is a grown woman. She can make her own choices."

"Yes, she is grown, and she can make choices. But tell me this. Have you ever presented yourself as a choice? She's never going to choose you if she doesn't even know that you're an option."

"Geez, man. You're not pulling any punches today, are you?"

"Actually, I am," he says. "If I weren't pulling punches, I'd tell you that your drinking and fucking around isn't helping you get over her like you think. And getting over her isn't what you actually want, even though you think it is. I know that's why you're doing it, even if you won't say it. You're a good guy, or at least you would be if you'd stop acting like such a fuckup. So stop being a fuckup and tell that woman how you feel."

"Well, shit." I run my hands through my hair and my tongue pokes out to play with my lip ring, a nervous habit that I can't seem to shake. "I can't tell her something like that. She has a boyfriend. It wouldn't be right."

"Normally, I would agree with you. But I get a bad feeling from that guy. I think Denise might be keeping him around because she feels like she's run out of options. I overheard her talking on the phone one day, upset about the fact that she's 36 already, and she's unmarried. I guess her mom's been after her about it."

"She can't marry Andrew." Just the thought of that makes me feel sick to my stomach. The three helpings of prime rib with all the fixings don't help either. "It doesn't seem like she even likes him."

"That's what I'm saying, man." Aiden gives my shoulder a little squeeze. "Just talk to her. You might not get to be with her, but maybe hearing she has other options will get her away from that guy before something bad happens. If we all feel the same way about him, it means something."

"He probably has a few bodies in his freezer or something." I laugh bitterly. It's supposed to be a joke, but Andrew is so creepy it wouldn't surprise me if he had bodies hidden somewhere.

On my drive home after dinner, I find myself parking in front of the liquor store. I'm not brave enough to go talk to Denise, but I also can't think about her with Andrew. A bottle of vodka sounds like good company for the night.

When I get home, I head straight to the couch with my vodka. Why dirty a glass? I drink straight from the bottle while I search for something to watch on Netflix, but nothing gets my interest, so I turn off the TV. It's totally normal to sit in the dark and drink alone, right?

No wonder the guys think I have a problem.

If I'm being honest with myself, I do have a problem, and it's gotten progressively worse the longer Denise has been with Andrew. That guy is so wrong for her, but she doesn't see it. Not that I'm a better choice, no matter how I feel about her. I'm such a fuckup that even if I got her to go out with me, she'd leave me, eventually. It wouldn't be the first time.

My brother and I were kids when my mom left. I was six, and Hunter was only three. I was hiding behind the couch when she came downstairs with a suitcase and told my dad she was leaving. Had I not been so curious, I wouldn't have heard what she told him as she walked out the door.

"I love you, Tom," she told my dad, "But I can't do this with those kids anymore. I never wanted them, and I still don't. I can't be their mother. I won't put off my life any longer because you wanted children. Goodbye. Don't look for me." And then she left.

She left because of us, me and my brother. Luckily my brother hadn't heard what she said, and he was too young to remember if he had. And I never told him about it. Even at six years old, I knew that would hurt him too much. I didn't even tell my dad that I heard it. He told us she had to go take care of her sick sister. Even after the way she left us, he didn't want us thinking badly of her. But I never forgot what she said. I never forgot that she left us kids, not my dad. Who abandons a child?

I had a few girlfriends when I was younger, but I always dumped them before they could dump me. After a while, I stopped dating and stuck to casual sex instead. Seemed to be an easier way to go about it. I never had to worry about anyone leaving because it would never be more than that one night, anyway.

And then I met Denise. When she walked up to me and the guys after a show we played at a friend's house party, I was instantly attracted to her. Her ice-blue eyes looked right through me, like I didn't even exist, and the need to make her acknowledge me consumed me. Even back then she wore a flower in her long black hair, pin-up girl style, and had a take charge attitude. Before she even started talking, I decided I would take her home that night to see what was under that wiggle dress and whether that take charge attitude transferred to the bedroom.

Obviously, that didn't happen.

She told us, "You guys have a great sound, but you won't get anywhere playing house parties. I'm going to represent you. I'll get you better gigs and together we'll take this thing to the next level." She was only twenty-one then, and she had balls of steel. After that speech, I knew I couldn't take her for only a night. If I took her home, I'd never be able to get enough. And that was too risky for me.

I tried to convince the guys that we didn't need her. And like an asshole, I did it right in front of her. Thankfully, the guys convinced me she was right. She'd had no clients before, but we took a chance on her, just like she took a chance on us, and now here we are. Next level, exactly like she said. The only price has been my never-ending heartache, because I've been in love with her since that day. A bargain, really, considering all she's done for the band.

So now I'm sitting here again, drinking by myself, wondering what it would be like if Denise actually loved me back. But I know she doesn't. I've done enough stupid shit in the last fifteen years to ensure that she would never take a chance on me now.

Instead, I get to sit here alone, drinking a toast to her happiness with Andrew, even though it means I will never get a chance.

Fucking Cheers.

BREAKUPS AND BARFING

Denise

After Andrew whispered in my ear during family dinner at Alex and Connor's place, again, I wasn't all that interested in having him come in and 'keep me very occupied', as he hinted to Ryder earlier. He's never made much of an effort with my friends at all, and it's really starting to bother me. Every time he leans over to whisper in my ear, my skin crawls. I have asked that he stop doing it and to say what he wants to say, but he continues with the whispering. It probably has something to do with the fact that he's always trying to get us to leave places early, or to say something rude about one of my friends. But it's fucking annoying.

"Okay, goodnight," I tell him as I practically leap out of his vehicle. I don't even lean in for a kiss first, which gets an irritated huff from him.

"No kiss?" He pins me with a suspicious look. "Is this about Ryder?"

What the hell? Why would that even be a question?

"No, of course not." I lean in the door. "It's about you whispering in my ear again and insisting we leave before I was ready."

"Your clients are... unsavory." The look of disgust on his face leads me to believe unsavory was the nicest way he could put it. "They're not the type of people I would normally associate with, and I don't think you should, either. They're honestly kind of trashy, Denise."

Well, that's news to me. He's never really gotten along with them, but this is the first time he's ever expressed this kind of distaste.

"Are you fucking serious right now?" I'm barely able to keep my voice down, but I continue quietly so I don't disturb my neighbours. "They are my friends, and they are all good people. There is nothing trashy about them."

He snorts out a laugh. "Oh come on now, Denise. They're musicians. They drink, they smoke, they're all tattooed and pierced. If they weren't wealthy, they would be the definition of trashy. Associating with them makes me look bad. If any of my accounting clients ever saw me with them, I'm sure they would drop me in a minute."

"How did I not notice how stuck up you are?" I huff in disbelief. "How did you ever bring yourself to lower your standards enough to get together with me, I wonder?"

"I didn't lower them necessarily. I always saw your potential. But I was hoping you would change the way you dress, at least when we are together. Your parents are nice upper-class people, Denise. When they introduced us, they assured me you would eventually settle down, and become more like them. I understand you dress the way you do because of your job, but you can't honestly think old band t-shirts are the most professional item to be paired with skirts? Or that those shoes you wear are the most feminine you could choose? They look like they belong in a dominatrix's closet."

I'm completely floored. I didn't know he hated the way I dress. I like to consider my look to be rocker-chick-meets-pin-up-girl with a little extra edge. And I love the way I dress. Even if my shoes do look like they belong to a dominatrix. Actually, it's probably at least partly because my shoes could belong to a dominatrix that I love them so much.

They are heels, though, and people usually consider heels to be feminine.

"My shoes? Do you mean the heels that I wear all the time? How are heels not feminine?"

"You know what I mean. They're just so... rock-and-roll looking. Big, flashy, and sometimes they even have metal bits on them. Women should be dainty. Submissive. You always look like you're daring someone to take you on."

I stare at him, eyes wide, mouth gaping in surprise. This is not the man I thought I was involved with, not at all. And right now I almost feel like daring him to take me on.

"Yeah... I'm going to go inside now. I'll talk to you later sometime. I think I need some time to think all this over." Before he can say anything, I slam the car door and run up the stairs to my house.

As I grab my keys from my purse, I hear him yelling my name from the open car window, but I refuse to turn around. Instead, I unlock the door, go inside, and lock it again right behind me. I was serious about needing time, but I'm pretty sure I've already made my decision. He thinks my friends are trashy, doesn't like the type of people that I work with, hates the way I dress, and is rude to the people I care about. The only thing I need time for is packing up the few things he has at my place and thinking about how to word the break up.

I refuse to stay with someone who likes nothing about me. The last thing I need is someone trying to tell me who to spend time with and how to dress. Thank you very much. My parents did enough of that when I was growing up. I'm a grown ass woman and I can take care of those things my damn self. I should have known better than to agree to go out with someone my parents set me up with, I guess. Even after all these years, they're still trying to turn me into Debutante Barbie.

Once inside the house, I get changed into some comfy joggers and a loose tank, ready to get to work packing up Andrew's stuff. I have no patience for a man who has been with me for almost a year, hoping that I would change myself the entire time.

I'm nobody's renovation project.

Andrew has very few belongings here and before long, I have one small box of stuff all packed up for him. I'll call him tomorrow to come over so I can break it off with him and he can take his stuff when he goes. No sense in prolonging the inevitable.

I'm starving since I didn't get to eat much at Connor and Alex's place. My fork tasted like it had soap or something on it, so I barely ate three whole bites before Andrew wanted to leave. I fix myself a cup of tea, grab a snack, and get settled in to watch something on TV. After far too long scrolling through my choices on Netflix, I settle on The Dirt. Nothing like a little Mötley Crüe debauchery to remind me how good I have it with my boys. Now anyway.

Sleeping Dogs went through a bit of a hard partying phase in the first few years, but it was never that bad. The worst thing I can remember is walking in on Ryder fucking a groupie in the women's bathroom at Rough Mix, in the very early days. It had to have been one of the first few times I'd ever booked them there. And it was a blessing in disguise, seeing Ryder bending that girl over the sink. Up to that point, I had more than a little crush on him.

It took longer than I'd like to admit getting over that heartbreak. Andrew was the first actual boyfriend I had since I'd realized that Ryder would never settle down, and if he ever did, it definitely wouldn't be with me. I spent almost fifteen years throwing myself into my work, making Sleeping Dogs the sensation they are today, and trying to deny that I had feelings for Ryder. I know I'm not the one responsible for their talent, but I got them in front of the right people and booked them into the right venues. That counts for something.

Fifteen years turning myself into the person I am now, a person who I love everything about, and the first guy I take a chance on doesn't even like me, apparently. I'm not normally one of those people that says fuck my life, but... fuck my life.

I stay up and watch The Dirt for a little before deciding to turn in for the night. I'll need a good night's sleep to deal with Andrew tomorrow and I haven't been feeling well for the last little while. Probably from working too hard. I usually wind up sick at the end of a tour and this illness feels like it's been coming since then. I'm not looking forward to the conversation with Andrew, but I refuse to stay with someone whose feelings for me depend on me changing who I am and how I dress.

***

When I wake up in my bed, it feels like only a few minutes later, but a glance at my phone tells me it's already after nine in the morning. I slept for over ten hours, but I feel like I haven't slept at all. I must be getting sick.

I am a firm believer in the concept of eating that frog, getting the worst tasks completed first, so I text Andrew to come over. Might as well get the shittiest part of my day over with as early as possible, so I can move on to something better. Like watching the rest of my movie from last night. Or buying more dominatrix shoes.

Me- Come over as soon as you can. We need to talk.

There, short and sweet. Well, not exactly sweet, more like short and to the point. He must have been waiting for my message, because he texts me back almost immediately.

Andrew- on my way

He'll take at least twenty minutes to get here, so I drag myself to the bathroom to have a quick shower before he arrives. I'm midway through shampooing my hair before my stomach roils with the sudden, unavoidable need to vomit. I jump out of the shower and throw myself to my knees on the bathmat only to wind up naked, dripping water, and throwing up into the toilet.

I guess that settles it then. I'm not getting sick, I am sick.

I flush and quickly rinse my hair in the shower, forgoing conditioner, opting instead to dry off and dress in my comfiest joggers and a big Sleeping Dogs t-shirt from the last tour. Andrew ought to be thrilled with this attire if he hates my skirts and band tees so much. There's nothing feminine about these baggy sweatpants and this oversized t-shirt.

The doorbell rings, announcing Andrew's arrival, right as I'm emptying my bathroom garbage can to bring to the living room in case I feel that overwhelming need to vomit again. I carry it with me when I go to let Andrew in.

"Hey," I mutter, turning and heading back to the couch. "Come sit. I'm sick so not too close." That's convenient too, since I have no interest in being close to him, anyway.

"Oh, okay," he says while lowering himself into the armchair opposite the couch.

"So I'm just going to say this. We need to break up." It's then that I feel my mouth filling with liquid, telling me I'm about to throw up. Good thing I brought my trusty trash can. I grab it off the floor and forcefully vomit up the rest of last night's snack.

"What? Why?" Andrew seems surprised, which doesn't make much sense to me after last night. He had to have been able to tell how unimpressed I was with his behavior. Plus, in my mind, this has been a long time coming. I probably wouldn't have been able to deal with his rude whispering for too much longer.

I grab a tissue from the box on the coffee table and wipe my mouth. "Really? You have no idea why—" but before I can finish that sentence I'm throwing up again, and Andrew takes that as his cue to leave.

"I'll call you later to talk about this," he says as he walks toward the door. "I don't think this is the right time to be having this conversation. You obviously have other things going on." And then he's walking out, slamming the door behind him.

"What a dick," I mutter into my trash can. "Didn't accept my breakup and then didn't even offer to help me when I am clearly sick."

I lay back and settle in for what I'm assuming will be a long day of throwing up when the doorbell rings again. I lean forward to get up, but that makes me throw up again. Whoever is at the door knocks and then opens it. I guess Andrew didn't bother locking it.

"Hello? Anybody home?"

Ugh, what the hell is Ryder doing here? Like I don't have enough to worry about today. He better not be here to tell me he got himself into some kind of trouble again.

Keep Reading in Face the Music (Sleeping Dogs Book 2)

Keep Reading for a Sneak Peek of Santa's Baby (coming late 2023)

Chapter One

Phoebe

Of all the ways I ever imagined spending the Christmas of my thirty-first year, I can say, with certainty, tracking down the Santa Claus who impregnated me was not one of them.

Yet, here we are.

"Oooh, this place is nice, Phoebe." Gavin walks into the living room and sets down a box marked *Lincoln*. "Maybe the owners will decide to stay overseas so you can buy the place. The furniture is pretty sick." My idiot brother flops face down on my furnished rental's overstuffed blue velvet couch and groans obscenely into the cushion. "Oh, man. You don't want to know the dirty things I'm thinking of doing to this couch."

It's not every day I rent a place sight unseen, so you can imagine the relief I felt when we got here and the place looked precisely like it had in the photos. That I found a furnished place on such short notice, right before the holidays, could be considered a miracle in itself. Finding a nice place in a safe neighborhood? Yeah, there had to have been some divine intervention involved for that to happen. Maybe I've had a visit from the Ghost of Christmas Present. Heh. Get it? Because finding this place had been a gift. A gift that I don't want defiled by my disgusting brother and whatever he plans on doing to my new couch, regardless of how temporarily it's in my possession.

"Ew, don't be gross, Gavin. And get your stinky ass off the couch. You're filthy."

"Hey! Is that any way to treat the guy who spent one of his infrequent days off both school and work carrying all your boxes into the house?" He drags himself off the couch. "Speaking of carrying boxes, didn't you promise me pizza and beer as payment for helping you move?"

"Ha! Nice try, kid. I'll order pizza, but you're sticking with soda until you're of legal age. Plus, you still need to drive home so I wouldn't let you drink even if you were old enough."

Gavin is only eighteen, my much younger sibling from my mom's second marriage. Two days after my mom gave birth to Charlie, and with a few months left to go before my second birthday, my biological father decided being a father wasn't really his thing, and he left. It took Mom a long time to find another man worth taking a chance on after that. She started dating Warren ten years later, and they married a couple of years after that when Gavin was born.

Like most teenage guys, Gavin is all raging hormones and unrestrained snark. But, despite his many annoying traits, he has a huge heart, and that's why he's one of my favorite people. No one was angrier than Gavin when I found myself waiting at the altar for a man I knew in my heart wasn't right for me. He spent that night a year ago storming around the hotel, hoping to run into my former fiancé so he could unleash his teenage fury. It's probably a good thing he never found him, though. I doubt it would have been a fair fight. Webster kept himself in excellent shape and would have been more than a match for seventeen-year-old Gavin.

Seventeen-year-old Gavin was a short, scrawny little shit. Eighteen-year-old Gavin is almost six and a half feet tall and packed with muscle. He's never said so, but I'm pretty sure he started working out after the wedding disaster, so he'd be ready if he ever saw my ex again. After a year of protein shakes and lifting weights, not to mention a huge growth spurt, Gavin is formidable. It still wouldn't be a fair fight, but the advantage would go to Gavin, not Webster. He took it pretty hard when I told him Webster did me a favor that day.

I almost felt guilty for not being as upset as Gavin about the situation. It had been a shock when I got the text telling me he wasn't coming, but not marrying Webster Day turned out to be the best thing that could have happened. It seemed like a dick move at first, but in the end, he made the best decision for both of us. I'd been considering making that same decision that morning as I sat through the hours of hair and makeup appointments required to turn me into a blushing bride. I should have done it, too. If we'd both skipped out on the wedding, I bet we'd have been able to get past it a lot faster. To this day, I've yet to speak to Webster face to face. The failed wedding incident has forced me to connect with my lifelong best friend through phone calls and the odd video chat only. Which sucks. I could have used his support when I found myself pregnant and alone.

"No way. Charlie said she would do the driving on the way home." Gavin jumps up off the couch and yells down the back hallway, "Isn't that right, Charlie?"

Oh, shit. Despite being one of my favorite people, I will still murder Gavin if he wakes up Lincoln. That thing they say about never waking a sleeping baby? Yeah, that's not just an old wives' tale.

"Shhh. Will you shut up?" I slap my hand over his mouth. "Lincoln is sleeping."

He looks so sheepish I could almost believe he felt bad about waking my baby if I didn't already know better. There's no way Gavin would leave here without saying goodbye to his nephew, even if that nephew is a baby who still hasn't figured out things don't disappear when he can't see them. Gavin is sure he has a special bond with my baby, though, and it's something he's incredibly proud of. I believe they have a bond, too. Lincoln always seems calmer when his Uncle Gavin is holding him. And Gavin never misses a chance to hold him, even when he has to make his own chances.

"Too late," Charlie says, coming out of the back hallway with a tiny baby snuggled in her arms. "The little guy was awake when I tried to sneak into the room to drop off a box. I think he sensed me because as soon as I walked in, an unholy rumbling started coming out of his little rear end. You'll need to do laundry, by the way. I rinsed everything and left it to pre-soak." She looks down at Lincoln with a grin and singsongs, "Isn't that right, Linky? Mommy has to do laundry. Yes, she does. She's lucky Auntie Charlie changed you and the sheets instead of running away and letting her deal with it."

My heart swells while I watch my little sister snuggle my baby, and not for the first time, I second-guess my decision to move back to Westborough. What am I going to do without my family around to help me for the next three months? Why did I follow through with this terrible idea? Oh, right. If I want Lincoln to have the chance to meet his father, this is where I need to be. And my sense of right and wrong won't let me entertain the thought of not trying to find his father. There's a man out there who doesn't know he has a son, and that doesn't sit right with me. There's still a possibility he will decide not to, but I want him to have the option to be involved in Lincoln's life. So, even if he ends up being a dickhead like my own biological father who wanted nothing to do with me or my sister, I'm going to find Lincoln's father and give him a chance to do better.

"Hey, hey. None of that now. I can see your brain working from here." Gavin is back on the couch, getting his sweaty teenage boy smell all over it. Whatever, I'll use a fabric refresher on it when he leaves. He can't stink it up too badly in such a short time, can he? "Everything is going to be fine. Tell her your news, Charlie. I can't handle seeing Fifi cry."

I rub my fingertips over my cheeks, and sure enough, they come away wet. "Sorry if my feelings offend you, you little twerp. I'm going to miss you guys, that's all. I'm allowed to be sad about that."

He jumps up off the couch and wraps me in a sweaty hug. "I'm going to miss you too, Fifi," he says. "But you won't have to miss Charlie."

I blink a few times and pull myself out of his embrace. "What's he talking about?" I ask Charlie, then repeat my question to Gavin. "What are you talking about?"

Gavin takes Lincoln from Charlie, snuggling him to his chest, and takes him into the kitchen. I hear the cupboard doors open and close and the water running in the sink. Sounds like Uncle Gavin is making his nephew a bottle.

"I didn't tell you because I knew you'd try to talk me out of it, but I'm staying with you. You have the third bedroom I can sleep in. I even got myself a part-time job at a coffee shop. I'm staying to help you with Lincoln so you can focus on finding his dad. It will be easier to track him down if you don't have to bring Lincoln with you everywhere you go. Plus, I can't be away from you guys for that long." Charlie's eyes are shiny with unshed tears. "You know I can't get enough of those midnight feedings," she jokes.

I chuckle. "Are you sure? You don't have to put your life on hold for me, Charlie. I love you for wanting to do this, but you don't have to stay."

"I know that," she says, wrapping her arms around me. "I want to stay."

"You're the best sister I could ever ask for," I choke through a sob. "I couldn't have made it this far without you."

And it's true. The seemingly endless months of my pregnancy would have been so much harder if it hadn't been for the help of my brother and sister, and, of course, my mom and stepdad. I'll never admit it to them, but after living back home with my parents for the last year, and having my family around all the time, I was a little scared to be on my own with Lincoln. I loved living here with Webster, but being on my own with a baby is different. The excitement of Westborough seems almost scary when I think about protecting my son from unseen dangers. I tried to play it cool, but I'm thinking I didn't do such a good job of it if Charlie covertly arranged to move here with me.

I've never been so happy to be such a shitty liar.

"Are you guys done with all the girly feelings out there? Me and the big guy want to come chill on that sweet-ass couch, but we don't want your emotional breakdowns cramping our style. It's hard to relax with all this crying going on."

Charlie and I both burst into laughter. After one more squeeze, I let her go.

"Yeah, we're done," I call out. "I'll order that pizza now so you can get on the road."

"Oh, yeah. About that," he says, walking back to the living room with my son in the crook of his arm. "Mom told me to spend the night and drive back in the morning. She doesn't want me driving alone at night in the winter. I don't know what she thinks I do after work at home. It's usually pretty late by the time I get out of the market."

Charlie sits next to him on the couch, her eyes on Lincoln. "There's a huge difference between driving five minutes in Fallbridge at ten at night and driving on the highway at two in the morning. Especially in the middle of winter."

"Yeah, yeah. Okay, *Mother*," he teases. "I'm already staying the night. Happy?"

"You bet," she says while ruffling his hair, taking advantage of the fact that he has his hands full feeding Lincoln. "We just wuv you so much, Gavvers," she adds in a baby voice. "It would devastate us if anything happened to you."

"Hey, no fair. Hands off the hair. Do you know how long it took to get it like that?"

They sit side by side, alternating between cooing over Lincoln and bickering with each other while I busy myself with ordering the pizzas. After I do that, I focus on unpacking my few boxes. The best part about finding a furnished rental is how little I had to pack to come here. It would have sucked if I'd had to move my furniture out of storage for such a temporary stay. Three months isn't long enough to justify renting a moving van.

I only hope three months is long enough to find Lincoln's dad.

The doorbell rings, and Gavin hops up to grab the pizzas. "Oh, thank god. I'm starving," he says, spreading the boxes down on the coffee table and flipping one open. "I'm a growing boy, you know." He grabs two slices and stacks them sandwich style.

I bring plates and napkins out from the kitchen. "We know, Gavin. You tell us every time you get even the tiniest bit hungry."

He wiggles his eyebrows, and grins before shoving the makeshift sandwich in his mouth.

"So, Phoebe. Why don't you tell me how you're going to find this guy? You didn't go into much detail when you announced you were moving here for three months to look for him. Do you even have any idea where he is?"

I heave a sigh. We've hit on the biggest problem with my plan. It sucks. Getting drunk and hooking up with a stranger after skipping your own wedding would be a lot easier to get over if you didn't get yourself pregnant in the process. Failing that, it would be nice if you remembered the name of the guy or any detail about him other than he'd been dressed as Santa Claus for a Christmas party being held at the same hotel as your wedding. The only things I have to go on are the luxurious red velvet coat I stole when I crept out, and a blurry photo I took of his face mashed into the pillow. Not great clues.

Why did I take his jacket, you ask? I guess I thought my walk of shame would feel less shameful if I covered my wedding dress with Santa's jacket. It didn't. But I made it back to my room without being seen, packed up, and headed home with no one finding out I spent what should have been my wedding night with a stranger.

Until a month and a half later, when two pink lines gave me the shock of a lifetime, ensuring that everyone would know exactly how I spent that night.

That's right.

My fiancé left me at the altar and the first thing I did was run out and get knocked up by Santa Claus.

Talk about Ho Ho Ho.

Keep reading in Santa's Baby

More Books by Chantal

SLEEPING DOGS THE COMPLETE collection

The men of Sleeping Dogs have had their fair share of women, but now that they're a little older, and a little wiser, they're looking for something more meaningful than the one-night stands typical of their past.

Second Chance (Sleeping Dogs Book 1)

She's an unemployed chef afraid of being burned by love again. He's a world-weary rock star tired of being used. Can a second chance at first love heal them both?

Face the Music (Sleeping Dogs Book 2)

She's a serious control freak of a band manager. He's a jaded joker of a rock star. Will a jealous ex and surprise pregnancy tear them apart before they start?

Skip a Beat (Sleeping Dogs Book 3)

She's a disgraced ex-cop looking for a career change. He's a moody drummer trying to keep his demons at bay. Can vandalism and ill-conceived revenge plans be the glue that mends their lives and binds them to each other?

Only the Best (Sleeping Dogs Book 4)

He's a romantic, guitar-playing tattoo artist looking for true love. She's an emotionally and physically scarred photographer who keeps people at a distance. When one wants true love and the other wants one night, can friendship and a fake relationship ever be enough?

Way off Base (Sleeping Dogs Book 5)

She's a single mom struggling to rebuild her life. He's a reluctant rock star tired of being alone. Can they repair a foundation of lies to build the life they both want?

Santa's Baby: A Hilarious Holiday RomCom

Last Christmas Phoebe spent what should have been her wedding night with a sexy Santa Claus impersonator she found in a bar. This Christmas, she's tracking down that Santa and introducing him to the son they conceived that night. The only question now is, what happens when she finds him and discovers he's more like the real Santa than she ever could have imagined, complete with a few naughty surprises of his own?

About the Author

Chantal Roome writes contemporary romantic comedies and is the author of the Sleeping Dogs series of cinnamon roll rock star rom-coms. She loves writing love stories with just the right mix of sweetness, humour, and sex. When she isn't writing, she's drinking way too much coffee, binge reading romance, and living out her own second chance romance with her husband. She's also a mediocre mom to two frustrating, but hilarious and endlessly loveable kids, one dog who has eaten every toy he's ever been given, and another dog who wants nothing more to use her tiny puppy shark teeth on any exposed flesh she can find.

Keep in touch with Chantal on social media

Visit Chantal's website at: www.chantalroome.com

Get the Roomie Review Newsletter chantalroome.com/newsletter

Join my readers' group facebook.com/groups/theromcomroome

f   facebook.com/chantalroomeauthor

instagram.com/chantalroomeauthor

pinterest.com/chantalroome

tiktok.com/chantalroomeauthor

twitter.com/croomeauthor

goodreads.com/chantalroome

bookbub.com/authors/chantal-roome

Acknowledgments

I'd like to extend a special thank you to Amie, my best friend of the last 37 years. Your encouragement and input were invaluable to me during the completion of this book. I literally couldn't have done it without you.

I would also like to thank Lorraine for making some brilliant suggestions and saying some really amazing things about me and making me feel like maybe I could do this after all. Not only were you a great boss at the deli, but you've been a great cheerleader for this writing thing I'm trying to do.

Special thanks also to Ashley for reading my book in advance, helping me work out some kinks, and for being one of my most vocal supporters. And thanks also for being my TikTok video buddy. You know the ones ;)

Renee. Well, you tried. Haha, just kidding. I love you. Thanks for reading the book and yes, I guess now you can say you know someone who "works in porn". Except you'll forever be the "slut" of this little whoremembers club :D

Thank you to Madison for offering your support and encouragement and your expertise in all things books. And thanks for letting me read for you, even though your writing is much smarter than mine and more than a little intimidating.

Lindsay, thanks for reading and for sending me helpful notes. I know you're busy with work and kids and the fact that you took time to read my book and let me know what you thought is so appreciated.

And last but not least, thanks to everyone else that read this book to help me sort it out. Thank you for your kind and constructive reviews. Many of you received copies after I published, but please know that I appreciate everything you've done for me.

www.ingramcontent.com/pod-product-compliance
Lightning Source LLC
Chambersburg PA
CBHW051213190726
48288CB00006B/1943